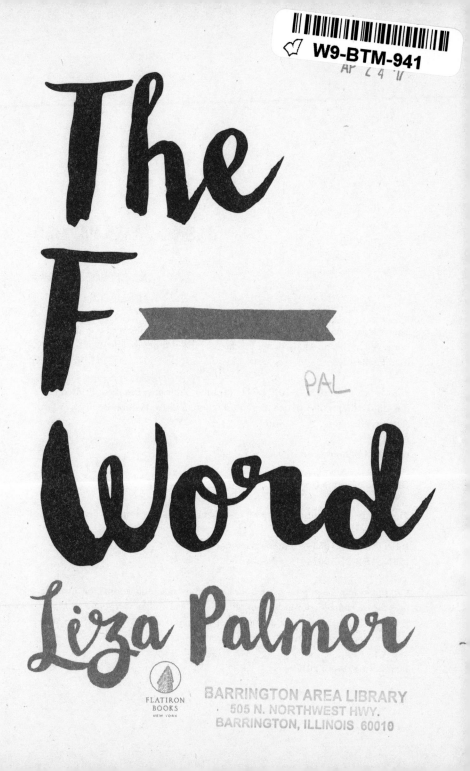

The F— Word

Liza Palmer

FLATIRON
BOOKS
NEW YORK

THE F WORD. Copyright © 2017 by Liza Palmer. All rights reserved. Printed in the United States of America. For information, address Flatiron Books, 175 Fifth Avenue, New York, N.Y. 10010.

www.flatironbooks.com

Designed by Anna Gorovoy

The Library of Congress Cataloging-in-Publication Data is available upon request.

ISBN 978-1-250-08347-0 (trade paperback)
ISBN 978-1-250-08346-3 (e-book)

Our books may be purchased in bulk for promotional, educational, or business use. Please contact your local bookseller or the Macmillan Corporate and Premium Sales Department at 1-800-221-7945, extension 5442, or by e-mail at MacmillanSpecialMarkets@macmillan.com.

First Edition: April 2017

10 9 8 7 6 5 4 3 2 1

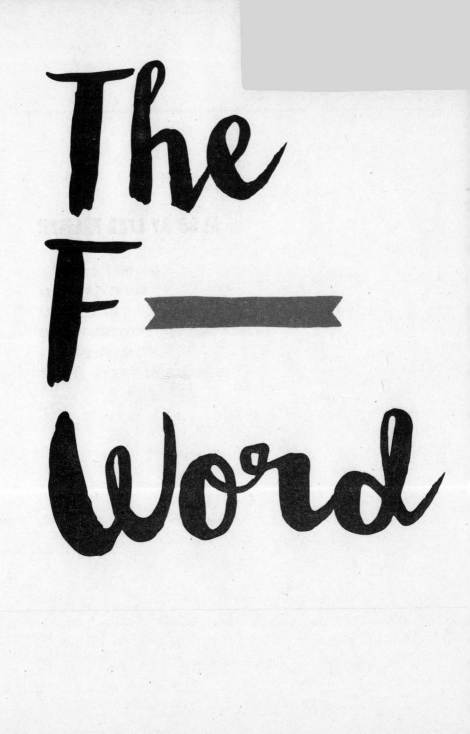

ALSO BY LIZA PALMER

I've looked at life from both sides now . . .

—JONI MITCHELL

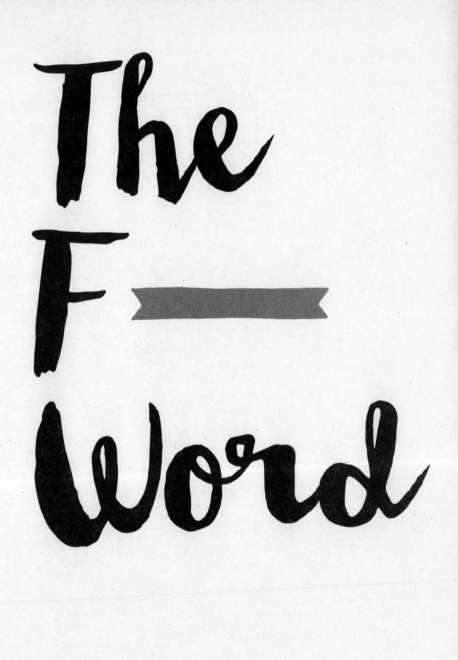

A THOUSAND POUNDS

"There's the truth and then there's the lie that people want to believe."

I'm sitting in my car in the parking lot of the coffee place near my house, on the phone with my assistant.

"The editor says they're going to pull the story," Ellen tells me. "She says the deal was that they had an exclusive and all that went out the window when she saw your client on the cover of *GQ* this morning. They were supposed to have the only cover of him this month." I turn my car off.

"Did you tell her it was supposed to be an inside piece that got moved up to cover last second?"

"Yeah, she's not buying it. I don't understand what the big deal is anyway."

"She's pissed they no longer have the get." I check my face in the rearview mirror.

"The get?"

"*GQ* was first, so by the time people read her interview with Gus it'll be old news. Literally."

"She's gotta know that *GQ* is so much better than her magazine."

"Well, that's her fear, for sure. Okay, she wants to believe this was a terrible misunderstanding. All we have to do is give her what she wants," I say.

"How do we do that?"

"We start soft. How hard this is on her. How sorry we are. How disappointed we are in ourselves. Are you writing this down? Then we talk about how we're okay with their story about our client being pulled or just relegated to digital content only."

"Are we okay with that?"

"Fuck, no." I grab my purse from the passenger seat and climb out of the car.

"Oh . . . okay. Right."

"Stay with me. Then, if that doesn't work we segue into how unfortunate it is that because of our unintentional—really stress that word—misstep, all of our clients will . . . how do I put this—" I open the door to the coffee place and stand off to the side for a quick second as I get my head together. Ellen waits. "Because of our unintentional misstep, their access to our clients will be blocked until we figure out how this terrible mishap came to pass."

"Blocked? All of them?"

"All of them." I walk over to where the line is forming and scan the food options.

"Okay. I'm on it," she says.

"And remember. She wants to believe you. And all you're doing—"

"Is giving her what she wants," Ellen finishes.

"Right. Talk soon. Oh, and Ellen? Send some flowers to the editor over at *GQ*. The cover is beautiful."

I hang up with Ellen feeling the smug satisfaction of someone who's just placed the last piece into the puzzle. I breathe a contented sigh as I drop my phone into my purse and fall into line right behind a father and his two daughters. The eldest can't be more than maybe six or seven—I'm not good with kids' ages, so she could be four for all I know. Maybe she's in high school. She's wearing a purple cottony dress and beat-up tennis shoes with giant flowers threaded into the laces. Her white-blond hair is messed up, and she's posing in a weird lunging position and looking at herself in the reflection of the stainless-steel base of the coffee bar. And she is having a very passionate, very detailed conversation with her father about carne asada tacos. He is holding the littler of the girls. She is gnawing on the top of a sippy cup and making an uncomfortably intense level of eye contact with me. I try a smile. Nothing.

"Honey, you're scaring the poor lady," the father says, turning around. "I have nightmares of waking up to that stare and just her little sticky hands tightening around my neck." He swipes the flame-red wisps of hair from her face with a sweet gentleness. The little girl doesn't take her gaze from me. I look at her father. Pins and needles radiate through my entire body. I try to regain control, but all my self-assurance and dignity have vaporized as if I've been walked in on in a public bathroom, pants around my ankles, helplessly reaching for the door and squealing some iteration of "someone's in here!"

"You're Ben Dunn," I say, before I catch myself.

"Do we know each other?" he asks.

"We went to high school together," I say. He looks exactly the same as he did in high school. The reddish-blond hair. The blue eyes. He was always so painfully masculine. I hate how well I know his face. I hate that I only know his face because Ben Dunn is as close as I've ever come to having an actual comic-book-level nemesis. How set his jaw was, how furrowed his brow, how that crooked smile told me if I was about to have a very good day or a very bad one. I studied him as if my life depended on it, because in many ways it did.

The last time I saw him was the day we graduated. He was surrounded by admirers and didn't even register me as I disappeared into the crowd.

That was twenty years ago.

"Ah," he says, his entire being deflating. "Well, let me apologize now, then . . . ," Ben trails off. He shakes his head, looks down at his oldest daughter, and with a long sigh finally speaks: "I don't think I remember your name."

"Apologize for what?" I ask, purposefully not answering his question. We all shuffle forward in line.

"For whatever terrible thing I did to you back in high school." His daughter looks up at him. "Daddy wasn't always the nicest guy, honey."

"Oh, I . . . you were always . . . you don't need to apologize," I stutter.

"What's your name?" the little girl asks. Ben shoots her a look. "What?"

"It's Olivia. Olivia Morten," I say. Ben's eyes jolt up to mine as if he's heard a loud bang. He looks away quickly, his face flushing.

"I'm Louisa." She points at the little girl in Ben's arms. "That's

Tilly." Death stare. Louisa points at Ben. He can't look at me. Won't look at me. "You know Dad." She sighs. A glance back over at her own reflection in the stainless steel. A quick lunge. She makes a bored staccato farting sound with her mouth.

"Olivia Morten," Ben repeats.

"I know. I've lost about a thousand pounds," I say, tucking a strand of hair behind my ear, unable to make eye contact. I clear my throat.

"A thousand pounds?!" Louisa says, laughing. "You can't lose a thousand pounds!" She stretches her arms wide and weeble-wobbles from one foot to the other. "A thouuuuuu-sand pouunnnnnds!"

Oh my god.

"Lou? Honey," Ben says, stopping her with a gentle hand on her shoulder and putting an end to my living nightmare.

"It's fine. It's actually a pretty spot-on impression," I say.

"A thousand pounds," Louisa repeats with a melodic sigh. "That's crazy."

"What can I get you?" the girl behind the counter asks. Ben and Louisa order as I quietly panic, Tilly's eyes now boring into the girl taking their order. He pays and Louisa takes the receipt and runs to an empty table. Tilly bullies her way out of Ben's arms and totters over to the table with Louisa, scrambling up into a chair of her own.

"It was nice seeing you again, Olivia," Ben says, tucking his credit card back into his wallet, one eye on his daughters.

"Nice seeing you, too," I say. He smiles and walks over to his table.

"Your usual? Chamomile tea?" the girl behind the counter asks, her pen hovering over the cup.

"You know what—" I glance over my shoulder. Ben Dunn

is cutting a sugar cookie in half with the precision of a surgeon as Louisa and Tilly eye him skeptically. I scan the food options once more. Louisa's impression of "a thousand pounds" burns through my brain and lands squarely on my chest. Flaky scones. Melty cookies. Even that wilty egg salad sandwich looks mouthwatering. "Think I'm going to splurge. How about—" Ben walks over and grabs a handful of napkins. "How about a small decaf Americano." Clearly disappointed, the girl rings me up with a sigh.

As I wait for my coffee, I can't help but stare at Ben. Each time I get caught. I shove my now clammy hand into my purse and tug out my phone. I scroll through work emails as I wait for my order. A text. It's Adam. He has to stay late at the hospital. Again. Thankful for the distraction, I make a quick call to that Thai place he likes and have dinner sent over, making sure they leave it for him at the nurses' station. My drink is finally called out. One last smile at Ben and his girls, and I'm finally able to leave that infernal coffeehouse. I beep my car unlocked, set the coffee in the cup holder, and close my car door. The quiet surrounds me.

"Ben Dunn." I say his name. I let my head fall into my hands and scrape my fingers through my hair. "Of all people." I look at my hands. Light pink nail polish. I isolate my index finger, grab the perfect fingernail, and pull. Pain. Blood. Immediately. I pull a tissue from my purse and wrap my finger in it. "Fucking Ben Dunn."

I put my keys into the ignition and let them hang there. Did I think he just ceased to exist? The smell of my decaf Americano has gone from inviting to rancid in mere minutes. "You're Ben Dunn." Why didn't I just think those words? Why did I have to say them? I see people from high school all the time, but it's not like they ever recognize me. Why didn't I just keep my mouth shut? And how is it fair that the sight of him can make me revert to exactly the same person I was in high school, as if that coffeehouse were the cruelest, most unfunny time machine in the world? No, you're going to forget you're a wildly successful, gorgeous, married woman and the time machine is going to plunk you right back down into your awkward teenage body where no one likes you.

"I AM A SIZE 2!" I yell to no one. "MY HUSBAND IS A DOCTOR!" A bearded man gives me a wary glance as he hurries to his car. "I RAN THE L.A. MARATHON!" It's not fair.

It's not fair.

Louisa's impression of "a thouuuuuusand pouunnnnnds" zooms to the front of my consciousness. Do I think I'm past all this? Safe? Do I? Do I still have to endure standing in front of Ben Dunn as his daughter weeble-wobbles around like a sumo wrestler? Let today be a constant reminder that I can never outrun her. But, it's not like I ever let my guard down. It's not like I ever feel safe in this new life. I am an interloper obsessed with honing my facade. I've built my entire life—my *new* life—around keeping my past a secret. My husband knows bits and pieces, but even the little bits he knows have been reshaped and colored by my persistent rewriting and massaging of the "facts." I shudder to think what would happen if he knew the truth of who I was. The whole truth.

"Stupid," I whisper. "Stupid."

No matter what I do, I'm always going to be her. It doesn't matter what I look like now or what I've made of my life over the twenty years since Ben Dunn saw right through me, all it takes is one run-in at a coffeehouse and I'm right back to being trapped inside the Sweaty Marble version of myself like it's some kind of haunted house. This is the moment I've been running from. It's the secret that flushes my cheeks when I even think about being unmasked: I was once really fat.

TAP TAP TAP

Gasping, I whip my head around toward the car window and see Ben standing there. I turn the car on, immediately silence the blaring music, and roll the window down.

"I'm sorry I . . . scared you," he says, crouching so he can make eye contact with me.

"Yes. Yes, you did," I say, barely catching my breath.

"I wanted to . . . I do remember you." He stands back a little from the car, peering into the coffeehouse. I look back to see Louisa and Tilly happily ensconced at a table filled with hot cocoas and a perfectly halved sugar cookie, not even aware their father is gone.

"Yes, we established that." I'm still replaying Louisa's unerring impersonation.

"No, I—" he starts. I shut the car off and open the door. Ben backs up as I swing it wide and climb out. I slam it shut with a forced sigh. Calm down, Olivia. I turn to face him. He continues, "Olivia Morten."

"Right." We stand there in the awkward silence befitting a conversation about high school.

"You still live locally?" Ben's eyes dart from me to his girls inside the coffeehouse and back to me.

"Yes, down by the Arroyo." I gesture toward a Metro station over my left shoulder as if that is "the Arroyo." It is not.

"I do, too. Well, not by the Arroyo. We live closer to South Pasadena than—"

"The Arroyo," I finish. He nods.

Silence.

"Are there guidelines for how to do this?" he asks. "Rules?"

"Talk in a parking lot? I think it's just about staying out of the way of cars," I say.

"Come on," Ben says, crossing his arms over his chest. "You know what I mean."

"Okay, then. Let's see if you're any better at taking social cues."

"How does that—"

"Just because you're ready to be absolved of the shit you said back in high school doesn't mean that I am." Ben takes a step back, his face draining of color.

"I wasn't the only one saying mean shit," he says.

"Are you saying that it was my fault?"

"No."

"That I made you say those things?"

"NO."

"How saintly should I have been? What fictional level of angelic would have been enough to make you take full responsibility for what you said?" He doesn't break eye contact with me so I can see every layer of this realization hit him.

Ben is quiet. Another glance back into the coffeehouse. The girls. Shoving sugar cookie bits in their mouths and laughing. He looks back at me. He puts his hands on his hips. Then stuffs them into the pockets of his jeans. And now he's crossing them again over his chest. He finally breathes.

"Don't blame me just because I beat you at your own game every once in a while," I say. He tears his gaze from mine and looks at the ground, shaking his head.

I am quiet. He starts and stops a sentence. Another one. I wait. When he finally speaks, his eyes stay fixed on the ground. "Do you ever wish you could erase whole parts of your life?" When he finally looks up at me, his eyes lock on to mine. His face flushes and then, "Just me?" A heartbreaking forced smile.

"It's not just you." A smile. A real one.

"It's not?" he asks. I nod in agreement. He steps forward. And I flinch. I hate that I do it, but it just happens. His entire being deflates. A breath. "I'm so sorry. For all of it."

"Yep." It's the only word I can muster. For everything I'm feeling, I'm not ready to forgive him. He just stands there.

"Yep," he repeats. "I'd better get back." I nod, fussing with the collar of my shirt. "You're bleeding." I look down at my finger. The blood is everywhere. "Here . . . just . . ." Ben runs over to a dull silver sedan parked two spots away, leans into the open window, and pulls something out. He hurries back over. "Give me your finger." I oblige him. He takes the now-bloodied tissue and wraps a bright blue and red bandage around my finger. "I try not to buy them only pink stuff, you know?" I nod. "These are superheroes. It's one of Lou's favorites. It's not just the one, though. They're a whole . . . it's a whole team."

"Of superheroes?"

"Of superheroes."

"This one is her favorite, though," he says, still holding my hand.

"And Tilly?"

"She likes the villain."

"Naturally," I say. He laughs. We both look back into the coffeehouse and Tilly is just staring at us, one single cookie crumb hanging out of her mouth. Ben waves at her and she flicks the crumb in her mouth and slides her gaze away from us slowly.

"Naturally," he says, noticing he's still holding my hand. As do I. And in that tiny moment it's like we both decide to 3, 2, 1 . . . let go.

"Thank you," I say, my finger held aloft as if I've just had an idea.

"You're welcome," he says, crumpling up the plastic bandage wrapper. "Nice seeing you again."

"You, too." Ben lingers. "See you around."

"Yeah. Yes. See you around." He waves one last time and with a final smile and a hint of a furrowed brow, he heads back into the coffeehouse and sits down at the table with the girls. I climb into my car, close the door behind me, and exit the parking lot, headed for home.

The streets of Pasadena. My driveway. Unlock the front door. Walk through the living room, straighten the dining room, and continue into the kitchen. Purse down. Workbag down. Set the coffee on the island and pull the fixings for a chicken salad from the fridge. I set my hands on the cold of the Carrara marble.

Quiet. Everywhere.

My legs feel heavy. I run my hand down the side of my body. Pinch the fat just under my bra. I close my eyes and am immediately bombarded with an almost seizure-inducing fireworks show of my past. Whole swaths of time I'd long had buried, now bursting out.

One memory, long entombed, burns brighter than the rest. And I fall into another unwelcome reverie. March 27th, fifteen years ago. My wake-up call.

I was a senior at Cal Berkeley, and one of my favorite things to do was to drive across the Golden Gate Bridge. The crisp San Francisco air that felt like I was inhaling life itself and the rhythmic thunks of tires on the pavement; the monolithic orange towers and the sweeping cables that seemed to cradle me at a time when I thought I couldn't be truly held by anything. Whatever the alchemy, being on that bridge made me feel weightless. And I'd have given anything for one second of that freedom.

I'd just gotten a new car and was there with my best friend at the time. It was cold. I remember that. I was wearing a bright yellow shirt, a cardigan with flowers on it, and khaki pants. I don't know why that night was different. I felt emboldened. The bridge made me do it? But, that night we got out of the car and began to walk. I remember talking excitedly about what I was going to do when I graduated. I remember feeling strong and alive. It was one of those nights. The kind where you feel like you can accomplish anything. I bent over the side of the bridge and just breathed in the night air.

That's when I heard it. A yell from a passing car. A young man's voice.

"Thar she blows!"

I remember my friend going through the usual Things People Say in a situation like that. Forget those guys and what do they know and some lighthearted joke to let me know it wasn't a big deal as she tried desperately to get the moment back on track, to a time before I was likened to a white whale by a carful of strangers. All I could do was take a deep breath.

I looked down at myself. As if for the first time. And I finally saw what they saw.

To them, I was just another fat girl on a bridge.

But that was never how I saw myself. Sure, people had made fun of my weight before. It was Ben Dunn's bread and butter. But, I never cared. Even then, I knew calling a girl fat was the go-to insult for every knuckle-dragging idiot who was just too dumb to think of something better. Being called fat never convinced me that I wasn't still valuable. But that night on the bridge was different. The punch landed. And I hated them for it. I loathed how superior they got to be in that moment. They weren't better than me, but because of The Fat, for that one fleeting moment they were. Being fat was a weakness. My only weakness. And I decided once and for all to sew that shit up. Tight.

My hands are in fists and I realize I haven't taken a breath in however long I've been lost in my not-so-distant past.

The bright blue and red bandage wrapped around my finger stands out against the white and gray color scheme of our house. I wash, chop and dice, grab a bowl from the cupboard, throw in the salad and the chicken, add some balsamic vinegar and a dash of olive oil. A fork. A cloth napkin. I take them both to the dining room table that's all decked out with its autumn tablescape: Gourds, pumpkins, and glass candlesticks trail down the center of the large wooden country table. I set everything down, find a place mat in the credenza, and set the salad on top of that. A trip to the wine cellar. A nice bottle of red. Pop. Pour myself a glass. Set that down on the corresponding coaster. Flip the napkin onto my lap.

I look at the bright red and blue bandage once more. I pull the napkin off my lap and walk down the hallway to the bathroom. I pull the bandage off and throw it in the bin next to the toilet. I rummage through the medicine cabinet and find the box of bandages that I bought at the store—regular, beige—and wrap one around my finger. I shake my head. Better. I close the medicine cabinet and walk back into the dining room. Flip the napkin onto my lap.

And I breathe. Home. This is who I am. There is no cruel time machine. I am not the Olivia that Ben Dunn made fun of anymore.

I'm not.

SWEDISH FISH

"The next step is one of those clip-on ties, you know?" I say, straightening Adam's tie that Friday night as we get ready to welcome our four dinner guests: the chief of cardiology and Adam's mentor, Dr. Jacob Peterman, and his new (fifth) wife, Nanette, Adam's college roommate, Gregory Werner, and his wife, Leah.

"You wouldn't last ten seconds with me in a clip-on tie," Adam says.

"I could."

"I can see it now: a huge gala event, everyone's watching as we descend the sweeping staircase, you look stunning as usual . . ." Adam pauses, pretending to wave at a make-believe friend.

"This is a rather elaborate fantasy sequence," I say.

"Oh, hello, Mr. President. Yes, I'd love to be photographed with you and the First Lady." Adam poses for an imaginary photographer and slowly luxuriates in adjusting his clip-on tie. He waves to another fictional person as I shake my head. Then, tragedy strikes as the imaginary clip-on tie comes off in his hands. He looks around the room in horror, his hands shaking.

"You're ridiculous," I say.

In the ten years I've been married to Adam, I've reveled in my old life fading away as my new life with him took center stage. His world was filled with everything the old me fantasized about: fancy dinner parties, vacations to tropic locations that didn't involve me making up excuses for why I needed to be fully clothed by the pool, hearing that sweet click as my airline seatbelt is buckled with no need to request a seatbelt extender.

"Ridiculous and right," Adam says, popping out of his performance with ease.

The light from the chandelier reflects and shines. It casts a glow over him that shadows his muscular upper body, the thick blond tousled hair, and that unnervingly perfect face. A face I've never gotten used to. In the beginning, in all of the pictures I took of him—and they were legion—he had this weary "another picture?" look in every shot. I was positive the people turning up in our pictures were actors hired to portray us in the movie version of my life. It's as if I had to keep convincing myself that this was real, that he was real. At the time, I hoped that Adam wanting to be with me meant I'd been accepted into this upper echelon. I now know it's far more complicated than that. The doorbell rings and Adam goes to greet the guests.

Even when I fantasized about Ben Dunn all those years ago, it's not like I really thought that we could have any kind of future together. My fantasies consisted of us gazing at each other from across a crowded room at some high school party—one of those teenage movie parties where the music is blaring and it's crowded and the intriguing outsider takes a chance and decides to go, but ugh, these people are so lame and . . . now the most popular boy in school is walking toward me with this look of wonder in those pale blue eyes. Isn't that how people in love talk about someone? As the bass dropped and the boy in a letterman jacket threw up into the ficus, Ben's pale blue eyes licked every inch of my pubescent shit show of a body. Where has this girl been? Ben would think to himself. How have I lived such an empty existence, he'd muse, absently setting down his red Solo cup of flat, room-temperature beer next to a passed-out party-goer. But the fantasy would always stop there, because That Look so terrified me as to what would come next, what Ben was capable of—what we were capable of together—and my out-of-control feelings, that all I did was replay the beginning over and over. The lock of our eyes, the smile, the walk across the crowded party as everyone whispered and gawked—the feeling that I'd finally been seen. I'd wake from the daydream feeling jittery and giggly but unable to continue beyond those initial moments. Beyond where I felt safe. Beyond where I was in control.

When the weight started coming off, I vowed—with every pound shed—that I would leave Her behind with it: the Fat Me. But, the Fat Me had infected more than just my body, she'd created a sort of filter in my mind that everything had to pass through. There was the world outside and then there was the version of the world the Fat Me would let me experience. In losing all the weight, I was merely flicking the bee off my arm, but its stinger was still deeply embedded under my skin. Poisoning. Corrupting. Violating.

Realizing I couldn't pluck the stinger from under my skin, I fashioned a rudimentary tourniquet and cut those parts of me off completely. It was just easier. By the time I met Adam, the weight was gone and so was the Fat Me: the forever alone, overly emotional, out-of-control embarrassment I'd been shackled to for far too long.

I became someone else. An Olivia Morten who was un-impeachable. An Olivia Morten that someone like Dr. Adam Farrell could love. Someone he would want to marry. And the Sweaty Marble who'd spent her youth invisible, unloved and untouched, who'd fought with and fantasized about Ben Dunn, disappeared. And the fantasies became a reality I could handle. A reality I could control. A reality I deserved.

And now, with one accidental run-in with Ben Dunn, I find myself unable to sleep, afraid that I'm one email notification that "so-and-so from high school has tagged a photo of you on Facebook" away from my entire new life crumbling down around me. I should feel amazing right now. I won. I WON. I used to dream of the moment Ben Dunn and I met up again and I looked amazing and he was, well, still him but you know, so sorrrrry for what he'd done and of course he'd be single and oh, look, SNIFF, I'm . . . sigh . . . I have to get home to my perfect husband and toodaloo, Ben. AND THAT SHIT ACTUALLY HAPPENED. I should be jumping for joy right now, high-fiving anyone and everyone, but instead I just feel exposed. Vulnerable. And there's no one I can talk to about this because, being the brain surgeon I am, I have exorcised every single remnant of that high school version of me from my life.

Everyone in that coffeehouse just thought two people were chatting in line. No one knows who I was. No big deal. I am alone with the weight of what happened yesterday. And it is killing me.

I force myself out of my reverie and walk, head high, into the dining room to join our guests. Jacob is pouring a glass of wine. Nanette wraps her arms around him as if the world is terrifying. Shaking off the remnants of my run-in with Ben Dunn, I loop my arm through Adam's. He pulls me in close and we watch as Nanette whispers something in Jacob's ear that I doubt he can make out since her baby voice can only be heard by dogs. Speaking of . . .

"If Nanette waxes rhapsodic about that gargoyle of a dog like it's her child, I can't be held accountable for my actions," I whisper. Adam leans in and kisses me.

"Sugar can only eat organic chicken, Liv, you know that," he says.

"Sugar can only go to a doggie daycare with an inside option because of her complexion," I say, mimicking Nanette's breathy little-girl voice.

"Aww, it's the American dream: penniless salesperson marries man who's old enough to be her father and spends her days bossing around the staff his last wife hired. I'm getting misty eyed." Adam wipes away an imaginary tear.

"Hopefully the twinkly lights from the chandelier will keep her distracted," I say. Adam stifles a laugh as we finally walk over to join the rest of the party. Leah is seated and checking her phone as Gregory mixes himself a vodka tonic at the bar cart.

I have to focus. *Ben Dunn.* I have to focus. *Sweaty Marble.* FOCUS. *A thouuuuusand pouuuuunds.* I take a breath. A long one. I'm here now. Ben is probably frolicking around South Pasadena with his adorable children and I'm here expanding in my lovely home every second. I wonder if my guests can see it. Smell it on me. The fear. No. NO.

I am still the same Olivia Morten I was last week. I am not invisible. I am not that Sweaty Marble. I am not the Fat Me. Another breath.

"You've outdone yourself again, Olivia," Jacob booms.

"It's my pleasure," I say.

"I keep telling Adam, you hold on to this one." Jacob slams Adam on the back with a hearty pat. "Don't make the same mistakes I have."

There is a chill as we all try to act like Nanette isn't the embodiment of Jacob's multitude of mistakes. Frozen smiles. An ice cube is dropped into the bottom of a glass.

"Olivia is the best thing that ever happened to me. I've come to terms with the fact that you all tolerate me simply because of her."

"And her coq au vin," Jacob adds.

"And her coq au vin," Adam repeats. I stand there. Smiling. "I'm not an idiot, Jacob. Or at least I'm not an idiot about this," Adam says, cutting through the tension.

"Not an idiot about this," Jacob repeats with a hearty laugh.

"Speaking of the coq au vin, I'd better check on it," I say with a polite smile. Jacob gives me a regal sweeping wave and I take this to mean I am dismissed.

"Right behind you," Leah says, joining me in the kitchen. "It smells amazing."

Leah is a makeup artist with a set of one-year-old twins and nowhere near the body you'd think she'd have because of this. Before I met Leah, Adam and Gregory would talk about her as if she were this incredibly smart, hilarious paragon of empathy who OH MY GOD was truly remarkable. And then I met her and realized that first and foremost, Leah was hot, thus making every excitedly listed character trait she possessed quadruple in magnitude. When a man says you're going to "really be surprised" by a new woman he's dating, he means that for someone so hot they're not a complete dipshit. And even then, it's debatable.

What I came to realize once the weight came off and I was allowed off the Island of Misfit Toys, was that women who look like Leah are so cherished by society that every nuance of their personality is highlighted and celebrated. Leah's intelligence, wit, and level of coolness in a woman who looked like I used to would make her a "fun work colleague" or "a hilarious sexless friend in whom I confide about my love life." But put those same characteristics in a super hot girl and you now have men falling all over themselves to crown her *Time*'s Person of the Year.

In the beginning, I thought Leah knew that her attributes were being amplified because of her beauty, but now I know that's not the case. She 100 percent thinks that given the opportunity she could lay out how outer space works simply because she saw half a TED Talk. But, she's a great orderer in restaurants, is unreservedly generous, and a great gossip, which I find are truly lovely characteristics for anyone to have, great beauty or no. Leah and Gregory met through friends. I imagine the introduction was something like, "Hey, he's rich and has a summer house in Montecito and she's a hot makeup artist who was a yoga instructor and can still put her legs behind her head." Aaaaand cue Mendelssohn's "Wedding March." But, she's married to my husband's best friend, so here we are.

Nanette comes into the kitchen with a glass of wine. Blond shiny hair, huge blue eyes, and a perfect figure that's both athletic and slim, Nanette Peterman is who the rest of us can blame for why the peasant top will never go out of style. We don't know Nanette that well, as her romance with Jacob was a bit of a whirlwind. I rely on this piece of information to ease my mind when I get nervous that Nanette Peterman is most likely the dumbest person I've ever met—and in Los Angeles that's saying something. When we were first introduced I asked her what her interests were and she answered, "I like outside." I politely pressed her thinking I'd misunderstood. No, not the outdoors. No, not *being* outside. I LIKE OUTSIDE. Then I asked what she did with her days. Vacant stare. Okay. What are you passionate about? At that question she shook her head like some kind of cartoon character. Finally, in desperation, I asked again what her interests were. And I swear to God it must have been half an hour before she repeated, "I like outside." And "I like outside" was her knocking one out of the park. Like she went home that night and thought to herself, Yeah, you DO like outside, Nanette. Nice one. When she and Jacob got married earlier this year, it sent a shiver down my spine. Guess I would have to learn to like outside, too.

I don't know if it's intentional that all my friends have a certain level of beauty. I'm thinking it's pretty intentional given my history. Having spent decades going unseen, I'm pretty sure I now populate my life with those who've never experienced such anonymity. I struggle to make this into something other than the shallow fantasy of a fat teenager, but if it walks like a duck . . .

"Caroline Lang," Nanette announces with the same inflection that makes everything she says sound like a question.

"What?" I ask, thinking I've misheard her embryonic peeps.

"The movie star. Style icon. Caroline Lang," Nanette says.

"She's a client," I say, taking a gulp of wine. "I'll pass along your—"

"No. Caroline Lang." I wait. Oh my god. "She's in your living room right now." I quickly set down my wineglass. "And she is just as elegant as I wished she'd be."

Why is Caroline Lang in my house? Shit. Something's wrong. I bark at Leah to watch the coq au vin and that I'll be right back. I push through the kitchen door and out into the living room where Adam, Jacob, and Gregory are crowding around the one and only Caroline Lang.

Caroline Lang is my top client. She is one of the biggest movie stars in the world and we've been together since the beginning. I took her from a fresh-faced twentysomething to box office juggernaut, and in return, she has made me one of the most sought-after publicists in Hollywood.

"I apologize for bursting in on you," she says, smiling as Adam hands her a glass of champagne.

"Caroline, you know Adam."

"Oh, sure." They give each other a friendly hug.

"This is Dr. Jacob Peterman and this is Mr. Gregory Werner." Caroline lets her gaze settle on each man as he is introduced. "This is Caroline Lang." Caroline smiles as they stare.

"Will you be joining us for dinner?" Adam asks.

"Oh. Actually I was . . . I need to speak with Olivia," Caroline says to me.

"We've got this, Liv. You can—" Adam eyes the den just down the hallway. "Take all the time you need." I notice that Leah and Nanette are watching the proceedings from the cracked-open kitchen door. I have to collect myself. Whatever existential pandemonium I've been swept up in has to disappear. STAT. I am Olivia Morten. I shake my head. The little round Sweaty Marble I was in high school rolls through my brain. No, not THAT Olivia Morten. I smooth my dress down over my body. This body. THIS OLIVIA MORTEN.

"We can speak privately through here," I say, guiding Caroline down the hallway toward the den. I push the Sweaty Marble Olivia Morten out of my head and hope she takes Ben Dunn with her. I open the door to the den and Caroline walks in first.

"What's up?" I ask.

"I'm so sorry, I know you're busy," Caroline says, shrugging off whatever persona she wore for the men in the living room.

"Don't worry about it. I've got like twenty minutes before that coq au vin goes off."

"Smells delicious." Caroline's voice is smooth and her diction is flawless. The Midwestern twang that gave away her humble beginnings is all but gone. Now she has the speech and manners of someone from the most elite echelons of society.

She downs her champagne, pulls a coaster over, and sets the empty flute down.

"Drink?" I ask, arching an eyebrow.

"Hell yes," she says, gathering her long blond hair to one side. I walk to the drink cart in the den and pour us each a gulp of the whisky I got from another client. I extend a glass to Caroline. "Bless you." I laugh and sit down opposite her, phone in hand, ready to jump into action.

"Hit me," I say. I discovered Caroline nine years ago. After weathering too many Sexy but Doesn't Know It parts in her twenties, Caroline was on the verge of obscurity. I poached her on the red carpet for some schlocky comedy she was in and by the end of business the next day I'd signed her. The first thing I advised—much to her agent's chagrin— was to take a smaller part in a critically acclaimed indie film rather than play some schlubby sitcom guy's nagging— but super hot—wife. It was the beginning of a lovely partnership.

"I left Max," she says. Caroline married Max Walsh five years ago. He was an up-and-coming director, it was an epic romance, and the tabloids ate it up. They've been a Hollywood power couple ever since.

"What? What happened?" I ask, trying to keep my voice even.

"What do you think happened?" Caroline asks, finally looking at me.

Shit.

"Willa Lindholm?"

"Willa Lindholm."

"I'm so sorry."

"She's not even twenty! Swedish. Has to learn her lines phonetically. Has legs up to here." Caroline shoots her thin, muscular arm into the air. She leans across and takes my whisky. "And I doubt she's the first." She downs it.

"Does Max know you know?"

"The better question is, does he care?"

"Are there photos? Do we need to pay someone off?"

"I don't think so."

"I can have Ellen sniff around a bit." I text Ellen a growing list of things that need to happen right now. The coq au vin isn't the only thing about to go off in the next twenty minutes.

Without looking up from my phone I continue, "We have a little over two months until *Blue Christmas* opens. Your marriage breaking up as you publicize a huge romantic comedy that opens on Christmas Day is not the best timing in the world." Caroline winces at the words "breaking up." A text back from Ellen. No chatter about Caroline and Max at the moment, but she's standing by. "Is Max interested in keeping this under wraps until *Blue Christmas* comes out? Even if he just walked the red carpet at the premiere. It would benefit both of you."

"Honestly, I don't think I can stomach standing next to him and smiling for the cameras." I nod.

"Okay . . ." My mind is reeling. Messages from Ellen are zooming in much like the CNN news ticker on the day of a natural disaster, although half of her messages are just emojis, so . . .

"You guys had talked about adopting, right?"

"Yeah . . ." Caroline is wary.

"Would you be open to pursuing that on your own?"

"I don't think so. I . . . I wanted it to be something Max and I did together," Caroline says. "Oh my god. I can't believe this is happening." She stands and pours herself a much bigger swig of whisky. Drinks it. And pours another.

"Because then the conversation becomes about what a survivor you are and look at the cute baby and booooo, Max, how could he . . ."

"No, I know." She walks back over to her chair. Her steps are careful. Right about now she's realizing just how drunk she is. She eases herself into the chair. "Feels shitty, you know? Baby as prop?"

"You wouldn't be the first," I say.

"Max is kind of adopting a baby." Caroline waits. "Get it?"

"Yep."

"That Willa is so young, that—"

"Yep."

"And they say I'm not funny." Caroline toasts herself.

"You're hilarious," I say.

"I've got a million of 'em," she says, her words slurring.

"So, you left Max? That was the order of things?"

"I left him after I found out he fucked the Swedish Fish, yes."

"So, he didn't leave you."

"I mean, he's cheating on me, so in a sense . . ."

"Have you already started the proceedings?"

"What?"

"Have you gotten in touch with your lawyer yet? To start proceedings?"

"Proceedings. Proceedings. Proceedings."

"I don't know what—"

"Such a funny word."

"Caroline?" She's still mouthing the word "proceedings." "Are you going to file for divorce?" The door to the den creaks open. It's Leah.

"So sorry. Some alarm went off? Is it—"

"It's the egg noodles." A look from Caroline. "Gluten free." A relieved nod. "Just take them off the stove top and put them through the colander already in the sink," I say.

"Egg noodles. Off the stove top. Colander. Got it," Leah repeats.

"And Leah?" She pops her head back in. "Can you turn down the coq au vin a smidge?"

"What's a smidge?" Leah asks.

"A hair."

"I don't—"

"Maybe one click on the dial. Like—" I turn my hand. "Like that much." Leah mimics my turn. I nod.

"Will do. So sorry to interrupt." Leah closes the door behind her.

"It's so cliché," Caroline says.

"Serving coq au vin at a dinner party?"

"I'm not the only one who's hilarious apparently," Caroline says, cracking herself up. "No, the whole Willlllllla Lindholm thing."

"I know."

"What's my cliché?"

"What do you mean?" Another text from Ellen. And another. She's acquired more information on Max and Willa, where they are, what they're doing, and has attached grainy photos of them right at this moment. They're together, but they're not yet *together*. It's at times like these that I am very thankful Ellen is on our side.

"What do I do now that people would go . . . oh, look at Caroline Lang, howwwww cliché," Caroline says, now slumped a bit over in her chair. "Now that I'm officially the woman scorned."

"You could go out to the hot clubs in age-inappropriate dresses and drunkenly hook up with whatever kid is bulking up to star in the newest superhero movie."

"Ugh, that just sounds exhausting. And sticky." Laughing, I finally look up from my phone. Caroline is studying the dwindling whisky in her glass. Watching it swirl around and around and around. "Do you think instead of going out to these clubs or whatever, this kid would want to come over to my house and watch TV in our pajamas? Please tell me that's what kids today are doing?" I look at her for a long moment.

"You're stalling," I say.

"If you told me Max was going through a phase, I'd believe you." Caroline meets my eyes. Pain.

"I know."

"So say it."

"We promised never to lie to one another."

"Ouch."

"Caroline . . ."

"I don't want a divorce, but Max doesn't want to be married to me anymore." Caroline doesn't know what to do with her hands. She finally folds her hands in her lap like a little kid waiting to have her school picture taken. "So . . ."

"Okay," I say.

"Have I ever told you how we met?"

"Caroline." I pull my chair closer to her and look her straight in the eye. "Are you ready to file for divorce?"

"I don't know." Caroline stands, sways, and then begins to pace. "Do you think Willa Lindholm knows that this is how it's going to be for her, too? There's always another Willa Lindholm. Always. I'm going to call her. I'm going to tell her. Help her. This is what they call leaning in, right?" Caroline bends over, digging through her purse for her phone. And then she stops. "I'm going to be sick." I help her back into her seat. "I can see the headlines now. *It's a Blue Christmas for Caroline Lang! PS: Did she get older and fatter overnight?*"

"You're going to be okay," I say.

"Sure doesn't feel like it."

"The whisky probably isn't helping."

"The whisky is the only thing helping, you mean." Caroline looks up and extends a hand. "And you." I take her hand.

"You're going to vomit, aren't you?"

"Yes." Caroline lurches to the bathroom and retches into the toilet just in time. "I'll get in touch with my lawyer tomorrow," she says, still kneeling at the toilet.

"Good," I say. Caroline stands, washes her hands, and rinses out her mouth. She walks back into the den a little worse for wear. "Is Richard driving you tonight?"

Richard is not just Caroline's driver. Two years ago, Caroline had a break-in at her house. Some nutjob was positive they were married in a past life. Richard Bernard, a former Navy SEAL, was hired the next day. For being someone who can kill you in less than three seconds—if that—Richard is a rather ordinary-looking man. No more than five foot eight, he's probably in his mid to late forties with salt-and-pepper, tightly cropped black hair and an always clean-shaven face. You don't even notice him. I guess that's the point.

"Yes," she says. "He's right out front." I nod and we make our way out of the den and down the hallway.

"I've got this," I say.

"I know you do." I smile. "I'm sorry I interrupted your dinner." Another smile.

"Maybe a new hairstyle?" I say. Caroline nods. "And tell your stylist that for the next two months we're going to go for color, youth, and a whole new attitude. But, respectful. You know what I mean."

"That it didn't get to me. You want me to be . . ."

"Plucky."

"Plucky," Caroline repeats.

"We just have to make it to Christmas Day," I say.

"I've always wanted bangs," Caroline says.

Caroline slurs her goodbyes to my dinner guests. Richard and I pour her into the awaiting Escalade and I'm back in the kitchen.

"So Caroline Lang," Leah says.

"She was one of my first clients," I say.

"No, I mean. I know why she was here."

"What have you heard?"

"The girl who does her makeup said something to me, but—"

"What do you know?"

"That they're having problems." Leah's voice sounds sad.

"So, it's just that? That they're having issues?" I ask.

"I mean—I've seen Willa Lindholm. The girl he's doing that new movie with? I did her makeup for this event earlier this year. She's really captivating. Perfect skin," Leah says. Nanette is nodding in agreement.

"What does Willa Lindholm have—"

"Oh, please, they're definitely sleeping together," Leah says.

"Did your friend tell you that?" I ask.

"She didn't have to," Leah says.

"Hm," I say. Leah and Nanette nod. Leah looks at her phone.

"The makeup girls start gossiping and it starts buzzing through the tabloids in—"

"Two days," I say. Leah looks up from her phone.

"Maybe three," she says.

"Shit."

"I feel a real connection with Caroline Lang," Nanette says, her palms up and outstretched. I nod. And then we stand in silence for the next several moments as Leah watches her mother putting the twins to bed from some app on her phone.

I sneak glances at Nanette and she looks utterly contented just to stand there. An elegant sigh here and a musing smile there, she couldn't be happier.

Nanette Peterman is the woman men describe as "sweet."

I won't do it, I say to myself. I won't do it. I can't. I . . . I look at the clock on the wall and see that the coq au vin won't be ready for another three minutes. I take a deep breath.

"So, how's Sugar?"

"We're still trying to get her an appointment with Dr. Mukhopadhyay, so . . ."

"Oh, no. I hope everything is—"

"Everyone says she's the best dog therapist in L.A."

This is my own fault. I should have fucking known not to ask.

The coq au vin bubbles away. I send Leah out with the salad and egg noodles. The crusty baguette that only the men will eat is sent out with Nanette. I tell them I'll be right out with the main dish but to go ahead and start serving the salad without me. I tap out several texts to Ellen about Caroline and plug my phone into the charger next to the toaster.

"Do you want red, Liv?" Adam asks, coming into the kitchen.

"Yes. Yes, please."

"Hey, good news."

"Oh?" One last text to Ellen. She zooms back with the running-man emoji with a puff of air behind him. I've learned that this is her "I'm on it" emoji combination.

"Yeah, Jacob has only asked me once how my wife 'keeps it tight,' so . . . we're right on track for me being utterly disenchanted with my hero come the end of the night."

"Oh, honey," I say.

"Please tell me I won't turn out like that," he says, leaning back on the kitchen counter.

"What? Of course not." I wrap my arms around him. He pulls me in tight and kisses the top of my head. I can feel him shaking his head. I pull away from him and look him straight in the eye. He looks away. "You hate dogs." A smile. He kisses me.

"God, she is an idiot. Like officially." I pat his chest and take the coq au vin off the flame. Adam brings down the serving dish from the top shelf.

"Thank you, baby." I transfer the coq au vin to the serving dish. I send it out with Adam. He gives me a wink as he disappears back into the dining room.

The quiet of the kitchen settles in around me. It's nice. I look at my phone. So many texts. From Ellen. She's checked with her sources.

The story is getting out. Caroline Lang and Max Walsh are dunzo.

"I don't want a divorce, but Max doesn't want to be married to me anymore," I repeat Caroline's words. Hear them aloud in the quiet of the kitchen. I say the line again. "I don't want a divorce, but Max doesn't want to be married to me anymore." I pick up my glass of wine. Take a long drink.

Caroline never mentioned love as she spoke about the end of her marriage. Not once. Whether she still loved Max. Adam calls for me from the other room.

"Just a sec," I yell back.

No, this is good. Love makes things messy. Caroline not factoring it into these proceedings works to our advantage.

TOMATO, TOMAHTO

"Oh, he's totally cheating. Wouldn't you?" Leah asks. The men avert their eyes, acting as though Leah's just speaking to the other women at the table. "Oh, come on. Can you imagine being married to THAT?" I drink my wine.

"Caroline Lang is a that?" I ask.

"It's just so relentless with her. She's so icy," Leah presses.

"I think she's gorgeous," Nanette says.

"Well, that's undeniable," Leah says, looking to Gregory for a reaction.

"Greg. I implore you. Don't say a word. Your life has never been more in jeopardy than it is right now," Adam says, laughing.

"I've always thought she was quite sexy, in that—I don't know, like it's kind of natural with her, you know?" Gregory says, pushing his glasses farther up his nose. I'm always surprised at how tall Gregory is. He seems so much smaller to me. Smartly cropped black hair, a wardrobe filled with oxford cloth shirts, and gaining an average of ten pounds a year, Gregory Werner is every wealthy man who is just attractive enough to have his pick of any woman. I've known him for going on ten years and I'm still not quite sure what he does for a living.

"Natural?? Are you serious?" Leah says, setting down her wineglass. Adam just shakes his head.

"You know, like it—"

"If you say 'effortless' right now, I may just have to throw this wine in your face," Leah says, only half laughing. I, of course, know that Leah will be mumbling "natural" to herself while scoffing and monologuing for the next several months, if not years. "Caroline has never had an effortless thought in her entire life." Of course, Leah is 100 percent correct. Caroline hasn't been effortless in decades. I keep this tidbit to myself.

"It's her job to look the way she does. She gains a pound and the tabloids start with the baby bump rumors," I say.

"I love those rumors," Nanette says.

"But does Caroline have to constantly remind us how hard it is to be that beautiful? You know? Have a piece of chocolate cake, why don't you?" Leah says.

"Oh, because you eat chocolate cake all the time?" The one time I bought gluten-free, vegan chocolate cake for Leah's birthday she took one bite, pushed it away, and pronounced it "too rich."

"You guys are really making me want chocolate cake," Adam says.

"I'm just saying, look up Joyless Ice Queen in the dictionary and there's a picture of Caroline Lang standing there with a bunch of kale and a yoga mat," Leah says. The table erupts in laughter.

What Leah wants is for Caroline to toe the party line like the rest of us. We Instagram pictures of lush, gluttonous brunches that we don't eat and make jokes about how our husbands better not want that last piece of a pie we have no intention of having and act like it's a spontaneous, last-minute choice not to have dessert. Ever. And while working out is definitely something we all do for the mental benefits as well as the physical, I doubt any of us will admit that our need for it borders on the compulsive.

The first rule of this new clique is that you can never, ever admit that you care about what you look like. It has to seem effortless. Natural. Oh, this old thing? Telling the truth about how single-minded and exhausting it is to look the way Caroline does equals being called a Joyless Ice Queen by a table of people who were friendly to you just an hour before. I've learned that what makes women truly beautiful is their own indifference to it, but no woman is beautiful and doesn't know it.

"I like kale," Nanette says.

"Awww, of course you do," Jacob says, nuzzling his wife.

"She can be off-putting, but—" Gregory allows.

"Off-putting? She's downright smug," Leah interrupts.

"She really is intelligent, though," I say. Leah just stares at me.

"I don't mind women being smart," Leah says, making sure to leave off the "as long as they're fat, ugly, and old."

"Weren't you saying that you love following the books she reads?" I ask.

"She posts some really good stuff," Leah allows. "But—"

"And that one book you've read how many times? The one she said was her favorite of last year?"

"Three times," Leah says.

"Didn't you email her about it?" I coax.

"I did," Leah says.

"And—"

"She wrote back a lovely reply thanking me for the email, asked what I was reading next and I noticed that she mentioned the book later on one of those talk shows. Said a friend recommended it to her." Leah clears her throat and sits back in her chair.

"She told me she really loved that you emailed," I say. Leah talked about that email for weeks and I've always held a soft spot for Caroline for taking the time to reach out to a friend of mine like that.

"Which is why it stings all the more when I hear her going on about her raw food diet like that's as hard as being a single mother holding down three jobs," Leah says. I collect myself and try not to launch across the table at my dear hypocritical friend who spoke about her in-laws failing to offer a gluten-free option at their last Thanksgiving like it was her own personal Holocaust.

"I know, I can totally see where you're coming from. But, I'm always astounded at how cruel people can be. Especially on the Internet."

"You're right about that," Leah says.

"And remember we were talking about how mind-boggling it was when those paparazzi shots of her and Max on the beach were released and people were going on about her thighs? And you were saying—"

"No, I know." Leah holds her hand up, conceding the point. Good. Because I can go on and on reminding Leah of all the millions of times she talked about Caroline like she was her savior, an infatuation that stopped just short of taping up a poster of Caroline in her bedroom.

"Never read the comments. I've told you that," Gregory says to Leah.

"I don't. I . . ."

"Don't look under the bridge and you won't see the trolls," Gregory says in an oddly singsong tone.

"I didn't look under the . . . how did we start talking about me?" Leah asks.

"Aren't we always talking about you?" Gregory says, laughing.

"Oh, my sweet, sweet husband," Leah says in a tone that I know means she has now focused her rage on Gregory. The rest of his night will be spent paying dearly for that one comment.

"More wine?" I ask. Leah holds out her glass. I pour.

"Thank you, pumpkin," she says. It's this endearment that catches me. I'm bent on defending Caroline because I think Leah is attacking me and that, despite my best efforts, I've been found out. But, she isn't. Leah is taking me at face value, an attribute I've always appreciated in her. As far as Leah is concerned, we're on the same team.

"But, no one deserves to be cheated on," Nanette says. She looks at Jacob like a baby startled by its own fart: Where did that come from?

"Of course not." Jacob sighs, looking at Leah as though Nanette's pain is her fault.

"I don't know. It's not like it matters to Caroline Lang anyway," Leah says, shaking her head. "What we think of her." Adam wraps his arm around the back of my chair.

"Well, she seemed pleasant enough," Adam says.

"You just want us to stop talking about it," Leah says, laughing.

"And is it working?" Adam asks.

"Oh, come on. I'm sure you've heard this before. Livvie must talk your ear off about Caroline Lang," Leah says.

"I try to keep the blood and guts to a bare minimum and—" Adam says.

"And so do I," I joke. Everyone laughs, happy to lighten the mood around the table.

"It's not like any of this matters," Jacob says.

"I'm sorry?" I ask.

"Movie stars. Hollywood. I mean, it's not like any of it matters," Jacob says.

"But it does," I say.

"To you maybe, hon. It's your job, but I don't give Caroline Whatever-Her-Name-Is a second thought," Jacob says, taking a huge bite of the coq au vin. I can feel Adam shift in his chair.

"But, that's where you're wrong," I say. Jacob slides his gaze from his emptying plate to me. He slowly dabs at the corners of his mouth.

"Enlighten me," he says.

"What was it that first drew you to Nanette?" I ask. Jacob looks warily from me to his wife. A wide smile.

"She just glowed—that blond hair was like a halo. I couldn't look away. I knew, in that moment, she was everything I wanted in a woman," he says. Nanette beams.

"But what I know is Nanette has her hair colored that exact blond because of a piece *Vogue* did on Caroline Lang back in . . . what was it?"

"Two thousand eight," Nanette says.

"Whether we like it or not, women like Caroline Lang set trends we don't even realize we're internalizing. When I was a teenager, I read this article about Winona Ryder going to a flea market and paying for everything with hundred-dollar bills. It was a throwaway line, but to me? It was everything. From then on, it became the thing cool girls did and I set it as my personal North Star. Being a woman can be such a mystery sometimes, we unconsciously look to these celebrities as surrogate mentors for our own femininity. They appear—as you said earlier, Gregory—to be so natural, that we look to them to set the standard. So when Caroline came out last year and said that she was worthless without her big cup of coffee in the morning, that simple statement allowed women to admit that—like the perfect Caroline Lang—they don't greet the day in full makeup and an unwrinkled silk nightgown like certain television shows would have us believe. Not only does this stuff matter, Jacob, I'd even go so far as to say that you owe your very marriage and current happiness to none other than Caroline Whatever-Her-Name-Is."

Silence. I take a sip of my wine. Jacob takes the napkin from his lap and tosses it on his now empty plate.

"Do you think you can ask Caroline where that patchwork blanket coat thing she was wearing in those pictures came from?" Nanette asks, cutting through the tension. Jacob clears his throat. "I tried sitting in a wheat field like she did, but it was actually really uncomfortable." Adam pours himself another glass of wine. Leah holds her glass up and Adam fills it as well.

"I can ask her stylist," I say.

"Stylist," Nanette repeats in a reverent whisper. I pass Adam the baguette. He tears off a portion and begins soaking up the coq au vin juices left over on his plate.

"What I think everyone is dying to know is what you two have decided Asher and Tiger will be for their very first Halloween," I say. As Leah and Gregory launch into the ins and outs of choosing their twins' first Halloween costumes, Adam leans over and whispers in my ear.

"I do so love watching you work." He gives me a lingering kiss on my cheek. "Work . . . annihilate." Adam gestures imbalanced scales with his hands, his face crumpled in faux confusion.

"Tomato, tomahto," I say. He laughs. The dinner party moves on in easy conversation as I nip away to the kitchen to ready tonight's dessert of baked pears. I put the kettle on for tea and switch on the coffeemaker should anyone wish to partake. As the water boils and the coffee percolates, I catch up on Ellen's texts along with one from Richard letting me know Caroline got home safely. We're all set to take this thing head-on.

As our guests enjoy dessert, I sip my tea and process the evening. I knew that Caroline was seen as icy. I knew people thought she could be tone-deaf at how rarified her life was, but I didn't know the extent to which her own fans loved to hate her until tonight. Her divorce is all they'll need to publically humiliate her. They knew it, they'll joyfully exclaim on their social media. She deserved it, they'll hiss to their girlfriends. She's not even that pretty/talented, they'll confess over SoulCycling.

It won't matter that Max is the one who's cheating with Willa Lindholm. No, what the tabloids will run with is the Ice Queen drove poor Max Walsh into the Swedish Fish's arms by being so damn unlikable.

In short, Caroline Lang had this coming.

I have two days to change the conversation. Two days before people are cooing over a "leaked" paparazzi photo of Max and Willa on some beach in Kenya.

I replay the debate later on that night as I clean up. Adam is back at the hospital and the house is quiet. It's Leah's last words that are the most telling and make me the most nervous. That Leah believes it doesn't matter to Caroline what The People think of her. That's the interesting bit. I dry and place the last wineglass in the cupboard and gently close the glass-fronted door.

Whatever flaws Leah will say Caroline has—She's smug! She thinks she's better than all of us!—Caroline's true crime is she's made Leah feel insignificant. She's made Leah feel like her words and opinions are beneath Caroline's notice. And if Caroline has made Leah feel this way, this will be the reaction from other women as well. Caroline Lang being cheated on will be like seeing a mean girl from high school finally get what's coming to her.

I drape the kitchen towel over the sink, unplug my phone from the charger, shut off the lights, and walk into the dining room. I straighten the table runner, snuff out the candles, and continue on toward our master bedroom.

Caroline Lang had it coming. I shake my head, as I get dressed for bed. Muttering to myself as I brush my teeth and wash my face.

The dark underbelly of being seen is that you threaten those who secretly fear they're invisible. I switch off the bathroom light and crawl into bed, remembering to plug my phone into the charger. I pull the soft blankets up and just sit. Smooth the blankets. Fidget. Shake my head. How do I change the conversation? Caroline Lang has spent too many years cementing the Smug Ice Queen persona to undo it now. We've tried to defrost her, but that only lasted for a few months at a time. How do I convince women that Caroline is one of us?

She's human and of the two people getting divorced, she's the one who deserves a bit of their compassion.

How do I recast her as courageous, yet benign? Because that's the ugly truth about women and gossip: We only talk shit about the women we're afraid jeopardize the things we have and want. That's why when I was fat, people made fun of me, but no one gossiped about me. Why? Because nothing of theirs was ever at risk of being taken by me, least of all their men. I could get great grades and get into Cal Berkeley and wear cute clothes and be from one of the wealthiest families in Pasadena and still never threaten their idea of themselves. I was never going to pull the attention away from them, because whatever I achieved would always be undercut by what I looked like. Admit it. You hear about some woman being successful and happily married and then you see a picture of her and she's fat? You say to yourself, "Good for her." Same criteria and you see the woman is thin and beautiful? "Ugh, what a bitch."

Last year, this UK tabloid took a poll on the most unlikable Hollywood stars. Caroline was fifth. But, that's not what bothered me. What bothered me was that she was listed between the drug-addled actor who pulled a gun on his fiancée and the singer who beat his girlfriend. And she had made the list simply because women thought she was icy.

I turn out the light and try to get comfortable, flipping onto my side, then my back. I see my phone light up and check it. It's a text from Ellen. She can meet with me tomorrow night. We'll come up with a plan.

"Everything is going to be okay. I've got this," I text back. Ellen texts back a set of emojis that would need the full power of the Bletchley Circle to decipher them. I reply with a simple "xo" and set the phone back down on my night-stand.

Icy. The word women use to cut someone they feel to be smug down to size. Saying Caroline is icy is the way women get back at her for making them feel like shit about themselves. Fine. If you think Caroline is icy? I'll give you something you can connect to. I'll give you the best friend you never had.

I'll give you fucking sweet.

ROOKIE MISTAKES

"We're not here to chat, ladies. We're here to make it burn!" Barb yells.

It's 6:30 the next morning and instead of dealing with Caroline Lang's impending divorce, I'm doing Swimtastics with my mother in the shallow end of a public pool to Dusty Springfield's "Son of a Preacher Man."

"I don't know if I'd call her icy, but I'm not so sure I'd want to be married to her either," Mom says under her breath as Barb leaps out of the pool to show us HIGH KNEES! HIGH KNEES!

Mom is now in her late sixties and has yet to slow down. She's just as heavily involved in charity work as she was when I was in school, running a nonprofit empire out of that same Spanish home I grew up in by the Arroyo. Her small, powerful frame has weathered the years well enough that I can still be in denial that she's getting older.

"Big steps, ladies! Really push it!" Barb leaps back into the pool and lets out a yawp. "It's good to be alive!"

I am the youngest Swimtastician by approximately twelve to thirteen decades. Mom and I have been coming to Barb's class ever since Mom had her hip replacement last year. In the beginning, I acted like I was so beyond Barb's crazy side-stepping antics, but then I got slapped into submission by the wraparound-sunglasses-wearing, zinc-oxide-smearing ex-hippie who can leap in and out of pools faster than a speeding bullet.

"I wouldn't want to be married to her either, but—"

"Olivia! I hear you!" Barb shushes me. "Arms out of the water! Punch the sky! Show 'em who's boss, ladies!"

"Sorry, Barb," I say.

"You should know better," Mrs. Stanhope says in an easy drawl, as she bobs by in her giant pink sun hat, a huge bandage stretching down her cheek from a recent skin cancer surgery.

"Yes, Mrs. Stanhope," I say, lifting my arms out of the water and punching the sky as Barb instructed.

"You need to stop getting me in trouble with Barb," Mom says with a wink. She speeds past me and catches up to Mrs. Stanhope, arms high in the air.

Ninety minutes later, Mom and I walk into the communal showers. My entire body is tired. I'm also the only one in here from Barb's class still wearing my swimsuit. All different kinds of bodies, all different kinds of women, and I still can't bring myself to join them in their collective nudity.

As I set our shower caddy on a plastic chair closest to our chosen showers, I can only envy the freedom of these older women. The blushing perfect-bodied teenagers of the club swim team try not to look at the round, powerful nakedness of Mrs. Stanhope.

I thought when I lost all the weight I'd be able to luxuriate in being naked. I'd finally be that carefree girl who flits around the house in nothing but a slightly open silk robe and a "come hither" look. First, those silk robes stick to your wet body and you have to peel them off like you're a human banana. Second, if someone could clarify the difference between a "come hither" look and a "where's your bathroom?" look, that'd be great. And third, no matter how much weight I lost, I realized I never learned how to simply look at my naked body. Just look at it. Not glance at it, or wince at it. Not pick it apart or judge it. Not groan at it or berate it. Just simply look at it. I am an expert in focusing only on what I perceive to be grotesque and I can target a single flaw with the sterile ruthlessness of an assassin's bullet. So, when I think about walking into those communal showers utterly nude, I can only laugh. Not even Adam has seen me naked. I know how bizarre that sounds. We've been married for ten years; of course he's seen me naked. Nope. It's been ten years of "romantic" candlelight and dim lighting, strategic sheet placement and zipping into the bathroom when his back is turned. I am a master at misdirection and will do anything to avoid having my own husband see me naked, to stand directly in front of him with all the lights on. Oh my god. Just thinking about that breaks me out in hives.

Mom peels her swimsuit off and rinses it out in the luscious hot water of the communal shower. While she's doing this, she's carrying on a lively conversation with Mrs. Stanhope and Joyce Chen about where to get the best Caesar salad in Pasadena. They've battled about this hot topic several times before. As Mom lathers up her body, she speaks animatedly about Julienne, saying that even their to-go salads are crisp and amazing. Mrs. Stanhope is a Smitty's woman. Always has been. Classic. Great croutons. Naked naked naked. And Joyce Chen argues for her favorite, Houston's, as she laces her wet suit over the spigot of her shower. Laughing and familiar, they wend their way through the day's schedule as I turn around, face the wall, and wash my hair, letting the hot water fall over my still-swimsuited "perfect" body.

"How's that husband of yours?" Joyce Chen asks, looking over at me.

"Busy. Always busy," I say.

"They have a tendency to be quite busy at that age," Joyce Chen says.

"Makes me downright nostalgic. Clay doesn't have anywhere to be, so guess where he always is?" Mrs. Stanhope asks.

"In your way," Joyce Chen and Mom say in unison.

"In my way," Mrs. Stanhope repeats, shaking her head.

"And you?" Joyce Chen asks.

"Busy. Always busy," I say.

"We did have a tendency to be quite busy at that age," Mom repeats Joyce Chen's line.

"That I am not nostalgic for," Mrs. Stanhope says.

"I do love a list, though. You can't take away our lists," Mom says, shutting off her shower. Joyce Chen and Mrs. Stanhope assure Mom that no one is going to be taking away her lists.

Joyce Chen and Mrs. Stanhope have known me since I was a little girl. As I entered adolescence, concern for my weight quickly became concern for my future. Attempts to set me up with their sons were painful affairs, but it was their loving excuses as to why their progeny hadn't been interested that stung far more. I know Joyce Chen and Mrs. Stanhope notice that I keep my swimsuit on when I shower. They also notice that I change into my street clothes under towels and back up against walls and coincidentally have to use the bathroom when the changing room gets particularly crowded and oh, I'll just get changed in one of the stalls, no problem. Mrs. Stanhope said something once. The exact quote was, "Why did you lose all that weight if you're never going to show it off, Olivia?" And I made that moment so unbearably awkward with my rambling excuses and stuttering explanations that no one has mentioned my weight since. Instead, they ask about Adam. As if he's become the embodiment of me losing all the weight. Which isn't that far from the truth.

Later that morning, I follow Mom up the hill from the Rose Bowl, wind around the Arroyo, and park behind her on Mission Street in South Pasadena. She beeps her car locked and I hold the door open as she walks into La Monarca later on that morning. Despite me waving it off, she still hands me money to pay for our order and finds a table near the back. I order two café de ollas, a croissant for Mom, and I splurge on a cup of fresh fruit for me.

"So, what is it that you think is going to happen?" Mom asks, taking the lid off her café de olla. She leans over and inhales the cinnamon and *piloncillo* scents wafting out of her coffee. "If she's already seen as icy, then how can this impact her career?"

"This could be the tipping point. She's always going to be a working actress, but if there's been this growing resentment of her—this could be the thing that pushes her out of that top tier," I say, forking a piece of pineapple. "She's already teeter-ing." I speak with my mouth full and the word "teetering" sounds like a mumbling mess. I swallow. "Teetering."

"And you think molding her into some—what was the word you used?" Mom asks.

"Sweet," I say.

"Sweet." Mom rolls her eyes. "Every time I think we're out of the 1950s . . ." Left by my father when I was little, Mom never remarried. Not only has she never remarried, Mom unabashedly celebrates her freedom like someone who escaped from a gulag. "And you don't think the simple fact that her husband cheated on her with a woman half his age will sway people?"

"No, I don't. I think women will think it was her fault. That she made him do it," I say.

"That's the same poppycock the women at the club say. Hollywood is no different than any other nest of vipers." Mom takes a sip of her café de olla. She closes her eyes and lets out a long "ahhhhh" afterward. "Oh, that's good."

"I have to remind women she's the one they should be rooting for," I say.

"So, is this where you concoct some big publicity stunt so the world can see how sweet Caroline is?" Mom asks.

"And now we're both going to have 'Sweet Caroline' stuck in our heads for the remainder of the day," I say.

"I do love Neil Diamond," Mom says, smiling and sway-ing back and forth.

"BAH bum bum," I sing.

"Maybe just play that song every time she walks around?"

"The Boston Red Sox might have a little problem with that," I say.

"So, what kind of publicity stunt would work?" Mom asks.

"People would see that coming from a mile away; no, this requires something a lot . . . smaller," I say.

"Smaller? How is that going to fix things?" Mom asks.

"I've got to find the things people don't consider publicity," I say. Mom looks confused. "A famous actress gives up her first-class seat on an airplane to a soldier and one of your girlfriends posts it on her social media with the post saying something about how this makes her like that actress so much more!"

"How is that . . . ?"

"All planned."

"How?"

"How was it an organic event when she was in full makeup and cameras were waiting for her at the gate?"

"Someone emailed it from the plane?"

"Exactly." I arch an eyebrow.

"Her publicist?"

"Yep." Mom smiles as if she's just answered a question right on a game show.

"That's so déclassé," Mom says, horrified.

"Pictures of an actress at the park with her kids? Set up. Those photographers were either tipped off or downright paid to be there by her publicist."

"But, why?"

"Because that actress thinks being a good mother is good for her brand."

"That's awful," Mom says, taking a careful sip of her coffee.

"Is it?"

"The kids . . ."

"Sure, that aspect of it. But, don't you warm to actresses

you think are just like you? You're more likely to see them as relatable?"

"I suppose."

"Everyone has a story about who they are. Not just celebrities. Look at social media—we're all pushing some version of the life we want you to believe. It's all just PR." I take a sip of my coffee. So good.

"Should I be terrified or proud of you right now?" Mom asks.

"Probably both," I say and we laugh. "I just have to figure out . . ." I stop. Think. "Well, figure it out." Shit. I run through all my old tricks, flipping through them in my mind. Did that, tried that, that flopped, that worked for a month. "This is going to take something different."

"Well, if we're still using the same playbook we've always used," Mom says. I look confused. "Betty Crocker cookbooks, three-piece suits, and signing your husband's name to birthday cards for his mother?"

"I think we are," I say.

"Fastest route? Charity," Mom says.

"Caroline started her I Made This Foundation, what was it . . . five years ago? It provides after-school programming in the arts," I say.

"That's something," she says.

"Yeah, but all it did was make people see her as this Lady Bountiful as she swanned into schools in white cashmere with gifts or whatever," I say.

"Then don't have her do that again." I laugh.

"It was a rookie mistake," I say.

"In the charity world, it's all about boots on the ground, you little darling."

"Right."

"It can't be about the photo op," Mom says, trying out some lingo.

"Photo op?"

"I know things, too." A wink. "What you're doing is providing hard evidence that she's a good person. So people will at least feel badly for gossiping behind her back," Mom says, taking a rogue grape from my cup.

"Maybe this is about people finally getting to see the real Caroline," I say.

"Ask her why she started her foundation. I've always found that people start the foundations they wish they could have had in a time of need."

"Hmmmm," I say, taking one last bite. I push the fruit over to Mom for her to finish it up. We sip our coffees.

"Myrna Dunn said that you ran into her son the other day." And I choke. "Drink some coffee. Honey?" Mom stands up and pounds on my back as I gasp for air. "Raise your arms over your head." I oblige as all of the patrons of La Monarca stare at the two women who have been transformed into professional wrestlers lurking in the back of the establishment. "Better?" Pound pound pound. "Better?" I wheeze a breath.

"Yes. Mom. I . . . good. I . . ." I put up a hand hoping she'll just sit down. This is almost as bad as her holding up a bra to my burgeoning chest in that department store when I was fourteen.

"Have something bready," she says, offering me some of her croissant.

"No, thank you." She rubs my back and finally sits. "I saw him and his two daughters."

"Three," she says.

"Three?"

"He has a daughter in high school," Mom says with a raised eyebrow.

"Oh. Well, he only had two with him," I say.

"You're blushing."

"I am not."

"You absolutely are." I shake my head. "You had such a crush on Ben Dunn in high school."

"We hated each other."

"Oh, is that what you're calling it now?"

"He was legitimately terrible, Mom."

"I don't think that mattered to you back then. Plus, people change."

"Do they, though?" I can't make eye contact with her. Mom doesn't know to what extent I've hidden my past. As far as she's concerned, I have nothing to hide. I'd love to think she's right, but I have too much evidence to the contrary. "So, he told his Mom he'd seen me? Did he mention how different I looked?"

"He did."

"Hm."

"He's back in town, you know."

"Yeah, I gathered that."

"So, just because we're talking about your teenage crush, does that mean you're going to revert back into the teenage version of yourself?" The Sweaty Marble version of me rolls through my brain. My stomach drops.

"God, no."

"Good, because I did my time raising a teenager," she says. I laugh, despite my growing anxiety. "Apparently, Ben's a principal now at some elementary school in South Pasadena. Oh, probably right around here, come to think of it." Mom turns around in her chair as if the elementary school is going to pop up within the walls of La Monarca. She turns back around and takes a sip of her café de olla. "Divorced." A cleared throat. Mom smiles at a passing patron on his way to the bathroom. "Oh, you know what, though?"

"What's that?"

"Maybe this is your . . . oh, yes. This could really work," Mom says, scooting to the front of her chair.

"What could work?"

"Myrna is in charge of the big Halloween fair up at Aster-house—a foster home in Altadena. Kids from all over are coming. She put Ben in charge of making sure all the kids have costumes, so maybe Caroline can help out with that. If her foundation is in the arts, she can . . . I don't know, say it's something to do with theater or . . ."

"No, that's actually perfect. This is perfect, Mom."

"Caroline could donate some costumes and then volunteer the day of," Mom says. "Everyone wins."

"I think this is a good place to start."

"And bringing some much-needed attention to the good work Asterhouse is doing is a lovely silver lining."

"This is so great," I say, pulling out my phone.

"No phones at the table, Liv." Mom eyes my phone and I tuck it back into my purse. "I don't have many rules, but I refuse to sit across from someone tapping away on one of those infernal devices."

"No, you're right. It can wait."

Mom reaches into her purse and pulls out a little journal with a pen attached. She flips through the pages and I can't help myself.

"You know that's just as bad, right?"

"Oh, shush—I'm trying to find Ben's contact information," she says with a smirk. She starts writing as I try to keep my composure. She tears off a slip of paper and there it is.

After twenty years, I finally scored Ben Dunn's phone number.

THE ADVENTURES OF SUPER HOBO AND SWEATY MARBLE

"Hello. Hi. Is this Ben Dunn? I'm Olivia Morten . . . this is . . . it's Olivia Morten. You know, A Thousand Pounds Olivia Morten? Maybe this'll help, just imagine . . . if you draw a face on a beanbag chair and then ignore it completely until you mock it in front of all your friends. Yeah, HAHAHAHAHAHAHA—maybe tell the beanbag chair she has a really pretty face?" I rest my hands on the top of the washing machine and breathe. "Oh my god." The laundry room closes in around me as I imagine actually talking to Ben Dunn on the phone. I've been picturing this moment for twenty-plus years, and I'm just as unable to craft a cool conversation starter as I was when I was fifteen.

Ben and I waxed and waned with our battles like most mortal enemies do. And then the football team's charity pancake breakfast happened. I went with Mom, as one does, and Ben was on the griddle, kitchen towel lazily slung over his broad shoulder and wearing an apron that read, "A rose is a rose is a Rose Bowl." The apron was tied twice around his narrow waist. It was early on a Saturday morning and there was something disarmingly intimate about how disheveled he was. He made charming, friendly conversation with everyone who came through the line. He quickly remade a little girl's pancakes that'd fallen on the ground and called her "sweetie" when he presented them to her with a heart-melting smile.

When I got to the front of the line, there was this split second before either of us spoke in which I allowed myself to finally and officially swoon. And then:

"Practicing on what will certainly be your future working in the fast-food industry?" I asked.

"Eating enough for twenty, I see," he replied.

And all went back to normal.

"Liv? Are you talking to someone in there?" Adam calls from the kitchen.

"Oh, it's just a funny cat video! I'm . . . uh . . . watching it on my phone," I yell through the door, hoping he won't investigate further. I frantically pull up a video of a cat swinging around on a ceiling fan that's actually hilarious. I watch it three times.

"When's your dinner with Caroline?" he says through the door.

"Check the calendar," I say. After one too many instances of "Hey, can you whip up dinner tonight for so-and-so from the hospital board," I hung a calendar on the side of the refrigerator in a desperate attempt to make Adam understand the concept of planning ahead and setting us (read: me) up for success. It's gone over about as well as you'd expect.

"Can't you just tell me?"

"No, I'm trying to get you in the habit of using the calendar," I say. The grumbling tantrum that follows implies that this mythical "calendar" and the details of my dinner with Caroline will have to be found at the summit of Mount Everest. In reality, it's approximately one centimeter from his face and all I'm asking him to do is gaze slightly to the left. Teach a man to fish and all that. I wait. And wait. And wait. "The dinner is at 6:30," I say, finally giving up. I don't have time to teach a man to fish right now.

"Was that so hard?" Adam asks. I hear him moving away from the laundry room door. I will myself to stop procrastinating. I hold the cell phone in my hands. Tight. Tighter. Just call him. JUST. CALL. HIM.

"You've got to pull yourself together. People change. This isn't the halls of our high school. You're an adult. He's an adult." I put the cell phone on the shelf and transfer the laundry from the washer to the dryer. "You had a crush on me, too? No, I didn't know that, Ben Dunn. I mean, I had my suspicions. So, all of that posturing was just to get my attention?" I pluck a dryer sheet from the box and throw it into the dryer. "I mean, I haven't really thought much about high school, you know? It's . . . oh, yeah, we've been married ten years. I know, he's very successful and good-looking, you're right." I slam the dryer door and set the timer. I pull the dark clothes from their hamper and load them into the washing machine. "You think I'm beautiful? No, don't feel bad for . . . you just had to tell me? What—" I pour the detergent into the washing machine, close the lid, and set the timer. "That you love me? That you've always loved me?"

I move the empty hamper out of my way and let the

whirring sounds surround me. I pick up my cell phone again and lean against the doorjamb. Okay, I dramatically collapse against the doorjamb. What familiar ground this is. I've been having imaginary conversations with Ben Dunn for as long as I can remember.

I can feel the flush in my cheeks that used to plague me. I can feel that old awkwardness tingling in my fingertips. That sinking feeling in my stomach that I've said something stupid is returning. That sickening vulnerability and the quick attack mode that always followed. My greatest fear is being realized.

She's waking up: the Fat Me.

I pick up my phone and check the time—4:47 p.m. Dinner is down on Beverly Boulevard, so it'll take me over an hour to get there. I have to call Ben now. I have to be able to pitch this plan to Caroline later on tonight. This is business.

I stand tall. Shut it down, Olivia. Tighten the tourniquet. I close my eyes. A deep breath. Tamp it down. Swallow it. The horizon straightens as the world comes back into focus, my ship finally righting itself. I push my shoulders back. Open my eyes. I turn and walk out of the laundry room, cell phone in my hand.

I shut the door behind me and stand in the kitchen. I open up my address book. Scroll through the names and find Ben Dunn right where I'd been obsessing about him earlier. I press his name and put the phone to my ear. Adam walks down the hallway toward the master bedroom.

"Hello?" Ben's deep voice crackles through the phone.

"Ben? Hi, this is Olivia Morten."

"Oh, hi. Hold on a sec," he says. I can hear rustling and some fidgeting. He muffles the phone and continues speaking to someone. Another word. A stronger word. Crying. A word that sounds like the last word. A closing door. "Sorry. Had to . . . Tilly took a toy and, well, it didn't go well for her."

"I can call back," I say, my stomach flipping.

"I'm afraid this is kind of the norm around here," he says. Another fidget. I can hear Louisa talking in the background. Ben is telling her he's on the phone. Some more talking. "Honey, the whole idea of homework is that you do it yourself. Me giving you the answer is . . . yep, I know." I can hear Louisa stomp off as Ben finishes her sentence. "I'm the worst dad in the world." I laugh. "Why did I think girls would be easier?"

"Because you don't understand women at all?" I blurt. My cheeks flush and my entire body tenses up. The next second of silence extends on for hours. And then Ben laughs. His laugh has this cracking, rollicking edge to it. It's the kind of laugh you'd hear booming from the back of a smoky bar where ZZ Top plays on the jukebox.

"You're right about that," he says. Silence. "So . . . what, uh, what can I—"

"Right, why did I call," I say, realizing that he's struggling.

"I'm assuming it has something to do with my mother running into yours at the Apple store the other day," he says.

"You mean when she was in there trying to figure out why the audio book she bought on iTunes wasn't being read in order?"

"It was on shuffle, wasn't it?"

"It was on shuffle."

"When my mom bought her new laptop, I signed her up for their one-on-one classes and knew I was in the right place when the kid—who seriously looked ten years old—started with, 'Okay, so take the computer out of the box.' I nearly started crying," Ben says. Another extended silence.

"Right, well, I'm afraid I've called about something far less exciting than IT assistance for our parents," I say.

"Oh?"

"I don't know if your mom told you, but I work in PR and—" I hear a crash in the background on Ben's end.

"Lou? Hold on one second. I'm so sorry." Ben sets the phone down. I wait. And I wait. I wipe the kitchen counter down. I load the dishwasher. And finally, "Okay, so we're at Defcon Two here. I would like to go on record as saying it's not usually this chaotic, but I'm going to have to cut this short. Can we—"

"The Asterhouse Halloween fair. Your mom put you in charge of making sure all the kids have costumes?"

"Delegation has never been something my mother shied away from."

"I would like to know if Caroline Lang can donate and volunteer the day of." My voice is clear and strong.

"Caroline Lang? As in . . . Caroline Lang Caroline Lang?"

"Yes. I can elaborate further if you'd like, but—"

"Monday morning I have office hours open. Eight forty-five. Come by and we'll speak further. It's a tentative yes, but I don't want this . . ." Ben stops. A moment. "I want to help you, Olivia. I want to . . . I'm anxious to make things right between us any way I can, but I also can't have this event turn into the backdrop of some reality show."

"It's not like that at all. Eight forty-five. I'll be there." Ben tells me the name of his school and gives me quick directions. I scribble them down on the back of a receipt.

"I'll see you then," Ben says.

"Yes, and thank you," I say.

"Don't thank me yet," he says. We sign off. I set my phone down on the counter just as Adam walks back out into the living room.

"That was Ben Dunn from high school. I was talking to him on the phone." My voice is robotic. I realize that had I spoken about my past to Adam at all, this announcement would have been met with much confusion. As it stands, the mention of Ben Dunn hardly registers.

"Oh?" Adam strides through the living room and into the kitchen.

"He's in charge of costumes for this Halloween fair and I asked if—"

"Cute," Adam says. "Hey, have you seen . . . there was a . . ." He sees my scribbled directions. "A receipt."

"Oh, shit. So sorry. Do you need it?" I ask, holding the receipt up.

"No, I . . . that's fine," he says. "There's a pad of paper one inch from your hand, but I'm sure the accountant won't mind your scrawls on the back of that receipt come tax time." Adam's hands are on his hips.

"Ben's mom and my mom ran into each other at the Apple store and—" Adam's phone buzzes. He picks it up, answers the text, waits, and texts again. "And then they started making out with one another and they're now lesbian lovers."

"You're doing that thing where you think I'm not listening," Adam says, tapping away.

"Just because you can multitask doesn't make what you're doing less rude," I say.

"But, if I'm listening to you and can answer this text, then . . ." He flicks his eyes up briefly. A smile. And back down at his phone.

"And this is where we start arguing about arguing. I've personally loved this portion of our marriage," I say with a sigh.

"Can it be labeled arguing if only one of us is doing it?" Adam asks, still tapping.

"I'm not going to do this right now," I say, walking past him.

"Do what?" he asks, finally looking up from his phone.

"Take the bait." He lets out a little laugh, and I will myself not to turn around. I have to get to dinner and I don't have time to have the same fight with my husband that I've had for ten years—where he avoids talking about what's wrong by telling me to calm down. Then I try—unsuccessfully—to prove to him that I am, in fact, calm by caring less and less about whatever it was I wanted to speak with him about in the first place. As I pull my keys from the hook, I realize Adam is correct about one thing—it's not arguing when only one of you is doing it. "I'll see you later on tonight." I close the door behind me and try not to follow the logic of this realization. Is it a marriage if only one of you is fighting for it? I shake my head. I'm being dramatic. I have to remember who I am. Not who I was, but who I am now. Who I really am.

Caroline, Ellen, and I are meeting at Escuela on Beverly Boulevard. I've asked Søren Holm, my boss at Birch PR, to join us. It was Søren's steadfast leadership that attracted me to his firm after moving back here from Washington, D.C., nine years ago. My excitement when Adam announced he'd found a position at a hospital right here in Pasadena was eclipsed by the prospect of having to transition back into the notoriously petulant Hollywood PR machine. But, Søren offered me a secure work environment, and in PR—with all of its nuclear moving parts—that's almost unheard of.

I push open the glass door and take a second to inhale the tantalizing, wafting smell of taco deliciousness. Escuela is a small restaurant that's always packed to capacity, with an open kitchen and a ceiling decked out with hanging vintage wooden shoe stretchers. The host makes his way through the restaurant and leads me to a table in the far corner. I thank him and settle in with the menu and some water. Ellen lopes in, a huge smile on her face once she sees me. Ellen Matapang is fresh out of UCLA and has more energy than I remember ever having. She's barely five feet tall and will probably have her own PR firm within the year. It's because of Ellen that one of the most-used characters on my cell phone is the smiling poop emoji and that I can now hold entire texting conversations using just pug photos.

"Okay, it's on some of the blogs, but only observational—I mean, they're not saying anything outright, just pointing out that Max and Willa are looking quite cozy these days." Ellen slides in next to me, looping her purse on the chair behind her. She starts flicking through some paparazzi shots of Max and Willa on location on her phone. Willa is sitting in his director's chair with her knees pulled up, little black Converses pigeon-toeing off the end of the chair. Max is standing over her, his worn Reds baseball cap pulled low. She's looking up at him in such an adoring way it's almost obscene. It's also exactly the picture the teenage version of me fantasized about—pulling my knees up and oh, I'm so teensy and cold and my sun-kissed hair falls over my shoulders, pouty lips with no lipstick on them and dewy skin glowing through the photograph. And I would look up at him like that and he would melt. I thought that's what love looked like. What love looks like. And apparently so do the gossip bloggers.

I see Søren walk in and wave him over. Lean and tall, Søren is every hot dad you raise your eyebrows at once they've passed you in the grocery store aisle. His wife of twenty-two years is incredible and their three kids are perhaps the cutest in the entire world. Basically, if he weren't such a lovely man I'd loathe him.

"We should have all of our meetings here," Søren says, his Danish accent chopping the sentence into a rhythmic staccato. He pulls out his chair and examines the room. "I assume you saw the photos of Max?" Søren pours himself a glass of water from the decanter on the table. Ellen passes Søren her phone and he flips through the photos disapprovingly. "Such bullshit. That girl is the same age as my daughter. He really is quite vile." He shakes his head and hands Ellen back her phone. "Please tell me you have a plan, Olivia."

"I just might. This is different. Bigger. Our next steps have to be as undetectable as possible. People have to come to know Caroline in a totally new way."

"No pressure," Ellen says.

"But, I have the first step," I say. "There's a Halloween fair happening next week at Asterhouse. It's a local foster home. My mom knows the woman in charge and her son, who's in charge of the costumes for the fair, is an old friend—" I catch my breath and scan the glazed-over eyes of everyone at the table. "And none of this matters, but Caroline can donate some costumes and volunteer the day of." Everyone nods. "On the PR side, I'll advise her to not wear too much makeup—"

"The natural look that takes hours and a makeup artist?" Ellen laughs.

"Exactly. Speaking of, can you call Maya? Caroline would post only a photo on her own Instagram. I'm sure her Instagram is being watched. Especially now. So we can expect the photo to get picked up."

"And what's the connection to the foster home for her?" Søren asks, waving the waitress over.

"Her foundation." Søren orders chips and guacamole for the table. I love watching an oblivious man order from all parts of the menu, not just the salad section. As Ellen walks Søren through the coverage on Caroline, I scan the restaurant. It's easy to see which couples are on their first or second dates because the girl is eating with abandon. She must show her new suitor that she's "not like those other girls" and shouldn't be labeled the dreaded "high maintenance." No, he'll tell his friends later, she really eats. She's super easygoing! She's just really sporty and healthy!

He won't question how a person who eats like a stevedore still manages to weigh less than one hundred pounds. He won't notice that she goes from eating everything at their dinner dates to eating nothing because she's "had a really big lunch." He won't notice that even though she talks about loving buttery popcorn and huge bags of M&M's, the only thing she ever gets at the movie concession stand is a bottle of water. When he does start to finally put it all together, she'll reveal just the bits she thinks he can handle. And when he uncovers the whole truth—if he ever does—he'll tell his friends that she wasn't like that when they started dating. Somehow during the course of their relationship she turned crazy; something that has nothing to do with him.

The man gets off easy in this scenario. Even within the confines of the relationship, he still gets to be himself. He still gets to be beloved for who he is and live the life he had planned for himself. It's the woman who sacrifices everything, perpetually terrified that her true self, if revealed, will be seen by her lover as some sort of demon that must be exorcised.

When a woman calls herself fat, she's voicing the deep fear that she is, in fact, unlovable. It's just easier to talk about juice cleanses and Cardio Barre than the deep abiding shame we fear is threaded into our DNA.

"We don't have time to waste," I say.

"But, we can't risk this looking like . . . well, exactly what it is," Søren says with a shrug.

"I like that it's a small local event not in Los Angeles or somewhere . . . you know," Ellen says.

"I like that, too," I say.

"What's the connection again?" Ellen asks.

"A friend of mine from high school is in charge of the costumes," I say.

"I keep forgetting you grew up here. So few people do," Søren says.

The waitress brings over the chips and guacamole and we order a selection of tacos, a little gem salad for Caroline, and one for myself. I also order some *elote,* which is grilled sweet corn with spices and lime squeezed over the top. When Caroline arrives she will be seated with her back to the restaurant, to lower the risk of a photo of her putting food in her mouth.

Just then, Caroline pushes open the door. She scans the restaurant as all the patrons try not to look at her. I put my hand up and she smiles. I watch as she moves through the crowded restaurant with a polite "Excuse me" here, a gentle hand on a shoulder there. She slinks and slides easily through. A restaurant like this used to be my nightmare. Tight. Small, wooden parlor chairs. Clusters of condiments on tables that could easily be knocked off by a passing ass.

Søren stands and greets Caroline with a hug. I give her a warm smile. Ellen, still starstruck, lets out an excited titter. The waitress comes over and Caroline orders a sparkling water.

"So, you've seen the pictures, then?" Caroline asks, shoving her purse under the table.

"Yes," I say.

"Could she look any younger? The black Converse? It . . . why aren't people commenting on that instead of . . ." Caroline trails off. She looks tired. She also looks like she's been drinking. She's wearing minimal makeup, an oatmeal-colored cashmere wrap, and jeans with a pair of booties. Her hair is swept up and she keeps brushing a rogue hair out of her eyes as she speaks.

"Instead of what? What have you heard?" I ask. Caroline doesn't look at me. "Did you read the comments?" She acts like she's looking for the waitress. "Caroline?" She shrugs and deflates.

"I know. I know, okay? You know I'm usually really good about that, but this whole thing is just . . ." She waves her hands around. "Throwing me off."

"I was saying the same thing, actually. About her age. I don't know why more people aren't bothered by it," Søren says in that calm, soothing voice of his.

"It's predictable, yet disappointing," I say.

"God forbid a woman leave her husband for a much younger man. What a wanton whore," Caroline says.

"However much we think we've progressed . . . ," I trail off. Caroline nods. The waitress sets down plate after plate of tacos. *Poblano*. Crispy beef and pickle. *Carne asada*. Pork ribs. *Jamón con queso*. Ellen scoots in her chair.

"I haven't eaten anything all day," Ellen says, flipping her napkin onto her lap. "Preparing for this very moment."

The waitress brings over our little gem salads. A quick snap of her eyes at Caroline. The waitress is about to . . . she wants to say something to Caroline, but knows she can't. Another smile. A lingering look.

"Can I get you something to drink?" she finally asks.

"I already have the soda water, but thank you so much," Caroline says.

"Oh, right?! Right . . . I . . . I'm so sorry."

"I could easily be talked into a whisky soda if you have that kind of thing," Caroline says.

"We do not!" The waitress laughs way too hard. "Okay! Let me know if you need anything else. Whisky soda?!" A nod and a bow and the waitress says her goodbyes. Søren pulls several tacos onto his plate, as does Ellen. I eat my salad and even allow myself a few bites of the *elote*. It's probably one of my favorite things in the world.

"Okay. I have a lead on something and wanted to run it by you," I say. Caroline nods, her mouth full. "There's a Halloween fair at a foster home near where I grew up. They're looking for costume donations so none of the kids will be left out, and maybe volunteer help the day of. I thought because of the work you do through your foundation, this might be something you'd be interested in."

"Would you be up for donating?" Søren asks.

"Oh, absolutely," Caroline says without hesitation. "That's really . . . I like this a lot." Caroline smiles.

"Good," Søren says, taking a huge bite of his taco.

"I remember—God, I must have been six or seven? Anyway, you know my home life wasn't the greatest. It's why I started the foundation. I would have killed for something after school. Especially something where I got to make stuff?" Caroline is quiet. Distant. "That would have been . . . it would have saved me." She takes a sip of her sparkling water as I can see her starting to get more emotional than she was ready for. Her seemingly idyllic, middle-class, Midwestern upbringing taught Caroline that keeping the status quo meant she couldn't tell the truth about how loveless her cold parents were to her and her siblings. "It was getting to be Halloween and my parents just couldn't . . . wouldn't . . . whatever, it got to the day of and I had no costume." I've never heard this story before. "We had one of those costume parade things and the morning of, I just panicked. I wrapped a towel around my shoulders, grabbed my little rollie-suitcase, and put some too-small cowboy hat on my head, and said I was a Super Hobo." I bark out a laugh and Caroline leans back in her chair, letting her head fall back. "Super Hobo!"

"Super Hobo," I repeat, gasping for breath.

"Why? Why did . . . why was that my go-to?" Caroline asks, wheezing with laughter, too. Søren and Ellen don't know quite how to react, so they're both wearing what can only be described as amused smiles. "But, I walked my Super Hobo ass proudly around that playground, telling everyone the story of my time on the rails."

"I love that," I say. Caroline's Super Hobo should meet my

Sweaty Marble. They've turned out to be quite the similar pair of ghosts.

"So, if I can save one kid from having to throw together their own Super Hobo costume, maybe something good can come out of this circus after all," Caroline says. This. This is the Caroline I want everyone to know. This is the Real Caroline Lang.

We finish dinner as we work through our whole plan of attack. Timelines. Social media campaigns. Polaroids and sketches from Caroline's stylist. The schedule for the *Blue Christmas* junket. Ellen gives us the most up-to-date intel from her Secret Underground Intern Army: Max's PR camp and what they're up to (stomping out fires as they come, playing up the Ice Queen angle), the buzz on Max and Willa's movie (bad) as opposed to the buzz on Caroline's new movie (good), and the groundswell reaction to the impending divorce (Caroline made him cheat). Ellen's voice shakes when she repeats this last one.

As we're walking out of Escuela, I see that it's started raining. Pretty hard, in fact. Caroline's driver, Richard, is standing by her waiting car with an umbrella. He's parked in the valet zone. Because Escuela is so cramped, a group of four people are forced to wait for their car outside. But the valet can't pull in until Richard moves the Escalade. Being in Southern California and thusly never expecting it to rain, the group is getting soaked as their car idles just a few feet away. With the crush of paparazzi, they can't walk around to get to their car. They are stuck and getting more and more drenched as Caroline eases her way out of the restaurant.

We finally get outside, and Richard immediately comes over and puts the umbrella over Caroline, and everything is happening so fast that when one of the paparazzi yells, "Why does everyone have to wait for their car but you?" I can't stop Caroline from saying:

"Because I'm Caroline Lang."

And just like that, we're in Damage Control.

YOU LOOK LOST

"Because I'm Caroline Lang?" I mumble to myself as I drive to Ben's elementary school after an utterly sleepless night. By the time we got home, the major gossip sites had *Because I'm Caroline Lang* as their headline, and some were already connecting the two terrible pieces of what is fast becoming an abysmal puzzle: Why is Max Walsh cheating with Willa Lindholm? . . . because she's Caroline Lang. It was a joke, by the way. That's what Caroline said. The actual line was, "Because I'm Caroline Lang, right?" It was her way of taking a dig at how even though she's the one getting cheated on, it's her fault because she's such an icy bitch.

Except no one heard the "right." And no one thought it was funny.

And it's only Monday.

It took me way too long to get ready this morning. I didn't want to look like I was trying too hard, or like I was flirting, or like I was desperate, or like I was fat or like I was too thin or like I was old or like I thought I was younger than I am. I wanted to find an outfit I felt good in, but everything I chose made me feel too . . . exposed, somehow. I ended up choosing a basic black skirt and a white shirt. Black pumps and a black bag. I have a black sweater if it gets cold. So, apparently one thing I wasn't afraid of looking like was that I'm on my way to a funeral.

I drain my morning smoothie just as I'm pulling into one of the diagonal parking spaces in front of the school. I search for the main office, skirting around little duckling lines of kids threading through the playground. There's a part of me—a very small part—that's thankful for Caroline's flub: As I walk to meet The Ben Dunn, the only thing pinging around in my head is "Because I'm Caroline Lang. Because I'm Caroline Lang. Because I'm Caroline Lang." Of course, that's not completely true. Every time I imagine seeing Ben again and really talking to him this time, I get so nervous I have to stop thinking about it. I still put one foot in front of the other but I'm sure my face is frozen in some haunting death mask of horror.

"You look lost," a woman in a flowing skirt and Birken-stocks says.

"I am. Desperately," I say.

"Who are you looking for?" She tells a little boy to slow down, shifts a stack of paper from one arm to the other, and focuses back on me.

"Ben Dunn?" His name. His goddamn name still ripples through me like electricity.

"Ah, yes." Is she smirking? Does she . . . does she think this is . . . what does she think is—

"I'm here on business," I say, my voice about eight decibels louder than it should be.

"Oh," she says. Again with the knowing smile. I will kill this woman.

"Is he . . ."

"Principal's office is through there," she says, pointing two doors down the hallway. A little sign reads FRONT OFFICE.

"Thank you," I say. The woman walks on as I smooth my skirt down, hoping to dry my clammy hands in the process. I will myself to walk. A deep breath. A slow exhalation. A swallow. Slide my purse back on my shoulder. And I walk into the front office.

A large counter anchors a tiny bluish room. Children's art covers the walls in joyful explosions: pictures of circle people with stick legs, their grins tracing from ear to ear, rainbows and fluffy clouds all atop shaky lines of green grass. The large windows on the back wall are frosted? Filthy? Both?

The little room feels like . . . real Cokes wrapped in tinfoil, and sitting by myself at lunch. It smells like being chosen last at team sports and packs of kids I wanted to be friends with more than anything making fun of me. It smells like wanting to belong and not understanding why I don't get to.

"You need to sign in." THAT. SAME. WOMAN. She swans past me and stands behind the counter.

"Oh," I say, eyeing the clipboard and pen with a giant daisy on the tip.

Olivia Morten   8:41 a.m.   Ben Dunn

"He'll be right with you," she says, settling behind a desk in the far corner. She motions to two child-sized wooden chairs like they're just perfect for adults to sit in. I glance around the room. A door emblazoned with PRINCIPAL BENJAMIN DUNN is just next to the two chairs. She motions again. Her lank brownish-grayish hair, sallow complexion, and all-around ennui bring back the frustration I had even as a kid. I knew full well that certain authority figures had no right telling anyone what to do. I look at her old-timey nameplate: JOANNE BLANK. It takes all I've got not to break into hysterics. Never has a person been so aptly named. I squat almost to the floor and finally find the seat of the tiny chair. My knees are pressed against my chest and right then Ben bursts in.

"Joanne, can you call Bryce, someone threw up by the baseball diam—oh? Olivia. Hi," Ben says, stopping in front of me. I try to stand, but I can't get any traction and the tight black skirt and the stupid fucking lowest chair in the world and can someone actually die from embarrassment and rage? LET'S FIND OUT. Ben extends his hand. "Little help?"

Oh my god. I hitch my purse on my shoulder. One more failed attempt to do it myself. "Olivia. Let me help you." In a fit of held breath and sheer unadulterated fury, I take his hand. Rough, strong fingers curl around mine, but I still don't trust him. So I try again to get up on my own, at which time he puts his other hand around my waist and hoists me up out of the seat. "You're as bad as Tilly." He loops my purse back over my shoulder.

"Thanks . . . I . . . my whole life passed before my eyes and it was apparently going to be spent sitting in that chair," I say, smoothing my skirt down again. Ben laughs. I look up at him smiling. Tall and looming, he's too close and his hand has yet to be unwound from my waist.

"Principal Dunn? What's a baseball dime?" Joanne asks in that unhurried, leisurely tone.

"I'm sorry?" Ben asks, finally letting me go.

"You told me someone vomited on the baseball dime, but I don't think I know what that is," Joanne says, smiling, the phone receiver in her hand. Ben's starched collar. The nick he got shaving this morning. The faint brown speckles in the pale blue of just his right eye. Chipping pink nail polish on two of his fingernails that I'm hoping was done by one of his daughters.

"The baseball diamond, Joanne. It's the baseball diamond," Ben says.

"Oh, yes. That makes much more sense," Joanne says, dialing the phone.

"Shall we?" Ben asks, pushing open the door with his name on it in black lettering. He waits for me to enter first and then closes the door behind him. "Joanne came with the job. People keep telling me she's an institution."

"Like the DMV," I say.

Ben laughs. "That's . . . that's it exactly. She's the DMV of people." He settles in behind his desk. He shakes his head and reaches for a mug that says *World's Best Dad* and takes a sip of what looks to be stone-cold black coffee.

"Thank you for seeing me today," I say.

"You're welcome, but as I said—"

"I assure you, it's not—I'm sorry, I should let you finish."

"Please. Continue," he says, sitting back in his chair.

"Mom mentioned that you were looking for donations for the Halloween fair at Asterhouse," I say, deciding to start at the beginning.

"I am."

"I can help with that."

"Hm."

"What?"

"My concern is that this charity will come at a cost and that makes me nervous."

"Caroline Lang can help. She wants to help." I sit back in my chair. Think. "She's a good person." Another moment. I look at Ben. He's listening.

"So where do I come in?"

"I want to show people the Caroline I know, and I think if she can donate some costumes and maybe just volunteer the day of the fair, it'll allow her to be seen in a different light. No outside photographers, no media circus. She'll post one picture on her own Instagram, but no kids will be in it." Ben moves his chair forward and leans on his desk, folding his hands. The two chipped pink fingernails are on full display. "I also think it'll be good for her. Personally."

"I'm having a hard time following—"

"She'd be just another volunteer."

"No, that I get." Ben unfolds his hands and taps his fingers. I wait.

"And the kids would benefit greatly."

"I feel like we're skirting around the biggest issue here," he says.

"I think her fame will bring much-needed interest to this charity."

"You hate me." Ben waits. "Right?"

"I . . . what?" First, I'm stunned. Maybe a little embarrassed. And then I get mad.

"And? You're not this nice," he says.

I lean forward in my chair. "I'm not this nice?" I repeat, making sure to hit the word "nice" with particular vigor.

"Yeah."

I'm speechless. I've never been so obviously hoisted on my own petard before. I knew this was a fool's errand, fueled by some teenage need to show Ben how much I've changed and how above everything I am now. Look at me, asking you for a favor. Yawn, let bygones be bygones. Ignoring the obvious: that our shared history should be toured like an old Civil War battlefield. Yes, and here is where Ben laughed when Olivia dropped her Lunchables. And if you turn to the left quickly, you'll see where Olivia asked Ben this famous question, "Which do you think makes you dumber, playing football or being a ginger?"

"I am not here to make you pay for who you were in high school. I am not here to humiliate you," I finally say. He clears his throat. Locks his eyes on mine once again. A furrowed brow.

"Why do I feel like that's exactly what all this is about?" he asks, his voice a low growl.

"You're not the only one who's haunted by who you were in high school."

We are quiet.

"I'm sorry," I finally say. "I'm sorry, too. I should have said it the other night."

"I don't know. Lou was talking with me about those superheroes and how sometimes you need a person who is kind of a villain to take out the bigger villain. And the kind of villain who is . . . what did she say, only bad because people had been mean to them."

"So my badness was only because of you? I don't buy it."

"No, not because of me. Because of something that happened before me. Your origin story, if you will."

"This is a very existential conversation about a bunch of people in tights."

"At least you're not the bigger villain in this scenario. The one beyond redemption."

"That's a bit dramatic, don't you think?" I ask. Ben laughs.

"Okay," Ben says.

"Okay," I repeat.

"No, I mean okay, okay—Caroline can come," he says, pulling a pencil out of a little tin, grabbing a pad of paper.

"Really?" I ask. Ben scribbles a list of names on the pad of paper.

"Really," he says.

"Thank you," I say, breathing easy. I smile. "Thank you." A pure, unadulterated smile. Ben rips off the top paper and slides it across the desk. He keeps writing.

"Here's a list of costumes some of the kids wished for and their sizes," he says. Falcon. Doctor. Belle. Train engineer. Batman. "Can Caroline take care of all five?"

"She'd love to." I remember her Super Hobo story. I think she's really going to love doing this. Ben stands. Caught off guard, I stand as well.

"Falcon is the superhero, not the bird." I nod. "And here's your list," he says, handing me another sheet of paper. "You're donating, too." I look at him. "And that's every kid accounted for. I can finally be taken off Mom's list. About this, anyway. I have yet to disclose whether my freezer can hold my parents' excess bacon, sausage, and ham." He smiles and I can't help but join him. He walks around his desk. "I have a meeting in ten minutes. I'm sorry to rush you." I walk toward the door reading my list. Rapunzel. Fireman.

"What's a Rocket? Like, a rocket?" I shoot my arm into the

air like a spaceship. Ben laughs as he opens the door, motioning for me to go first.

"No. That's Rocket Raccoon. He's . . . it's hard to explain. Just Google him." Joanne doesn't look up as we pass through the front office. She's misting some dying plant that's next to her computer. The water misses the browning leaves and hits the keyboard.

"Rocket Raccoon," I repeat, folding the papers up and putting them into my purse.

"He's kind of amazing." Ben folds his arms across his chest and stops just outside his office. He scans the hallways—his domain. Little kids chirp their hellos as they carefully pass, giggling and speeding up their pace as they get out of range. "The details for the Halloween fair are also on the paper. When and where and all that." He smiles. "Let me think a bit about what booth she can work." I pull a card from my purse and hand it to him.

"That's all my information, so you can let me know?" I ask, seeing that the fair is this Friday. Which is going to be tight. All hell may break loose before then. But, this is the right way. This is the plan.

"See you Friday, then," he says.

"Friday," I say, standing there. Awkward. "Okay. I'll let you get to your meeting." He extends his hand and I take it. "Thanks again."

"Drive safe," he says. I nod. We let our hands go. Another nod. I wave. He waves. I walk down the hallway. I look back once. He's still there. Another wave. I wave and turn back around and hurry out of the school before I make him wave again. Only when I get to my car do I see Ben continue on to his meeting. I close my car door and let the silence surround me.

"What the fuck is a Rocket Raccoon," I mutter. I file away the day's events. I can't think about . . . My face flushes as I remember my words. No. Don't think about it. Remember? That was the . . . *You're not this nice.* A sigh. I put the key in the ignition and take my phone out of my purse. Texts from Ellen. A missed call from Søren. I sit in the car and catch up on what was apparently the wrong twenty minutes to leave my phone in my purse. Putting out more fires. Setting up meetings. Putting in a call to Caroline's agent and another to her manager. I schedule a time to speak with Caroline later on this morning.

I reach over my shoulder for my seatbelt. It tangles and twists around my hand and my shoulder. It gets stuck. Pull . . . stuck. Pull . . . stuck. And I pull harder and . . . stuck. Stuck. Stuck. Stuck.

"SHIT PISS FUCK," I yell. The rage comes exploding out of me in the silence and calm of my car on this emptied-out street. "Shitpissfuck." I bury my face in my hands. Make it go away. Make it all go away.

What am I doing here? In what world does my only plan for Caroline's redemption involve Ben Dunn, a man famous for saying that his high school conquests had "been done by Ben Dunn." To what lengths am I willing to go to prove that my past is truly behind me? Mean shit? You better believe he said a lot of mean shit. And what? Just because he lets his adorable daughters paint his fingernails pink, he's no longer the same person who tormented anyone who couldn't chug a beer or throw a football?

Why do our teenage crushes hold such sway over us? Even as adults, these crushes continue to hold a place in our hearts that we would never bestow upon them as the people we are now. But, oh, to be the object of a teenage girl's affection. Our crush's mere presence will reduce a grown woman to rubble simply because he represents the ideal of something much too complicated to grasp as a teenager: True Love.

I loved Ben Dunn at a time when he could be the only thing that mattered. I could pine away for him twenty-four hours a day because I hadn't yet begun to exist. Factor in the worrisome amount of disagreement I received at the hands of my One True Love and you've got yourself quite the after-school special. Of course, I didn't see that at all. I was taught—through movies and television—that if you argued with someone as much as Ben and I did, that you actually loved one another. I hate you! No, I hate you! (Cue passionate make-out session.) These unrealistic expectations, coupled with the glimpses I'd get of Ben being a good person (to other people), and I was hooked. We were meant for one another. He just didn't know it yet . . . even though he totally did deep down.

Loving him was simple and bewitching and in my dreams of us I was beautiful. He was my savior at a time when I didn't know I could be my own.

I could give him everything, because I didn't yet know that I should save some for myself.

But, that was then. Just because I had a crush on him when I was a teenager doesn't mean I have to be shackled to him for the rest of my life. I can stop this. I can send one email to Ben, untangle this entire mess, and then never see him or anyone from high school ever again. But, I'm not the old Olivia, and even if he's still the same old Ben Dunn, it shouldn't matter. I can do this. I've got this. I'm not the Fat Me anymore. He can't make fun of me if I don't allow it. He can't make me feel like shit if I don't give him permission, right? That's how this works. No. I have to go forward with this to prove to myself that I've changed. Ben can't get to me like he once did. He can't.

I won't let him.

ROOMMATE ISSUES

The rest of the day is a blur. Coffee. Phone calls. Meetings. Ellen running in and out of my office. At one point she has four phones in her hands. More coffee. More phone calls. I inhale my usual lunch of cottage cheese, fresh berries, and a dash of cinnamon. I make myself take a lap around the office.

Thanks to my tip-off, Caroline is photographed leaving a Starbucks in Zuma, and she Instagrams a photo of her coffee with the name "MARILYN" scrawled across it. Her caption is, "So maybe not everyone thinks it's because I'm Caroline Lang." Now, that's funny. The public's sentiment tilts just a bit in her favor as people Regram her quip.

At the end of the day, after a particularly grueling meeting with a new client, I retreat to my office. And sit. We survived. Caroline told me her lawyer is finishing up the paperwork and she'll be ready to file right before the courthouse closes on Friday—just in time for everyone to have gone home from work and not be in front of their computers. She seemed . . . distant. I wanted to ask if she had anyone she could be with tonight, but I didn't. Maybe what she wants is a bottle of wine, some bad television, and her 8 o'clock pants. Or maybe that's what I want. Let's face it, that's what we all want.

As the office empties out, I take the opportunity to do a quick Internet search for Ben. I troll the various social medias. Nothing? Who has nothing? I find an old article about him from when he was the backup quarterback at USC. He was charged with drunk and disorderly and was let off with a fine. The photo that goes along with the article is prime Ben Dunn. He's just taken off his football helmet and his thick reddish-blond hair is swooped up in a messy tangle. Sweat and dirt cover his face. That face. Boyish yet utterly masculine. Hooded blue eyes, just the right amount of freckles, and a crooked smile that's almost cliché in its roguishness. Ben is everything your mother warned you to stay away from. And as is always the way with men, he's only gotten better with age.

"It's not fair," I say, closing out of the article.

"What's not fair?" Ellen asks, rushing into my office.

"Life, my dear Ellen. Life," I say, sitting back from my desk.

"Sometimes it's kind of fair," Ellen says. I look up at her. "Take, for instance, this example." Ellen shows me her phone. On it is Max Walsh photographed with another young stunning woman that is neither Willa Lindholm nor Caroline Lang.

"He really needs to stop wearing that bright red baseball cap," Ellen says.

"You're only as faithful as your options," I mutter, scrolling through the pictures.

"No one knows who she is, but . . ." Ellen takes the phone

back and flicks to a particularly flirty-looking picture of Max and the Unidentified Blonde (as she will come to be known). "Come on." She hands me back the phone. "What a dumbass." The photos look like they're at a dive bar probably somewhere around where they're filming. The pictures are grainy. A telephoto lens was used or someone took them on their phone. This required some patience. The photos also mean that the tabloids are now willing to burn their bridges with Max and Willa's publicists just so they can be the first to provide further proof of the crumbling Lang/Walsh marriage. Usually you can control tabloids by threatening that their access to your clients is worth their patience—or outright silence in some cases. These photos are evidence that the tide has turned.

"Caroline's filing Friday, these will help us. Do we know where these pictures are going to be posted?" I ask, gathering my purse and coat. Ellen rattles off the usual suspects and I nod.

"You look exhausted," she says, her fingers flying over her phone's keypad.

"It's been a long day," I say. I walk from behind my desk and follow Ellen out into the bull pen. There are a few assistants still here and I see Søren in the conference room with a handful of people. I give him a wave and he smiles, giving me the international gesture that he'll call me later. I nod. "You'll text if you hear anything from your army of informants?"

"First rule of informants," Ellen whispers.

"Right. Sorry. Don't talk about informants," I say. Ellen puts her finger to the side of her nose and quickly walks back to her desk. "You scare me sometimes," I yell to her.

"Good!"

An uneventful elevator ride down to the gym on the ground floor of our building. I change into my workout gear and do an hour of cardio followed by thirty minutes of weights. It feels good. No phone. No email. No urgent calls from Caroline. No leaked photos from Max. Just terrible pop music pounding in my ears as I run on a treadmill and watch the muted nightly news.

As I do my sets of sit-ups, I replay the morning with Ben, convincing myself that this is what closure feels like. And up. This is what it feels like to not care about someone. And up. He's part of my past. And up. Working with him on this Caroline deal is only proof of that. And up. And up. And up.

I lean back on my hands and sit cross-legged in front of the mirror as my abs burn. Her. The woman in the mirror. That's who is unaffected by Ben Dunn. That's who will walk away from this situation with her shoulders pushed back and head held high having, once and for all, rewritten history. She's the woman I've become. She's who I am now.

He's really sorry. A whisper. In the back of my head. Tiny. High-pitched. I get ready to do push-ups. Plank. And down. And down. He's really sorry. And down. And down. No. If I acknowledge his apology, that means it still hurts. And down. And it doesn't. Down. The girl he made fun of is long gone. Long gone. And Ben's apology about some mean shit he said doesn't mean anything because whatever it was he said is long forgotten. And down. AND DOWN AND DOWN AND DOWN. I let my knees fall to the mat and lean back, my head falling between my outstretched arms.

"I'm not her anymore," I whisper to the sweaty mat. I sit back on my haunches and repeat the words in my head. *I'm not her anymore.* I try to make myself see the woman in the mirror. That's who you are now, Olivia Morten. Look at you. Look at you. But, I can't. I just look at the sweaty mat and push myself up to a standing position and walk to the changing room.

Back in my car, sweaty and noodle-armed, I put my purse on the floor and the paper with the directions to Ben's school flits down after it. I pick it up and set it on the passenger seat. I start my car. A quick glance to the paper.

Wait. What? A receipt for the Post Ranch Inn. It's dark in the parking garage. I pick up the paper, my own writing seeping through from the other side. The Post Ranch Inn in Big Sur is where Adam and I went on our honeymoon. It's the place we go to get away. It's the place we go to forget the real world. Everything is always perfect at the Post Ranch Inn. The receipt is for the Coast House. It's for just a . . . I swallow. It's for just a couple of weeks ago. When Adam was supposed to be at a conference in Denver.

Yesterday. Adam staring at the receipt after I cavalierly wrote the directions for Ben's school on the back of it. That's right. That's how it got in this car and that's why he was none too keen that I'd commandeered it. I put the piece of paper on the passenger seat of my car and reverse out of my parking space. This is easily remedied. I won't let this become some weird misunderstanding. Adam is at the hospital tonight. I'll just go ask him.

My mind is clear in that eerie calm-before-the-storm kind of way. I won't think about it. I will drive. I listen to my steady breathing. The breathing begins to muffle in my ears as it gets harder and harder to focus on just driving. I blink. And blink. Clear my throat. It's like my body is giving me errands to run so I have something else to think about. I pull into the hospital's parking structure. Grab my purse. Grab the paper. Stand there. Fold the paper and put it in my purse. Arrange my face. Collect myself.

And I walk through the maze of the hospital. Long hallways. Elevators. Another long hallway. Get buzzed in. Two lefts and a right. Tight corner and I approach the nurses' station that my husband calls his home base. The foam containers with the Mediterranean food I ordered from work earlier this evening litter the nurses' station.

"Olivia?" Nurse Brenda Cawley. Has seen everything and can just as easily take your temperature as bring you back to life. Wiry, blond, and leather-faced, she comes out from behind the nurses' station. The other two nurses look at each other as she walks toward me.

"Is the . . . is that my . . . the dinner I sent for Adam? Is he here? Dr. Farrell?" I ask. The two other young nurses busy themselves so poorly that it's almost embarrassing.

"Come here, hon," Brenda says, her head twitching toward a private corner.

"If you can just point me to where Adam is, or is he in surgery?" I ask.

"He's not here," Brenda says, folding her arms across her chest. She watches me.

"Oh," I say.

"I don't know how much of this you're going to wanna know," Brenda says, her voice clear and strong. Brenda is very comfortable with giving people terrible news. I ready myself. I hesitate. I start and stop a few sentences and Brenda watches me drowning. "The dinners. Let's start there. My theory? You send them when he tells you he's working late?" I nod yes.

"He's not. We eat them." Brenda motions over her shoulder to where the other two nurses are watching. They jump back into "looking busy" mode. "They're very good and I just never knew how to tell you. How do you say thank you for something you're not supposed to be eating? We felt terrible."

"The dinners were for you guys," I say.

"Olivia, you—"

"A thank-you from me to you. For all the hard work you do for Adam." I back away from Brenda.

"Okay," Brenda says, resting her hands on her hips. "Well, thank you for them."

"You're welcome," I say, with a smile. "I'd better get on home. Adam's probably there now."

"Yeah, okay," Brenda says, her voice flat.

"Okay. Okay, then. Enjoy the food and hey, how's your oldest doing at college?" I ask, beelining for the exit.

"She's good. Having some roommate issues, but who doesn't."

"Who doesn't," I repeat.

"You take care of yourself," Brenda says.

"I will," I say.

"Bye, now." Brenda tucks back behind the nurses' station. The two younger nurses gather around her and I can't even watch. I press the elevator button. Again. Again. Again. Again. Again. It finally comes and my head is pounding as it descends. Through the maze of hallways, various lefts and rights and I continue past the sick and grieving. At least here I fit right in. No one questions why a woman is near tears as she speeds down a hallway. I'm among friends.

Graduation cards. Christmas presents. Flowers for weddings. I've known Brenda as long as Adam has been a surgeon at the hospital. I've seen the other two nurses at various holiday parties and company events. They seem nice enough. Efficient, Adam says. I burst out into the crisp night air and I'm back in my car.

What I didn't tell Brenda is that I know. I've known all along. And not just about this last woman Adam is cheating on me with. I've known about all of them.

I just didn't want anyone else to know.

WHAT THE STAINED SHIRT SAYS

There's a bench on this winding street that overlooks the 110
freeway. I always notice people sitting on it as I drive home.
In a time of so much digital stimulation, the view from this
simple bench is just as compelling as any streaming television
show. Which is why I finally stopped there on my way home
from the hospital to drink the single can of beer I bought at
a corner liquor store and try to figure out what to do next.

I park the car, stow my purse—phone and all—under the
passenger seat, grab the beer still in the small brown bag, and
walk over to the bench. A young man and his dog are walking along the low stone wall that separates the winding road
from the steep drop-off into the Arroyo. The young man looks
at the paper bag, then at me. A respectful nod as he walks
past. I sit, crack open the beer, and take a long drink.

As I've known for almost a year, her name is Nicola
McKesson and she's an orthopedic surgeon who works at the

hospital. This time around, I made the conscious decision not to stalk Adam's newest fling on social media. I don't want to put a face to a name, nor do I want to cast the role of the woman who's currently bedding my husband. Nonetheless, I can hazard a guess as to what this Nicola McKesson looks like. She's neither pretty nor ugly; she's what I call Pageant Plain. On the beauty pageant spectrum—wholesome pretty, not slutty hot—but unremarkable. She's the woman you'll drunkenly tell your friends, "But, I'm so much hotter than she is," and you'd be right. But, he still chose her over you. I take another swig of the beer and watch the red and white lights of the cars on the freeway snake through the valley just below.

Adam was my first. Everything. I'd never had a boyfriend, I'd never even dated, let alone had sex with anyone. I'd never even held hands with a boy before him. No, I had unrequited crushes on boys who were way out of my league (see: Ben Dunn) and built out my fantasies until they felt as real as possible. Another swig. I went from a thousand-pound virgin weirdo to whatever this version of me is, all the while expecting myself to catch up on the myriad intricate relationship lessons you're supposed to learn in your teens and twenties.

So when I found out about Sarah—the first woman Adam cheated on me with, about a year into our marriage—I thought our marriage was over. But, the other shoe never dropped. Margaret was short-lived and made a few tragic phone calls to the house. Then there was Amber—whom I caught sitting outside our house on more than one occasion. Then Kate—a dim-witted brunette who taught us Pilates for a time. As they came and went (literally), I began to understand that these dalliances had little to do with our marriage or the life we were building together. These women were essentially the golf of Adam's busy schedule—a hobby I wasn't interested in and was happy he did with other people.

But, lately I've begun to fear that Nicola is different. Adam has been seeing her for going on a year and I'm beginning to worry that whatever he has with her will start affecting us. Am I losing him? Why would he take her to the Post Ranch Inn? That's our place.

That's our place.

I twist the pop top can opener off and flip it around in my hands. Our honeymoon at the Post Ranch Inn was the closest my life ever came to my teenage fantasy. The rose petals on the bed, the candlelit dinners, and the bathrobes that actually fit were all secondary to the overwhelming feeling that I'd finally crossed the finish line. I'd made it. I'd been chosen. So, I have to believe that it's not the same for them. Any idiot can go to the Post Ranch Inn. Even Nicola.

Because, as always—nothing about him has changed. He is the same man I married. There's been no ebb and flow with his attention, he hasn't started working out or dressing better. He is Adam. Another swig. My Adam. Our Adam? His own Adam, apparently.

This is fine. This is manageable. This is marriage. Ten years down the line, a good marriage is less about lust and flipping stomachs and more about unwavering things like last-minute dinners for hospital board members and getting a serving dish down from a high shelf. In the end, I have to believe that marriages like ours last longer than the seemingly exciting, more volatile ones that soon fall prey to the whims of love.

Maybe this fling with Nicola is about the deal Adam and

I made not to think about kids until we'd been married for ten years. We wanted time to ourselves as husband and wife before we took on the next chapter as parents. So, Nicola feels different because maybe he's thinking she'll be the last dalliance before he truly settles down.

My marriage is solid. I am happy and fulfilled.

I chug the rest of the beer, drop the pop top can opener inside, crumple the can up, and toss it toward the bin. I make the shot.

"See? My luck is already turning." I let out an incredibly loud burp. It echoes into the valley below.

I shift on the bench. Clear my throat. Watch the red and white lights.

He's never out-and-out lied to me before.

"Of course, he has," I say out loud.

Of course, he has. I just never found out before. Okay. Hold on a second. I'm forgetting the most important thing. I am his wife. Not Nicola. Let's remind everyone of that, shall we? Including Adam.

I put my feet up on the stone wall and slip down a bit on the bench.

"I can't lose him," I say in a whisper so it won't echo.

I can figure this out. I will figure this out.

Thanks to that light beer being basically colored water, I'll be okay to drive home after just a few more minutes. I sit in my car scrolling through my text messages and emails. Gus Ford, my youngest client and current *GQ* cover boy, who's just landed a starring role in the newest superhero movie, is apparently having a meltdown at Chateau Marmont. Ellen is on it, but there may already be some photos of him on social media. I give her the name of their security guy and have her send champagne to the rooms closest to Gus's with a note of apology. As I drive, I call his manager and we circle the wagons. By the time I get home, Ellen has confirmed that the only photos are blurry and it just looks like he's having a good time at the bar. I tell her to get him in my office first thing tomorrow.

I walk up to what I know will be an empty house and think about how slowly tonight's events unfolded. It wasn't this explosive! shocking! humiliating! discovery. Have I been as much to blame for Adam's dalliances as he has? I unlock the front door and walk through my enchanting silent home. I make my chicken salad. Set out a place mat, flip my napkin onto my lap, and eat dinner alone. I wash my face and get ready for bed in a haze of shame and regret with a chaser of rage and determination. I can't think clearly right now, tonight's events just keep replaying on a manic loop in my head.

I plug in my phone and crawl into bed. As I struggle to fall asleep, I get a text from Ellen with a screenshot of Caroline's latest Instagram post: a photo of a silhouetted girl dancing at sunset with the quote "Not to decide is to decide" written over it.

"Borderline," I type back.

"Should we have her delete it?" Ellen texts back.

"Too late now." I put my phone back on the nightstand and pull the covers up to my shoulders.

Adam didn't come home last night. I knew he wouldn't. As I tossed and turned, I started putting the pieces together. And the result was this giant middle finger I never saw before. Or only caught glimpses of.

I shake my head as I wait to pull into the parking structure early the next morning. The dinners and the late nights. Is he hiding his infidelities in the cracks of a busy life? Hell, am I hiding his infidelities in the cracks of my busy life?

I leave for work at 7:30 a.m. and don't get home until well after 8 p.m. When I do finally get home, I make dinner and prepare for the following day: pack my gym bag, get my work clothes ready, make my lunch, and gather the ingredients for my morning smoothie. When I don't fall asleep watching television, I crawl into bed looking at my phone until I'm startled awake when it drops on my face.

I wave my parking permit in front of the machine. Again. Again.

"Come the fuck on." I press it against the machine. "Better? Do you see me now?" The machine reads, "One moment, please."

"Pull back," the parking kid says. "Pull it back."

"It's not—" I pull the parking permit back and the boom barrier lifts. "Going to be quite a day." The parking kid smiles and I drive through.

I wend my way through the parking structure, trying to find a spot and it dawns on me that Adam didn't really try to hide his infidelities—busy schedule or no. We never had a conversation about having an open marriage, but he's got to know I know.

He has to know I know, right?

I find a parking space, gather my stuff, and step into the elevator as that single question haunts me. I grunt hellos and offer distracted smiles as I walk through the office. About halfway through, I lock eyes with an intern and it's her look of jealousy and utter fear that zooms me back to the here and now. That's right. Just like no one here knows about the Sweaty Marble version of me, they also don't know that my marriage is going through a rough patch. Unlike Caroline, there aren't paparazzi taking blurry photos of Adam and Nicola canoodling at the Post Ranch Inn while their editor scours my old year-books for photos of me taking up an entire cafeteria table as I devour a breakfast burrito by myself. No, I can be the same Olivia Morten who inspires and intimidates, just like I was yesterday. I straighten up and smile brightly at the intern and she stutters some rambling morning greeting. This pleases me.

"Is Gus here yet?" I ask as Ellen rounds the corner.

"No, you would have heard swooning amongst the interns if he was," Ellen says, handing me a coffee.

"Thank you. I don't know if you'll ever come to under-stand how much I appreciate this coffee." Ellen just looks at me. Shit. Wait. No. Don't be earnest, you fool. "I'd like to thank the Academy . . ." I hold my coffee in my hands and look out onto a make-believe audience. "My parents who never gave up on me—well, my mom at least . . ."

"Speaking of . . ." Ellen walks into my office and plops down into one of the client chairs. Okay. We're back in busi-ness. That can't happen again. No room for humanity in public relations. I follow her in. "One of those ridiculously pre-tentious websites that we hate?"

"Right," I say, settling behind my desk and booting up my computer.

"Yeah, well—maybe we need to start liking them. One of them saw a rough cut of *Blue Christmas,* don't ask me how, and said that Caroline's performance in it was 'Oscar worthy.'"

"They used those words?"

"They did."

"Holy shit."

"I know."

"Has it been picked up anywhere?" I ask, clicking on the email Ellen sent me about this very subject. I follow the link and sure enough, there is the offending navel-gazing website. I scroll down to find their mention of Caroline as Ellen reads the quote aloud.

"In a film one might dismiss as the usual rom-com fluff—"

"Is this entire thing a backhanded compliment?"

"No . . . well, kind of," Ellen says. I slump back in my chair. "May I?" She holds up her phone. I nod. "In a film one might dismiss as the usual rom-com fluff, Lang offers a surprisingly layered, Oscar-worthy performance as a woman who must come to terms with a life that's not quite how she pictured it," Ellen says, letting her phone finally drop into her lap. "This is amazing, right?"

"A layered, Oscar-worthy performance," I repeat. "Okay, this is very good, but I am going to burst our bubble for just one second and then we can celebrate quickly before Gus arrives."

"Go on," Ellen says.

"I don't know if this is quite the year we want the scrutiny of an Oscar campaign. You get nominated for an Oscar, or not even that—you're rumored to be in the running to get nominated and you're expected to attend Q&As and special screenings and appearances and luncheons and junkets and round tables and festivals and at every one reporters want Caroline to be 'Oh, am I in the running for an Oscar? Little ol' me?' So she has to stress being authentic and super relatable and down to earth and off the cuff." I make sure to stress that last one.

"Off the cuff. Eesh."

"Right, so if someone comes at her with 'Mrs. Lang, how did you find and cultivate the darker aspects of this character in regards to her disintegrating marriage?'"

"Oh, no. No no no." Ellen stiffens.

"It's not like we can do anything about it, nor would we want to. I just had to say that out loud one time," I say, taking a long drink of my coffee.

"Understood," Ellen says.

"We'll just be extra vigilant."

"There's a higher gear than the one we're already using?" Ellen asks, unadulterated fear crossing her face.

"Apparently we're about to find out," I say. Ellen shudders. "Okay. First things first, we control the story as long as we can. Can you set up a call with Rachel Hatayama? She's that *Vanity Fair* writer we like." Ellen looks at me as if I've forgotten myself. "I know you know who Rachel Hatayama is."

"It's like that coffee meant nothing," Ellen says.

"The greatest gift ever bestowed on me, you mean?" I cradle it to my breast. Ellen laughs. "Set up a call and we'll offer her an exclusive—letting her know that some shit is going down and she'll want to pick up what we're putting down, you know?"

"Pick up what we're putting down?" Ellen asks.

"Yeah, you know," I say. Oh my god. What is happening? First the earnest over-the-top gratitude about a coffee, and now I'm some kind of weirdo goofball. Fat Me is really trying to break through today. She senses a chink in my armor and is going for it. Oh, Olivia, are you feeling low and vulnerable? Huzzah—I will make a terrible joke and then you'll start your period in front of the boy you like!

Take that! I regain myself. "But, we're going to need the cover."

"But—" Ellen says, typing away on her phone.

"I know it's last minute, but they can post a photo and at least part of the article online before the magazine comes out." A knock on my office door and an intern pokes her head in.

"Gus Ford is here," she says. Ellen rolls her eyes as the girl is unable to keep from sighing.

"Oh, thanks," I say. Ellen stands and begins to walk out of my office.

"No, you don't have to leave. I'm taking Gus on a little adventure. We're going Halloween costume shopping for that fair I'm taking Caroline to."

"Genius," Ellen says, staying put.

"I know," I say, striding out through the bull pen, last night's events dissipating like a fog.

Happy for the distraction, I open the door to the empty waiting room and see Gus's lanky frame huddled over his phone, San Francisco Giants baseball cap pulled low.

"Come on, kiddo. We're going on a field trip," I say.

Gus looks up, quickly pocketing a phone that was merely a prop so no one would approach him. He's wearing an old flannel, ripped jeans, and vintage Air Jordans. His overgrown dark brown hair flips and curls from under his baseball cap and it looks like he's trying to grow some kind of adorable pubescent beard. Of course, I'll get him to shave it off STAT.

But, it's his face. That heavenly face of his. The one he's been trying to hide since it was slapped across every bus, every billboard, and became the face that launched a billion-dollar tent-pole-movie franchise.

"Look, I know I'm in trouble. I just—" He tries to keep up with me as I exit the waiting room and push the button for the elevator. "I had too much to drink and was being super lame. I'm sorry, okay?" The elevator dings open and we step in. It's thankfully empty. Gus's earnest, yet completely hollow apology is the true hallmark of life in your twenties. It's a decade marked by belligerently misguided proclamations announced as if they're both bold and revolutionary. But these same bold and revolutionary pronouncements are never backed up by careful research, work experience, or other boring things like letting oneself learn and be humbled by someone who might know better. No, step aside! Here comes a twenty-five-year-old with all the answers!

"What happened at the Marmont is only a symptom," I say.

"A symptom? What . . . what does that even mean?" He crosses his arms over his newly bulked-up chest. To me, he looks like a little boy wearing one of those superhero Halloween costumes that comes with built-in muscles. He clears his throat.

"It's the stained shirt at Comic-Con," I say.

"Oh my god, we're back to the stained shirt at Comic-Con. That was three months ago!" Gus's voice cracks in frustration. He pulls his baseball cap off his head and runs his fingers through his dirty, mussed hair.

"Because that's when this whole thing started." The elevator dings open at the parking garage and we walk to my car in silence. Gus is shaking his head the entire time, figuring out what to say next, but trying to choose his words carefully. We load into my car. "Seatbelt." He obliges.

I can barely think about myself in my twenties without groaning. A decade of bad dye jobs, awful crushes, and dressing my newly thin body in trendy clothes that make me cringe just thinking about them. Whenever people talk shit about the millennial generation, I always point out that we were all assholes at that age. We've just done the only thing we could to survive; blocked out that whole period of our lives except for those few curated moments we've saved for our highlight reel.

"Sometimes a stained shirt is just a stained shirt," he says, as we pull out of the parking garage.

"Listen, Freud, it's what the stained shirt says, and that's what I've been trying to make you see ever since."

"What the stained shirt says? That doesn't even make sense."

"You were in Hall H at Comic-Con. Not because you borrowed money from your parents, shared a shitty hotel room with six other people, and took time off from a job that pays you barely minimum wage, just for the chance to sleep out overnight to maybe get a seat. No. You were flown down there, picked up in a luxurious town car, and put up at the best hotel where your every need was seen to. And you show up in a fucking stained shirt. So, what that stained shirt said to all of the people who had to scrimp and save and sacrifice to be there was that you didn't give a shit."

"But, I do give a shit. I give all the shits."

And right there is the secret all twentysomethings don't want you to know. Underneath all of that enraging bravado is a scared kid who doesn't want to be an adult anymore and just wants to come home. The beginning steps of the adventure into one's life are as exhilarating as they are lonely. It takes years to get a good night's sleep away from your own bed at home and far too long to learn how to feed yourself in a way that's not completely depressing. And the loneliness you feel on those nights spent by yourself in your twenties is unparalleled.

An unwelcome slide show of my own twenties flickers in the back of my mind. The sad, heartfelt pep talks I gave myself. The series of well-decorated hovels I tried to make feel like home and the constant nagging fear that there was something unfixably wrong with me. I clear my throat and focus back on Gus.

"I know you do. I do. I also know that you reeked of weed and your stylist had to buy some of the loaner designer shirts you tried on because you hadn't showered in what . . . days?" Gus is quiet. We stop at a red light. I look over at him. He's still shaking his head, but I can see from under his Wayfarers that he's started to cry. The light turns green and I pull over on a small tree-lined side street.

He takes off his sunglasses. "No one tells you that when you get famous, you're going to get all this cool stuff, but . . . ," Gus trails off, completely choked up. The sobs escape from him in such waves that he looks terrified by them. "I feel trapped. I'm trapped." I undo my seatbelt and reach over to hug him as he cries. His baseball cap falls to the floor as he hugs me back, tucking in tight. The erupting pain of Gus's beckons my own and I tug it back like it's a child about to run out in front of a car.

"It's okay . . . shhhh." I rock him back and forth trying to soothe him. "Shhhh."

"Why am I so miserable? I have everything I've ever wanted," he sobs. I knew he was having trouble, but I honestly didn't know how much he was struggling. Gus jumped from a niche actor in a cable series to a movie star in less than one year. He went from being able to walk his dog every morning down the Silver Lake street he'd lived on for years to holing up in a new empty rental house in some soulless gated development with twenty-four-hour security that he never even had time to properly move into. My mind races. Where do we go from here?

Gus is currently surrounding himself with a crop of dip-shit star-fuckers who he thinks are his friends, when actually they just want access to the VIP section of clubs and to post a photo with him to their Instagram feed. I'm sure it was one of them who tipped off the paparazzi about Gus's antics at the Marmont. For a price. But, he does have a solid family up in the Bay Area. Always has. We break apart and he sops up his tears and snot with the sleeve of his flannel. I offer him a tissue. He smiles and takes it.

"I'm sorry. I really am fine," he says.

"It's okay not to be fine," I say. Gus just laughs. "I know. I don't think I even believed it as I was saying it." I laugh, too. It's good to see him laughing, even if it's at our shared crippling perfectionism. I slide back into the driver's seat and think. He watches me. Waiting.

"What?"

"I think we need a new plan." I start the car up. "Seatbelt." He obliges. That painful slide show from my twenties taps me on the shoulder as Gus and I talk logistics all the way to the costume shop. Junkets. Filming. Push away the fear of losing Adam and being alone again. Teams of people. Expectations. Responsibilities. Don't you dare give yourself another one of those ardent pep talks. Mental health. Breaking points. You're not the same Olivia Morten from your twenties. Pros and cons. By the time we find parking, I think we've got some semblance of a blueprint for the coming months and I'm officially at war with myself.

"First thing? We're going to get you out of that rental agreement. That house is slowly killing you." I beep the car locked as Gus pulls his baseball cap down low, scanning the deserted parking lot for paparazzi. "We're in North Hollywood in the middle of the day. We should be fine."

"Yeah, right," he says, picking up his pace toward the costume shop. I follow him in, willing myself to leave whatever unwelcome turmoil I'm experiencing out here in this shitty parking lot. The lot looks like somewhere they'd find a dead body on one of those procedural dramas on television. A fitting place to leave the memory of my twenties, then.

The costume shop is a giant open warehouse peppered with slightly worn mannequins in loose-fitting slutty maid's outfits and sagging superheroes. There are a few workers shuffling around in red vests, but other than them, we're on our own. I show him the list that Ben gave me and we get to work.

"So, what's this for?" he asks, pulling a fireman costume down from a rack. He turns the costume around again and again, then puts it back. He grabs another one. "How old are these kids?" I hand him the list and he scans the sizes and ages. A quick nod. He puts the fireman costume back and grabs a more authentic one as if he knows exactly what this kid wants.

"There's this Halloween fair for Asterhouse—it's a foster home in Altadena—that Caroline and I are going to. We're bringing costumes," I say, looking through the racks for a Rapunzel.

"Can I come?" Gus asks, not looking at me.

"Sure," I say, smiling.

"Do they need me to bring anything?" Gus finally chooses a fireman's outfit, rechecks the list for the size, and carefully drapes it over his arm. "Rocket would be over here, although this kid really is going to need a Groot." I follow him as he walks to another part of the store.

"I don't know what half those words mean," I say.

"Rocket and Groot are a superhero team. They need each other. And it's from a comic book. A comic book they just made into a very popular movie that you should see because this is your business."

"I shall do my due diligence." An arched eyebrow. "I promise."

"Uh-huh." He takes a few steps and turns. "Hey, tell Caroline I'm sorry. About, you know . . . what's going down." He starts and stops at each aisle, scanning its contents and then rushing to the next one.

"What's going down with Caroline?" I ask, once I finally catch up with him.

"Yeah, you know," he says.

"How do you know about 'you know'?" Gus continues on down the aisle. I follow, and find him at an endcap completely overrun with Rockets. This many raccoons in one place would be my mother's worst nightmare. She says it's their little hands. She "doesn't trust them."

"A guy I know dated Willa or, you know, tried to date Willa," he says, his lip crooking as he tries to hide this guy's less than honorable intentions.

"And?"

"Her and Max Walsh, right?" He turns around, three Rocket costumes in his hands. A little shake of his head and he whirls back around, puts two Rockets back, and flicks through the rest of the rack.

"Ugh," I say, pulling my dinging phone out of my purse. A text from Ellen.

"Rachel Hatayama is in." And then a thumbs-up emoji and a party hat emoji.

"That's great. Get details to Caroline," I text back. I scan the emojis, panicking about which one connotes gratitude for Ellen's awesomeness, while keeping a safe distance from the Fat Me's latest attempts at taking center stage and the insistent tapping of my own highlight reel—which is really more of a tragic black-and-white French movie where just the large pizza box is in color. As my finger hovers over the screen, I accidentally hit and send four poop emojis. "No!"

"Everything okay?" Gus asks, walking over with all three costumes draped over his arm.

"I just sent four poop emojis to my assistant for no discernible reason."

"Oh, she thinks there's a reason."

"There should really be a three-second delay on texting," I say, staring at the little text bubble that indicates Ellen is crafting her response.

"Has she written back?" Gus asks, making his way to the cash register.

"She's still typing," I say, riveted.

"That's a long time," Gus says, buying the costumes before I tell him he doesn't have to.

Finally Ellen texts back the frog face emoji and the steaming teacup emoji. I show it to Gus and he barks out a laugh. "What? What does it mean??"

"Well, the origin of that particular combination is this tea ad with Kermit the Frog—"

"Wait, there's an entire backstory for this? How deep does this shit go?"

"You'd be surprised. But, what it's come to mean is that what you just typed is none of her business. She's just sipping her tea. Get it?" Gus has never been more serious as he tries to explain this to me.

"That's just great. That's great," I say.

"Aaaaand now I want some tea," he says. "Can we drive through somewhere?"

"Yeah, fine. You know what, I'm just going to act like it never happened," I say, dropping my phone into my purse.

"That's what most people do with texts like that," Gus says, laughing. I look over at him as we walk through the empty parking lot toward my car. His chin is high. His shoulders are back. He's playfully twirling the big plastic bag full of costumes. His entire demeanor has changed in just the little bit of time we've spent in here, away from the stained shirts of Hall H and the drug-filled nights at the Marmont with his dipshit friends. This is the Gus Ford I signed. So I know what to say next.

"You've been in the monkey-house too long."

"I've been in the what now?" Gus asks, waiting for me to unlock the doors. I beep my car unlocked and we both climb inside. He buckles his seatbelt without my prompting. I turn on the car and pull out of the parking lot.

"The monkey-house. You don't smell the stench anymore,

so it's only by leaving it and walking back in that you can truly smell—"

"The shit," Gus finishes. He pulls his phone out of his pocket and swipes it on.

"Right. How bad it smells and what you've gotten used to."

"So L.A. is the monkey-house," Gus says, trying to find the nearest place to get tea on some app on his phone.

"The L.A. you're trapped in right now is. I mean, I'm from here and know that this city can be more than just the movie industry. Home, for one," I say.

"Turn left at the next light," he says. I nod and put my blinker on. "So where do I go? Wait. This isn't some kind of intervention, is it? You're not driving me to some ridiculous rehab place for spoiled shitheads in Malibu, are you?"

"No, of course not."

"Oh, okay." His voice is wobbly as he guides me to make another left.

"I'm thinking more like going home," I say. He looks over at me. "Your real home."

"To Marin?"

"Your parents would love it," I say.

"It's right here on the—" I pull into a drive-through Starbucks. "Yep." He slips his phone back into his jeans pocket.

"Take a road trip up the coast of California—"

"After the foster kid thing, right? I can still come to that?"

"Of course." Gus and I are silent as we inch forward in the Starbucks drive-through line. I look over at him. His cheeks are flushed and I can see his jaw muscle pulsating as he tries to keep his composure. "This isn't a punishment." He won't look at me. "Gus?"

"Feels like one. You're essentially sending me to my room."

His voice is barely a whisper. I reach across the center console and take his hand. He grips mine so tightly. I feel his pain like a gut punch. I have no delusions that by sending Gus back home, all of his problems will be solved, but it's a first step.

"I don't want to get a phone call that you've OD'd." He hangs his head, and once again, I see the tears stream down his cheeks. "It's much worse than you're letting on, right?"

He nods.

"You can't go on like this," I say.

"I know." We inch forward in line and somehow pull it together long enough to order our teas.

"It's okay not to be fine," I say again. He looks over at me and just shakes his head, a smile curling across his face. "Still not going for it, huh?"

"You can't even say it with a straight face," he says, laughing and wiping his tears away with the sleeve of his flannel.

"I know," I say. "What about, 'It's okay for you not to be fine, but not for me because I have to be perfect'?"

"Yeah, that feels more organic."

"Feels more organic? God, you have got to get out of L.A. Like, now." I push Gus's money away and tell him to get my company card from my wallet.

"Maybe I'm *like* not the only one in the monkey-house *like*, you know?" Gus teases.

"Maybe not," I say, laughing. But as I go through the motions of paying for our teas, the car begins to close in around me. The sounds of the busy Starbucks from the drive-through window muffle, as does Gus's playful chiding. My eyesight starts to darken around the edges like I'm seeing the world through some kind of old-timey-vignette filter. I take a deep breath. Another one. My breath doesn't catch. Even as I panic,

I manage a smile at the girl as she hands me one piping-hot tea after the other. I think I say thank you and am pulling the car forward to find a parking space just as my throat closes. The last thing I remember is Gus's hand on my back and him asking if I'm okay, if I'm okay . . .

PETTY

Drowning.

Breathe.

Water in my throat. Fuck. Pull. Up. Pull. Up. Breathe. Hands grabbing me. Someone's calling my name. So far away. I'm right here. Please. Help me. I'm pulled under again. Breathe. Something is on my chest. Get it off. Off. Let me up. Let me up. Why can't anyone hear me?

Black.

Floating.

Black.

What is that? Far away. I can't make it out. Reach. It disappears. Reach. Wait!

Black.

There it is again. Hiding in a darkened corner of my mind. Stairs. Water. Reach. Almost. Almost. Shit, wait. No.

Black.

Urgent voices. It's right around this corner. I know you're there. I recognize you. I know you. Please. Let me . . . let me just see you. I turn the corner . . .

And then I'm ten years old and roller-skating down my old street, bent over and swinging my arms to and fro just like the Olympic speed skaters did. Hoping the streetlights don't come on before I win my heat and can move on to the finals to face the Dutch front-runner. I can feel the wind on my face. The freedom. Every part of me is alive as I cross the finish line. I throw my hands up and in my best sports commentator voice say, "Morten has done it! What a race! Against all odds, Olivia Morten has won this one for America!" I wave to the invisible crowd and make the sound effect of an audience cheering as I take my victory lap. This is me. The Real Me. I am finally able to gulp a full breath, but as the memory fades I get pulled under again.

Black.

"Olivia? Honey?" The cold metal bar of the hospital bed. I jolt awake. The tubes and monitors trap me.

"Where am I? What . . . what's happening?" I feel my own body like I'm in an unfamiliar dark room.

"Livvie, you had a panic attack. A pretty bad one." I focus. Mom. *That* was a panic attack? It felt like I was dying. Mom bends over the hospital bed and takes my hand. I scan my surroundings and try to process the bustling emergency room that hazily comes into focus around me. Doctors and nurses speeding from bed to bed, patients in various states of pain and suffering, worried loved ones kept at a safe distance.

"We were getting a tea," I say over the din. I can't put the pieces together. Shit. "Where's Gus?"

"Right here," he says, walking over to our little corner with two bottles of water.

"Thank you, dear." Mom takes one of the waters. "What a lovely boy."

"What happened?" I ask. "Did I pass out in the parking lot? Did you see my underpants? Oh my god. How bad was it? If I peed myself or whatever, you need to never say a word, okay? Just don't tell me. This is my nightmare." I pull at the oxygen tubes in my nose. "Ugh. Is this necessary? What time is it?"

"It's not even dinnertime," Mom says.

"When can I go home?" I ask, trying to sit up. Gus finds the bed controller.

"Hold on, I've been dying to do this," he says, pushing the button to get me to sit up straight. Ellen strides into the hospital room.

"Ellen, honey. Do you need a water? Gus can fetch you one if you'd like," Mom says, perfectly comfortable bossing around a child millionaire.

"No, thank you, Ms. Morten," Ellen says, rolling over a stool for my mother to sit on. My mother thanks her and sits.

"Call me Polly, please." Ellen beams and settles in next to Gus.

"You seem to have adapted to the new surroundings well enough," I say, as Mom takes a genteel sip of her water.

"Oh, hush," Mom says with a wink.

"Does Adam know I'm here? We should probably tell him before I'm discharged. I imagine that will be happening soon. Where's my cell?" I ask, trying to get comfortable. I take a long, slow, deep breath. It catches at the top and I finally feel like I'm on the other side of whatever this was.

"He does. They called for him immediately and I believe Ellen has your cell phone," Mom says.

"Oh, good." Ellen waggles my cell phone around and goes back to texting furiously on her own.

"Adam is talking to the ER doctor who admitted you. He's trying to get you discharged as soon as possible."

"Oh, good. I mean, it was just a panic attack. It's silly I was admitted at all," I say.

"You didn't see it," Gus says. This catches me off guard and I can only muster a self-conscious nod in agreement. There is a lull in the room. Ellen, Gus, and Mom exchange looks.

"What? What happened?" My mind steamrolls through every humiliating scenario that's awoken me in the middle of the night with a flop sweat since I was a teenager. We're all just one fainting spell away from public incontinence, is my take-away from all this. Must be more vigilant. No more panic attacks. Not that I could have stopped it if I wanted to. "Do you guys want me to have another panic attack? Just tell me!"

Ellen turns her screen around to reveal the headline *Gus Ford: Real Life Superhero!* Underneath the headline is a grainy cell-phone picture someone has taken of Gus walking through the backlit emergency room doors, carrying me in his arms like some, well, to quote the headline, real-life superhero. Thankfully, my hair is fanned just enough to obscure my face. I scan the article quickly and can tell that Søren and Ellen have been hard at work making sure my identity stays hidden.

"Did you sell them that me staying anonymous played into the whole damsel-in-distress thing?" I ask.

"It didn't take much convincing," Ellen says.

"Good. Good, they're mentioning his upcoming movie

every time," I say. I rearrange the oxygen tubes in my nose and pull Ellen and the laptop closer. "Can you put me up a little more?" I ask Gus. He presses the button and the bed moans upward. Mom just watches me. Drinking her water.

"Søren gave them a quote from Gus if they agreed to keep you anonymous and mention the upcoming movie," Ellen says.

"This is great. Really great work," I say, smiling up at Ellen. She looks over at my mom and then back at me, finally reciprocating a small smile herself. "And where is this?"

"Everywhere," Ellen says, rattling through various gossip sites and news outlets. "It's going viral."

"I didn't know what to do. I thought you'd had a heart attack or some kind of seizure. I did the first thing I could think of and drove you as fast as I could to the nearest emergency room," Gus blurts.

"Did you think I'd be mad?" I ask.

"I mean, it's very public," Gus says, not looking at me. I take his hand. "I was so scared. I thought . . . I don't know . . . I just wanted you to be okay."

"Hey." I playfully shake his hand back and forth. "You were perfect." He snaps his eyes to meet mine for one brief second and then looks back down at the ground. "Thank you." He finally looks me in the eye. I smile. "Thank you." His face flushes. "But, now we need to get you out of here. Ellen?"

"I'm on it. The front of the hospital is crawling with paparazzi, but Adam has given us access to an exit where no one will be. There's already a car waiting. He didn't want to go until you woke up." I smile at Gus again as Ellen gathers up her things. She hands Mom my cell phone.

"I'll see you Friday," I say to Gus. He nods.

"It was nice meeting you, sweetie," Mom says to Gus. "Lovely seeing you again, Ellen." They both smile and disappear into the maze of hospital hallways, leaving a scrum of paparazzi disappointed.

"That picture is actually just what we need," I say, shifting in my hospital bed. "The goodwill from it will propel Gus through the next few months and he can get out of L.A. and back home, where he can recharge and find the foundation he's been missing this last year."

"Okay, kid. We're done talking about work or Gus or whatever else. Are you going to tell me what really happened?" Mom rolls closer to me, her little legs barely able to touch the floor.

"Must have been the stress from all this Caroline stuff," I say, adjusting my blanket.

"Don't lie to your mother."

Ugh. Fine. I try to remember. "The last thing I recall was talking about the monkey-house," I say.

"The monkey-house?"

"It's a long story, but I was telling Gus he had to get out of L.A. because he couldn't see how bad his life had gotten. That he'd been in the monkey-house so long he couldn't smell it anymore."

"Ah."

"I'd already been thinking about my twenties—which, as you know, were not that great—" Mom nods. "So when he made a joke that maybe he wasn't the only one in a monkey-house, I don't know, it just all went black and I have no idea why."

"So it was the idea that he wasn't the only one in a monkey-house."

"Yeah."

"That you yourself were in a monkey-house of your own."

"I guess."

"And then you had the panic attack."

"Apparently." I can't get comfortable. This fucking bed. And all these tubes. Can someone turn on a fan or open a window? Before I know it, a piercing beeping wails throughout the ER. Mom stands just as a nurse rushes over.

"Olivia? How are you feeling?" The nurse checks my blood pressure and does a full once-over.

"I'm fine. I'm fine," I say, smiling at Mom. My mom smiles back . . . after a few seconds.

"Okay, try to breathe deeply for me. Can you do that?"

"Of course. Yeah, that's . . ." I try to take a deep breath and it doesn't catch. Oh, no. The panic is immediate. Again. "You're almost there, Olivia. Let the oxygen do the work. Just give me a deep breath." I focus on Mom and I wait for it to feel like I'm drowning again, then deeply inhale as much as I can. The cold oxygen in my nose feels good and my breath finally catches. The beeping subsides. I breathe again. And another.

"There you go. Good job," the nurse says. Adam turns the corner and hurries over to me. Mom rolls her little stool back from the bed.

"Okay, okay. Gus and Ellen are safely away," he says. I smile, taking another deep breath. "Liv?" he asks, brushing my hair back from my face. "You scared me." His hand rests on the side of my face. His touch feels changed. This is the first I've seen Adam since my run-in with Nurse Brenda and the Uneaten Dinners. I must acknowledge that what happened with them might have something to do with whatever this panic attack was.

I try to calm myself. I don't want that stupid beeping to

continue acting as some kind of tattletale truth serum. Adam drops his hand from my face as I blather on about Caroline and stress and work and Gus and things that I now know are bullshit.

I can't look at Mom. Her words bounce around my brain like a loose rubber ball wreaking havoc. Which monkey-house am I stuck inside? Is it Adam and his many women, or is it just that I don't want anyone to know about Adam and his many women? Was it the realization that he took Nicola to the Post Ranch Inn? Was that what did this? That I now have actual proof that he is out-and-out lying to me, plus the added bonus that people are starting to know? Or does this go back to seeing Ben Dunn again? Is that what's unsettled everything? I feel my shoulders creeping up. Okay. So, it's seeing Ben again that started all of this? I shift in the bed. No. That's not all of it. The Sweaty Marble Me rolls through my consciousness and my entire face flushes like I've been caught cheating. And all of a sudden, the look of respect and awe-struck fear from that intern this morning melts away. The other shoe has finally dropped. After all these years, I've finally been found out. They know. I was once a big fat loser who all but shoved her perfect, successful husband into the arms of an un-told number of women, and no matter how many weepy pep talks I gave myself, I'm not perfect or fine and you should take your admiration somewhere else, young lady.

And that's when I realize that I wasn't worried about what happened to me in that parking lot this morning so much as what it looked like. Could you see my underpants? Did I em-barrass myself? Then the beeping. THE BEEPING. Adam im-mediately leaps into action. Calling for a nurse and pleading with me to take a deep breath.

The Fat Me is waking up like some long-dormant vol-
cano.

"Take a deep breath, my love," Adam says. I try to smile
for him. I'm fine, I hear myself wheeze again. The beeping.
Beeping. "Everything is okay, Liv. Liv? Can you look at me? It's
going to be okay." I keep trying to fake being okay for Adam
and this stupid traitor of a beeping machine. But, it's not
working. It's not working.

Back in the day, people always cheerily told me to fake it
'til I made it. Feel awkward about that new exercise regimen?
Fake it 'til you make it. Feel vulnerable about walking into a
crowded room alone? Fake it 'til you make it. Not sure someone will ever truly love you? Fake it 'til you make it! So, I came
to understand faking it until I made it as knowing that I may
be a fucking train wreck on the inside, but as long as I looked
perfect on the outside, I could be happy! And I thought I was.
I really did. I thought I was finally accepted and admired as
someone who was to be cherished. I thought I was loved.

I thought I was happy.

I look past Adam and see Mom. Watching me. I focus on
her. Wait until my lungs hurt, press the oxygen tubes into my
nose, and inhale from the deepest part of myself. It doesn't
catch. Adam calls for a nurse and I steel myself. Okay. Shit.
Something real. I can count to ten. Just count to ten. I can do
this.

One. Two.

Breathe.

Three. Four. Five.

Think about the roller-skating.

Six. Seven.

My shoulders drop and my fists slowly relax.

There's the finish line, Olivia. Think about the cheering invisible crowd as I speed-skate to victory for America.

Eight. Nine.

Now breathe. It catches.

Ten.

The beeping subsides. Adam smiles and Mom finally sits back down on her rolling stool and takes a long drink of her water. She's trying not to look worried, but come on. She's not fooling anyone. Apparently neither am I.

Turns out you can fake it 'til you make it for only so long before it backs up on you like a clogged toilet.

And that shit goes everywhere, whether you like it or not.

"What is that?" I ask, staring at the monstrosity that's hanging on the back of my office door.

"That's a Groot," Ellen says, barely able to hold back her smirk. I examine the costume more closely. The main component of the Groot costume is a leisure-suit-adjacent cylindrical trunk with two cut-out armholes. The fabric—or whatever this hard unyielding material is they've used to make the costume—is airbrushed to look like bark. In an accompanying plastic grocery bag, they've given me a brownish long-sleeve spandex shirt, a pair of twiglike gloves, and an oversized wooden head with black marble eyes.

"No, *this* is a tree."

"Right," Ellen says.

"No. Okay. Seriously. Who's the superhero that's kind of dangerously sexy and where's that costume?"

"That is literally every other superhero except Groot and you don't get to have one of those because you explicitly asked for this costume. If you'll recall, you were leaving the hospital and texted me in no uncertain terms that Rocket needs a Groot. And Groot is a giant tree."

That's right. I got discharged from the hospital with exaltations about Groot and Adam drove me home. I made my follow-up appointments, got into my pajamas, texted Mom that I was home safe, plugged my phone into the charger, and went to sleep. When I woke up the next day, my chest hurt like it did back when there used to be smog alerts in elementary school. It felt like some new and terrible hangover. But, I got up, showered, made my morning smoothie, and met Caroline for her *Vanity Fair* interview with Rachel Hatayama at Le Petit Ermitage like I said I would.

Adam said I should take the day off, adding that my "workload" was starting to "take a toll" on me. I said I was fine and that once I got the photographer's schedule, I'd let him know when the shoot for the Christmas card would be. He just nodded, kissed my forehead, and laughed.

"I actually don't know if you could survive without your elaborate lists," Adam said, looking down at me with a smile.

"Well, I know you couldn't, so . . . ," I said, tilting myself back just enough to look him in the eye.

"Oh, I'd do just fine," he said.

Rage came first. At myself. This is the future being "so laid-back!" bought me. Ten years down the line and my husband is condescendingly looking at me because he literally has no idea how complicated and demanding it is to run our home, let alone do my job. To him, my lists are adorable little manic trifles and not the important kinds of things he has to worry about.

"You'd do just fine because there are legions of women around you who keep lists of the things you need without so much as an acknowledgment from you," I said.

"You're tired." A wink. A pat on the arm.

"I am tired."

"That's what I just said." He picked up his workbag and his travel mug, and started walking toward the front door.

"The brass link on your workbag was broken. Do you remember that?"

"Of course."

"And now?" I waited.

"Honey, if you're trying to prove to me that you're still on top of things . . ."

"It's fixed. Did you even notice?" He looked annoyed. "You said you liked that travel mug, so I ordered it. And the coffee in it? It's the kind we liked when we took that road trip up the coast to Cayucos. They had it at the Brown Butter Cookie Company. Do you remember?" He let out a long sigh. "You're about to grab your keys, right?"

"This is silly," he said.

"They're on that same hook by the door because, do you remember how you kept misplacing them?"

"This really is petty, Liv."

"It's not petty . . . it's not petty to want to be acknowledged and respected for making our home life something to be proud of. Is it so hard to look around and just say thank you?"

"Well, while you're buying hooks for keys and telling starlets what to say over soy lattes, I have a quadruple bypass this afternoon." He opened the front door. "Maybe you need to see someone. Talk to someone—a professional—because whatever this is?" His eyes hit me like a punch. "Simply won't do." And he closed the door behind him.

I stood there staring at the closed door. I wanted to scream. I wanted to run after him and rub his nose in the new fall porchscape I'd put together that he'd yet to notice. But, I didn't. I just didn't.

"You were pretty drugged up," Ellen says, bringing me back.

"I'd just had a panic attack, so . . ."

"So, here we are. Rocket gets his Groot. Now hurry up, you've got to be there in—" Ellen checks her watch. "Shit. Yeah, you've got to get that on now and head out. The traffic is going to be terrible. Caroline is meeting you out front at 3:30."

"Thank you," I say, looking at her. Ellen looks up from her phone. "You do a lot for me. I have lists, but your lists put mine to shame." I thought Ellen would think less of me after the whole panic attack thing. But, all that's happened is that she's gotten kind of nicer. Which—in the dark of the night—worries me because she's probably planning my downfall.

"It's my job," Ellen says.

"I know. I know . . . I just really appreciate it."

"Oh. Well, you're welcome." Ellen stands there. Uncomfortable.

"But I'm not driving to Altadena as a tree. That's just patently unsafe."

Ellen looks relieved. "Fine. Where's your gym bag?"

"I have the fair tonight, so I worked out this morning. All my workout clothes are sweaty and gross." I point to the offending bag over in the corner of my office like it's a pile of vomit.

"I have some workout gear you can wear underneath.

Why don't you change into that?" She hands me a reusable bag that says "Talk Nerdy to Me" and inside I find a pair of yoga pants and a sports bra.

"This is barely any clothes at all," I say.

"It's what one wears under a tree costume." Another look at her watch. Ellen takes the Groot costume down from the hook, drapes it over my arm—it weighs around seventeen thousand pounds—grabs a cheesy T-shirt from the goodie bag of Gus's movie premiere, stuffs it into the bag, and opens the door to my office. "Text me if you need anything. I'll be over at Gus's putting his stuff in storage."

"This is a very bad idea."

"It's a wonderful idea. That kid is going to love it. Everyone needs a Groot, just like you said."

"How did I choose the one non-sexy superhero?"

"Just lucky, I guess." Ellen closes the door to my office as we head out through the bull pen and finally get to the bathrooms. I go into one of the stalls and change into the workout gear. I pull the tight spandex brown shirt over the sports bra. The tight stall. The tree outfit. The spandex sticking to my now-sweating body. I'm panting as I contort my body to pull and tug and heave the costume on.

"Caroline's lawyers say they'll file her divorce today as close to five p.m. as they can," I say through the stall door.

"That's good. Hopefully the holiday weekend will buy us something," she says. I fold my work clothes and pack them into the reusable bag.

"She'll be at the fair when it's filed, so if it does start going viral she'll be in good hands," I say. I throw on the T-shirt and roll its sleeves up so they won't be visible outside of the costume's armholes.

"And *Vanity Fair*?" she asks. I put on my sneakers and tuck my heels into the bag as well.

"An exclusive snippet along with some shots from the cover shoot will go live on Monday."

"That's good," she says. I come out of the bathroom stall now clad in workout gear, a shiny grotesque brown leotard and an oversized T-shirt with Gus's face on it.

"Let's get this over with."

ROCKET NEEDS A GROOT

"What on earth?" Caroline asks, making no effort to hold back her laughter. I shift the Groot head to my other hand and we have the most awkward side hug ever.

I stomp behind Caroline through the full parking lot packed with cars, their trunks open and full of Halloween decorations and candy. Volunteers excitedly ready things for the Trunk or Treating that will be happening not soon enough for these kids.

"Oh, so Super Hobo is calling out Groot?" Caroline does a little spin. Her beach towel cape, the miniature cowboy hat, and tiny rollie-suitcase are finished off by what looks like pajamas and Wellington boots. Hilariously, the Super Hobo Costume 2.0 probably cost somewhere in the thousands. The towel alone.

"I figured I'd bring back an old classic," she says.

"How are you?" I ask.

Caroline deflates slightly. Just how ridiculous we look discussing something so serious is not lost on me. "Not good. Of course, he's been texting. And, of course, I love that he's been texting and then I hate myself for it."

"Have you been texting back?" I ask, loathing that I'm thinking more about the possible leak of her texts than her actual well-being.

"Of course not."

"Right. I'm sorry." I tug on the tight collar of this costume.

"They should be filing any minute." Caroline checks her phone. "They said they'd call."

"Yeah," I say.

"I feel like I should receive some kind of letter saying I've grieved enough and I'm ready to move on," Caroline says, only half joking.

"What, like: Congratulations, Caroline Lang! Your test scores look great and you've clearly learned from this experience. We are granting you admission to the next phase of your life. You are now relieved of any and all feelings you once had for your ex-husband." I speak in as newscastery a voice as I can. Caroline laughs. "Please see admissions about the lovely man who's been assigned to take you on an adventurous romp through the exotic locale of your choice. While you're there you will be able to gaze out onto the body of water of your choosing as you cry sublimely, remembering what you've endured."

"Cue music." Her smiles fades. "We've been watching too many of my movies." She spins her towel cape around just a bit.

"It's going to be okay."

"No, it's going to be different. We have yet to see if it's

going to be okay." I just nod. Caroline doesn't need a pep talk right now. She just needs to be sad. Or mad. Or all of it. "He has yet to move his stuff out, so that's something to look forward to."

"Mrs. Lang?" A volunteer dressed as Dorothy from *The Wizard of Oz* approaches us.

"Yes?" Caroline asks, turning to face her.

"Hi. I . . . uh . . . I'm in charge of the booths. I'm supposed to help with yours?" She extends her hand to Caroline and the wicker basket with the stuffed Toto that's looped over her arm hurtles toward Caroline. "Oh, god. I'm . . ."

I try to bend over to pick up the basket and realize too late that there'll be none of that with this costume. I almost lose my balance. I grab on to Caroline's arm and she hoists me back up, steadies me, picks up the basket, and hands it back to the poor woman.

"Thanks. Thank you." The woman takes the basket and can't stop apologizing and shaking her head. "I'm Katie. I'm one of the teachers here. I'm a huge fan."

Caroline extends her hand to Katie. Katie carefully takes it. And I see Caroline disappear into Movie Star Mode, a welcoming smile spreading across her perfect face. Meanwhile, her entire life is falling apart.

"So great to meet you. I hear I'm in charge of the photo booth?" Caroline asks.

"Yes. We thought you'd be great for getting the kids to strike silly poses and all that. You know, because that's kind of what you do . . . for a living." Katie's words just hang there. "Not that that's all you do. I'm . . . I'm just so nervous."

"It's totally fine. I'll follow you, then?"

Katie nods and starts walking toward the field that's just

past the main buildings of Asterhouse. Caroline gives me a wave. "I'll let you know when they call," she says, holding up her cell phone. I nod.

"I'll find you," I say, shifting the Groot head again to my other hand.

"I imagine I'll see you coming," she says with a wink. She turns to follow Katie, her little rollie-suitcase trailing behind her. And, just beyond Caroline, I see Ben turning the corner dressed in his football uniform from high school. Number nine.

Fuckkkkkkkkkkkk.

It's a cruel, cruel turn of events, universe.

Whatever gratitude I felt that I saw him first, and not as I lumbered (heyo!) across the field only to be peed on by some overly zealous dog, evaporates as his eyes find me. Or they kind of do, then he tries to process why I'm a giant tree and this smile overtakes his entire face. As he walks over to me, I'm fifteen again and imprisoned in this goddamn tree just like when I weighed a thousand pounds. My breathing becomes shallow. No. Oh, god, no. Please don't let me pass out and become incontinent inside this tree. Not in front of Ben Dunn.

"I almost didn't see you," he says, motioning to the row of trees just behind me, his helmet in his hand. The muscles in his forearm are taut as the weight of the helmet ebbs and flows with the motion.

"I'm not just any tree, I am Groot," I say.

He laughs. "You don't get why that's funny, right?"

"I grasp why this whole thing is hysterical, but no, not that part specifically."

"It's his one line. It's . . . never mind," he says. We stand in silence.

"Thanks again for letting Caroline join in," I say.

"Oh, no problem. All the costumes you guys brought are great. The kids were so excited."

"Dad! Daaaaaaaaaad!" Louisa hurries over to Ben, dressed in some kind of wrapped linen getup and carrying a giant walking stick. Trailing just behind Louisa is a tiny Maleficent, holding upward of ten plastic bags filled with water and a single goldfish each. I see Ben's smile fade as he takes in what's in Tilly's hands. "Grammy told her she couldn't play anymore, but she won't give 'em back." Tilly rumbles over and leans on me. I'm pretty sure she thinks I'm a tree and not a person. Maybe we're all just trees to her. Ben kneels down and starts talking quietly to Tilly. She instinctively hides the school of goldfish behind her back.

"What's your costume?" I ask Louisa.

"Rey," Louisa says, striking a pose.

"I don't know who Rey is, but I love all the linen," I say. The look on Louisa's face is a combination of disbelief and disgust. I've rendered her speechless.

"Linens? Like how when Dad says to put our towels away in the linen closet?" Louisa is absently touching my costume, her tiny chocolate-smudged fingers working their way across the faux bark.

"Kind of."

"Rey is in *Star Wars*. She's a Jedi." Louisa's tone isn't mad. Just disappointed.

"Oh. Oh. Right—"

"Do you know movies?" Louisa's follow-up question doesn't sting as much as her tone. She's talking to me with the terrified kindness of someone who honestly doesn't know what the monster in front of them is capable of.

"I know movies. In fact, I'm Groot. From . . . from that one movie," I say. Shit. Louisa's eyes narrow. She knows. She waits. Ben stands back up and is now holding all but one of Tilly's goldfish.

"Which one movie?" Ben asks, absently redoing Louisa's elaborate ponytail configuration. Tilly pulls her black dress up, tugs a piece of candy out of her little jeans underneath, and then sits down next to me.

"It was actually a comic first," I say, stalling. Tilly sighs, pops the candy in her mouth, and leans back against me.

"Oh, good. They found you," Myrna says, walking up in a Snow White costume.

"Mom, you remember Olivia Morten," Ben says.

"Yes, honey. What about her?" Myrna asks, taking back all of the baggies of fish from Ben.

"Would you like to say hello to her?" Ben asks, gesturing to me. Myrna's look of utter disbelief as she turns her gaze to me is less about me being dressed as a tree and more about me no longer weighing a thousand pounds.

"Oh, yes. Yes. I'm so sorry." Myrna collects herself and re-groups. "Of course. Hello again, Olivia." Myrna extends her hand and I shake it as best I can.

"Thank you for making a place for Caroline," I say.

"It's our pleasure. She's been lovely," Myrna says. Myrna looks at the little girls. "You ladies ready to head back?" Tilly hands the candy wrapper to Ben and lifts her one remaining goldfish high.

"No more playing at the goldfish table, Señorita Tilly-weather McStubbins," Ben says. Tilly smiles wide and hugs him around his neck.

"Señorita Tillyweather McStubbins is not her real name."

Louisa is concerned. I nod. "It's just a nickname," she whispers. "Dad makes up crazy nicknames all the time." She's leaning on her little staff as she speaks.

"What's his nickname for you?" I ask.

"Commander Louisa Smarty-pants of the Seventh Brigade," Louisa says, saluting.

Oh my god.

"That's a good one," I say. Louisa beams.

"The kids are loving Gus," Myrna says, motioning to the field. Tilly's dress is still hitched up above her jeans as she takes her grandmother's hand.

"Oh, so sorry. I forgot to tell you about him," I say, looking from Myrna to Ben.

"His people called," Ben says.

"His people?" I ask.

"I know. I say things like that now because of you," he says.

"Lovely seeing you again, Olivia. But, it seems we have a cakewalk to get to," Myrna says, as the girls go wild. I smile and wave as they begin to walk away. Louisa looks over her shoulder. She comes running back and takes my hand in hers.

"*Guardians of the Galaxy*. That's the movie you're from," she says. "In case anyone else asks." Louisa nods. "Bye, Dad. Love you." Ben leans down and Louisa gives him a quick kiss. Louisa catches up to Myrna and Tilly and we follow them down to the field where the fair is.

As we make our way to the field, I can't look over at him. I actually can't. It's too much. This—well, not exactly this—is the fantasy I had in high school: Ben and I walking into an event somewhere. He's wearing that uniform and I'm thin and beautiful and, you know, not trapped in a tree. But, even

now as we make our way down the stairs, he's talking so easily with me. He's animated and familiar. That part of the
fantasy feels almost eerie. I knew he'd be like this. Friendly
and open. Not the sarcastic bro version of him from high
school. Of course, I'm not making fun of him either, which
might also be a factor.

"Gus dressed up as his character from the movie. The kids
love it. He brought tons of toys and stuff," Ben says. We get
to the bottom of the stairs and the whole fair opens up in
front of us. "Put on your head before the kids see."

"Oh, right." I plop the head on. "Um. Okay. I . . ." I fiddle
with the head and finally get it situated so I can see out of the
weird black marble eyes. "I can barely see anything."

"Here." Ben takes my arm. "I got you."

Shit. Shit. Shit.

"Before I check in with Gus and Caroline, can you take
me to Rocket?" I ask, my words muffled.

"She's right over here." Ben's hand clamps around my arm
and I let him lead me through the chaos of the fair. As we
walk, I realize that being stuck inside this costume mutes all
of my senses, except for my hearing. And the only thing I can
hear is what it must be like to be Ben Dunn, even for one day.

"Looking good in that uniform, Ben," a woman coos.

"Oh, you know, gotta pull the old relic out from time to
time," Ben says, his voice laced with sugar.

"Well, you've definitely still got it," the woman says. Ben's
hand shifts and tightens on my arm as they exchange what I
can only imagine are sexy, wanton glances at one another.
All the while ignoring the enormous tree he's dragging along
with him.

My breath echoes around in the giant tree head. Quick,

shallow breaths as I sink into the old familiar invisible status of my youth. How quickly this sensation returns. I wobble a bit in the costume. Ben is quick to catch me.

"You okay in there?"

"Yep," I say, instead of blurting out I am having quite the mental breakdown. One of many, apparently. Cue: hysterical laughter that no one could hear because I'm trapped in a motherfucking tree. I start walking. The faster I meet up with Rocket, the faster I can take this infernal costume off and the faster I can get back to whatever is left of the life I've built over the last ten years.

"We'll take it slow," Ben says. I nod. He takes my arm once again and I can feel his other hand on my back, steadying me. We are getting ever closer to the fair. Finally. And right on cue:

"I wish it were Halloween every day." Another woman. "If it means I get to see you in those pants."

"Now you've got me all embarrassed," Ben says, his voice loud and confident, not embarrassed at all. I can't help but scoff at that one, which probably sounded like a low elephantine bleat from where Ben and the lady are standing.

"My friend still asks about you," the woman says, now farther away. "You never texted her back."

"Ooh, gotta go!" And I can feel Ben motioning to me.

"She really likes you!" The woman's voice fades. And then all I can hear are the kids going crazy for my costume.

"Wave. Wave to the kids," Ben says. I let go of Ben and the kids mob me. I take several pictures. I even strike a few poses. Tree poses, sure, but I'm getting better at this and it's helping. The ghost of my past is receding as the joy of the right-now takes over. "Okay, guys. Let Groot find Rocket." The kids love this.

"Rocket's over there!!!!!!!!" they all shout. I wave my good-byes, Ben takes my arm once more, and we head over to where Rocket is apparently doing the cakewalk. And then I hear it.

"Groooooooooooot!!!" A little girl. Somewhere off in the distance.

"Steady yourself. She's running toward you right now," Ben says.

"Take a picture. Take a picture," I say, handing him my cell phone.

"I'm going to let you go, okay? Okay?" Ben asks.

"Yes. I've got it. I think—" He lets go and I see this blur of brown and black and orange coming at me.

"I knew you'd come, Groot! I knew you'd come!" And I feel her hugging my legs. So tight. I lean down—or really it's more like falling down ever so gracefully—and wrap my arms around her. I manage to kneel down. And when I do . . .

"Thank you for coming," she says into my ear. I can finally see her little face. Her hair is in braids, each one held together by a brightly colored barrette. Her skin has been painted to look like a raccoon, the gray muzzle and whiskers now streaking a bit from sweat. The raccoon ears are crooked from running around and the costume that Gus so lovingly picked out fits her perfectly.

"Let me get a picture of you two," Ben says. "Jordan, sweetie." Jordan is just staring at me. "Sweetie, look toward the camera." She begrudgingly turns to Ben. "Okay, now smile." Her little arm feels so tight around my waist. Then Ben takes another picture and she's now striking a very superherolike pose. "That's great! Do you want to see it?"

"No! I know it's beautiful!" And with that, Jordan skips off.

"Asterhouse tries to place the kids with relatives if they can. My mom said that her aunt flew in last week from Houston. That whole side of the family didn't even know about her," Ben says, taking my arm and lifting me back up into a standing position. I see Jordan bolt over to a young woman in a flowery dress. Jordan is pointing over at me, pointing over at me! The woman nods and smiles, then hands Jordan a *raspado* that's colored Dodger blue, bright red, and sunlight yellow. Jordan leaps into the air, punching her fist to the sky.

"My favorite!" She takes the *raspado* from her aunt and dives into the delicious shaved ice.

"Please tell me—"

"Oh, absolutely. She's already started adoption proceedings," Ben says.

"Thank god. Because . . ."

"I know."

"Is that really you in there?" asks Gus. His superhero outfit is spectacular in real life. He's all muscular arms and molded body armor. I nod and he laughs. "I can't believe you actually did it."

"You said Rocket needs a Groot."

"I know! Didn't know you'd go through with it," he says.

"I wish I'd known what a Groot was before I did!" Gus lets out a giant belly laugh.

"Hey, man. Can you take a picture of us?" Gus hands Ben his phone.

"Sure. Sure."

"Nice costume. Looks real," Gus says to Ben.

"It is real," Ben says.

"Hahahaha, right. So's this," Gus says, motioning to his superhero costume. Ben lets go of my arm and takes the phone from Gus. His motions are jerky and rough. I'm waiting for Gus to come get in the shot, when I see Ben ever so slightly come up onto his tiptoes. Gus bounds over to me, but I stay focused on Ben. Lips pursed. Jaw tensed. As Gus tucks in next to me, Ben settles back into the height I've always found perfectly lovely. Apparently he felt he needed to be a little taller standing next to Gus Ford.

"Can you get Jordan?" I ask. Gus calls over to Jordan and she comes running. A crowd gathers and we pose for several photographs. I want this picture of Gus in his superhero costume + cute kids to make Caroline's divorce news slide even further down the gossip food chain and not unintentionally start a rumor that just because Caroline and Gus were at the same event, they must be sleeping together. I make a mental note to text Ellen later so we can track that. Jordan says her goodbyes to us and runs back to the booth where she can win one of the goldfish Tilly decided to return.

"I'm heading out right after this," Gus says.

"Good," I say, nodding.

"From now on, you should do all of your inspirational talks as a tree," Gus says, lunging into me for a hug. Ben walks over and hands Gus his phone.

"Oh, thanks," he says, taking it. Gus laughs. Like really laughs.

"What?" I ask.

"Tree hugger. Get it? I'm a tree hugger." I can't help but laugh simply because Gus thinks this is hysterical. I see Ben roll his eyes. "I'll check in before I go, but until then I have some kids to beat at Skee-Ball." A quick wave to Ben and Gus is off.

"He's something," Ben says as we walk around the fair. I nod. "Taller than I thought he'd be."

We walk in silence toward the photo booth. Caroline looks like she's having the best time in the world. Of course, I'm not sure if that's actually what she's feeling or if she's just acting. She sees me, holds up her cell phone, and gives me a thumbs-up. The look on her face is one of someone who's done something they can't take back. Her divorce has been filed, it's all over the Internet, and all she can do now is focus on making sure a little kid who's dressed up as a fireman gets the picture he wants. I wave my giant tree arm at her. She laughs, of course. Because I'm a hilarious animal.

"Is there somewhere I can change out of this?" I finally ask.

"Oh, sure. Up here." Ben pulls my arm in whatever direction. More pictures. More near stumbles. I'm sweating so profusely at this point the slick spandex long-sleeve shirt has now rolled all the way up my back. Another set of stairs and now we're inside. "Mom set aside one of the conference rooms for the volunteers." Ben opens the door and I immediately pull the Groot head off.

"Finally," I say. My hair is stuck to my forehead and I'm positive every ounce of makeup I carefully applied this morning is running down my face. "Can you?" I turn around. "Unzip me, please?"

"Oh, sure," Ben says, stepping forward. Asking Ben to unzip me is the fantasy I didn't even know I had. It sounds so sexy and like it should be in the movies. Instead, I'm in some wood-paneled, musty conference room surrounded by women's purses, folding chairs, and card tables, asking him to free me from a tree costume under which he'll find a sweaty T-shirt, some yoga pants, and a body that only I have seen completely naked. He unzips the back of the jumpsuit and the fresh air feels so good. I shrug my shoulders forward and loosen the costume as coolly as I can.

"Thanks," I say, turning around and trying to find some darkened corner or angle where Ben won't be able to see if things go wrong. But, I'm stuck. The harsh fluorescent lighting and nowhere to hide forces me to take the costume off no matter what the clothes—or I—look like underneath. And Ben just keeps talking to me—like nothing earth-shattering is happening. He's pacing around the conference room, going on and on about Gus and his generation and when he was their age—which wasn't that long ago, he'll have me know—as I peel off the costume, then carefully unthread the spandex long-sleeve shirt from underneath the oversized T-shirt, making sure it doesn't ride up on my bra, exposing my belly with its stretch marks and surgery scars, faded and healed as they may be. Once I'm safely out of the costume, T-shirt smoothed down and hair tamed somewhat, I jump back into the conversation.

"You're just pissed he said that thing about your football uniform not being real." I "fold" the costume as best I can and place the head on top of the unwieldy pile.

"What?" Ben's head snaps around as if he's just realized there was another person in the room.

"Because you were fine about Gus and the next generation while those women told you how hot you were in that outfit," I say.

"How hot I am in this outfit?" Ben asks, hitting the word "outfit" with particular disdain. What I don't say is, I'm no different than those women: I think he looks hot in that outfit. Always have.

"I wish it were Halloween every day so I could see you in

them pants," I repeat, my voice high and lilting. He flushes. "I get it. Getting older is tough." I comb through the tree detritus and find my phone. I start scrolling through texts from Ellen. Gus is all moved out. Caroline's divorce is hitting the Internet along with a few candids of her at the Halloween fair. Gus's photo posing with Jordan and me is also making the rounds. I text about the whole Caroline+Gus thing and she says she's already on it. She thought of that like a week ago, she'll have me know. I let out a laugh and am about to text something else, when I notice Ben has stepped closer to me. I look up just as he's setting his football helmet down on the table with a stern look on his face. Now, that's the Ben Dunn I am used to.

"This is not about getting old," he says.

"It absolutely is," I say, settling right into our old patterns. "He's a little shit who—"

"Made you feel old," I say. "Just admit it."

"Must be nice to know utterly everything."

"It is, actually." I step forward. Ben laughs. "So, you're not the most popular boy in school anymore. So what?" Ben's smile fades.

"Okay. That's not what this is about, so . . ."

"If you say so." I pocket my phone, tuck the costume under my arm, and extend the Groot head to Ben. "Can you hold this?"

"Just because you want everyone to forget who you were in high school, doesn't mean I have to," Ben says, snapping the head away from me.

"Just because I want everyone to forget who I was in high school? What are you talking about?"

"That's what this really is about, isn't it?"

"No, it's not."

"If you say so . . ."

"Very funny." I step closer to him. "You were a terrible person in high school. You really shouldn't be painting that time in your life like it was the glory days."

"You don't know what you're talking about."

"I actually do, though. You may have been popular or whatever, but you were legitimately awful," I say.

"At least I had something to be proud of," he says, elaborately tucking in his jersey.

"Yeah, making fun of fat girls and being able to throw a ball should make you swell with pride."

"And what about you and that time you said I should be thankful that I could play football because there was certainly no other way I was getting into college."

"I did not say that."

"You absolutely did. We were in Mr. Moore's English class and it was right at the end of the period. We were presenting our *Crime and Punishment* papers, remember? And I mispronounced fucking Dostoyevsky. You yelled the correct pronunciation from the back of the room and everyone laughed. As I was walking back to my seat you followed that up with the doozie about me not being able to get into college without football."

"Yeah, and then I went back to being me and you went back to being king of high school."

"What does that have to do with anything?"

"Context is everything."

"Are you still trying to wriggle out of taking responsibility for the things you said?"

"'Wriggle.' What an adorably condescending word."

"Why can't you just say you're sorry?" Ben is getting more and more upset. Whatever suave polish he had earlier in the day is all but gone. "And actually mean it this time?" Then Ben's entire face changes. "Oh, wait. Shit. Okay, I get it. I get it now."

"What?"

"When you talk about high school, you—"

"I don't talk about high school."

"Fine. When you think back on high school, then."

"I don't think back on high school either."

Ben is about to speak and then doesn't. Another strangled start and stop. He takes a deep breath and finally speaks. "We were both terrible." His voice is soft. Different. My throat burns as I swallow through the emotion. We are quiet. For a long time. We were both terrible. I say it again and again inside my own head. Looking to Ben for some reason why that statement is so true but has never been spoken until this moment. Maybe birds of a feather flock together because they have to. Everyone else thinks they're awful. Am I still terrible? I allow a tiny nod. He watches me and is about to say something else, but . . . doesn't.

I used to think Ben was perfect because he was the only one who challenged me. He was the only one who waded in and wasn't afraid. Turns out, he was just the only other jerk who spoke the language.

"Good thing we've left that firmly in the past," he says.

"Yeah."

Quiet.

"I really loved playing football." He looks down at himself, his eyes skim over the uniform and his own body. I watch as the shame infects him.

"You can still play."

"It's not the same."

"Does it have to be the same?" Ben's eyes lock on to mine. "I don't know, we may have been younger back then, but apparently we were giant assholes."

I set down my costume and take a step toward Ben. He leans slightly to one side, his head tilting so we can see eye to eye. I don't know what to do with my hands. Or moreover, I want to do everything with my hands, but won't. I place them as platonically as I can on his upper arms. I feel his biceps tighten and move underneath the slippery jersey material. I take a deep breath and smile.

And just as I'm about to say something chastely motivating and wholesomely inspirational, Ben kisses me.

And. It. Is. Good.

HAMBURGER NIGHT FOR VEGANS

Warm tingles break out everywhere, bursting across my body like fireworks. I follow the detonations like a curious detective. Goose-pimpling skin. His unshaven jaw. My body and his body. Just the heat. The heat. No. Too much. I can't breathe. My fists tighten around his jersey as if the teenage version deep inside of me is already throwing a tantrum because I'm about to ruin this for her. And she propels me deeper into him. I want more. No. I hear myself let out a painful, yearning moan that comes from somewhere so hidden it scares me. Frantic, I break free from him.

"I'm so sorry. I . . . I shouldn't have done that. I'm so sorry." Ben steps back. And then farther back. "Shit."

"We'd better get back out there." I turn around and gather the costume in a wad. "You ready?" I whip the Groot head around with enough pent-up energy to hurl it all the way over the San Gabriel Mountains and motion to the door.

"Right behind you," he says. And of course now every-thing he says is sexual and I feel my face flush and I hate it. I have to get out of this musty conference room. Now.

As we walk down the hallway, I start and stop a thousand sentences. All of them horrifying. I congratulate myself on realizing they're horrifying before I say them. The worst of-fender being some blurted version of, "My husband was right behind me last night, if you know what I mean." Which is both super tacky and 100 percent false. My husband hasn't been "right behind me" in years.

Years.

Years.

Adam and I and sex . . . it just never clicked. I jiggle too much. I'm too heavy. My body doesn't work right or some-thing because it never reacted to Adam how he wanted. How I thought it was supposed to. Is this right, I'd be thinking? Is this what sexy is? Is this what love feels like? And I would miss it. He would finish and I'd still be wondering. When I found out about the other women, it didn't surprise me. If I'd been good at sex, Adam wouldn't have had to go looking elsewhere for it. No, I did this. This was all my fault.

But, that kiss was something new. Although, right now the shame and embarrassment for how uncontrollably greedy I felt and that no matter the state of my marriage, I am in fact still married, is eclipsing any big questions or even the fantas-tical high-fives that finally, after scoring his phone number just days ago, Ben Dunn kissed me.

I open the door to the outside and hold it open for Ben just as Myrna comes walking down the hallway with Louisa, Tilly, and five cakes between them.

Fuuuuuuuuck.

Ben quickly glances back and looks as horrified and flushed as I do. For such a teenage fantasy moment, it seems apropos that his mom would almost walk in on us.

"Ten goldfish and now five cakes. What else? A partridge in a pear tree?" Ben asks, throwing his hands up.

"Dad, that's nuts. You know that's not how the song goes." Louisa laughs, struggling to hold her two cakes. Louisa looks over at me. "We sing it all the time. He knows the words." Louisa says this as if she's concerned his little joke will besmirch his good name in the Christmas carol community.

"Señorita Tillyweather McStubbins, please tell me you're done fleecing this poor charity event for the day?" Ben asks, unable to keep from smiling. Tilly hands Ben a cake and puts her hand on his cheek and then ambles on into the conference room.

"She just kept winning," Myrna says in a haze of wonderment.

"She's got to give them back," Ben says.

"Can we have cake for dinner?" Louisa asks, poking her head out from the conference room.

"It's hamburger night, but we can have cake for dessert," Ben says.

"Five cakes for dessert?"

"No, a piece of one cake." Louisa stomps back into conference room and breaks it to Tilly. Tilly looks from Louisa to Ben. Her icy glare sends a chill down my spine. While she stares at Ben, she casually runs a finger along the pink icing of the nearest cake and licks it.

"I've got this. You guys look like you're in the middle of something important," Myrna says.

"No, it's—" Ben stammers.

"I'm just going to go put this in my car." I hold up the Groot costume as if Myrna has just won it on a TV game show. She nods and heads into the conference room. Tilly closes the door behind Myrna.

"I'll walk you," he says.

"No need," I say, my pace quickening.

"It's really no trouble," he says.

"Fine." We walk in silence through the parking lot. "I'm just right over here." I point to the side street. I look back and Ben nods. Understood. Yes. You are parked on that side street. Noted. I find my car. Beep it unlocked and place the Groot costume in the backseat. "Thank you."

"Olivia—"

"I should head back. Check on Caroline and Gus," I say, starting to walk back toward Asterhouse.

"What were you going to tell me? Earlier. Before I—" Ben cuts himself off and stops walking. He puts his hands on his hips and stands there. "What were you going to say?" I turn around and walk toward him. He watches me. He's about to say something, but cuts himself off again. "Please."

"That you should be proud of what a great dad you are." I am about to step closer to him, but stop myself. "Your girls are amazing." He nods. I can hear him breathing. It's loud. And I can't help but smile.

"I know. I'm a loud breather." He doesn't lean this time, probably because it led to something we would both rather not repeat (ish). Instead he stands up straight and looks down his nose at me—not in a snobby way, in the actual literal way. The sunlight gleams through his eyelashes. Which is ridiculous.

"Is it allergies?" I ask. We continue back toward Asterhouse just as the kids are set loose on the Trunk or Treat portion of the day's events. The kids swarm car trunk after car trunk as volunteers help them fill their pillowcases and plastic pumpkins full of candy.

"I got my nose broken as a sophomore and then again senior year. It hasn't been right since," he says. He turns his head to the side. "I think this is the problem." He slides his finger over a crooked bump at the bridge of his nose. "Super attractive, huh?" I see Caroline across the parking lot and wave her over.

"Oh, I love your nose," I say absently. My stomach drops. My face flushes. Goose bumps slither down my spine. I try to think of something to say. Anything. Instead, I just stand there with my mouth hanging open—weird noises gurgling and oozing from it like some sort of petroleum seep.

"Good to know," he says. I force my mouth closed. "Good to know." Caroline walks over to us.

"Caroline Lang, I don't think I've introduced you. This is Ben Dunn. He was the person in charge of the costumes." Caroline and Ben shake hands. "Nice to meet you's." "Pleasure's." I'm still wondering how "Oh, I love your nose" slipped out of my mouth.

"Such a lovely event," Caroline says.

"Ben's mom, Myrna, is actually the one in charge," I say. Caroline smiles.

"Speaking of, I'd better check in. See if she needs anything," Ben says. "Great meeting you." A nod to Caroline. "Olivia." A lingering nod to me. And we watch him walk away. For a while. A long while.

"I do love Halloween," Caroline says.

"It's definitely growing on me," I say.

"Rachel Hatayama sent over the photos they'll be using on Monday along with some of the pull quotes. I'm sure they're not the only ones they'll be using, but I thought that was nice of her." Caroline is speaking quickly. I can definitely appreciate a woman who just doesn't want to talk about it. Right there with you, sister.

Although . . .

As time passes and my hunger dissipates, I'm starting to remember more details of our kiss. Ben's lips. His one hand at my waist pulling me into him and the other at the nape of my neck, tilting my head just as he needed it. His mouth fast on mine. Warm. Wet. Soft. I bring my fingers up to my own lips.

"Olivia?" Caroline. Shit.

"I'm sorry. I zoned out."

"Is there anything I should be doing tonight?" Caroline asks again.

"What do you want to be doing?"

"I don't know." I wait. "I think I want to go home. Unplug. Watch more of that mystery series about the hot vicar."

"Sure," I say, smiling.

"Hey. It's really good," she says.

"I'm sure it is."

We fall silent, watching the kids.

"You okay?" I ask.

"No." She forces out a perfect Hollywood smile. Underneath, though. Pain. Fear. Her smile fades. She looks at the ground and starts speaking. "I hate that this is going to be part of my biography. That sounds so stupid, but there it is. Every time someone introduces me, every time someone talks about me—amongst all of my accolades they'll always mention that

I am divorced." She looks up at me. "I am divorced." I watch as those three words buzz around her like wasps. "It's so . . . is it scary? Is that the right word? No. Sad." Quiet. "Sad."

"I'm so sorry," I say.

"This is bullshit. I finally get noticed for awards season the year this happens? Because you better believe it's not going to be about my performance or the film or the script. Nope. How did the divorce color your performance? Did you sense something was off in your marriage and pour all of that into the role? Has Max seen the movie? How hard is it coming to these events by yourself? You're so brave."

"Those are one hundred percent going to be questions people ask you."

"Oh, I know. Rachel already asked one of them."

"Which one?"

"How the divorce played into my performance."

"What did you say?"

"I said that I use everything. 'That's what actors do. That's why we're all so'—and I leaned in and whispered—'so crazy.'"

"I bet she loved that."

"She did. And then I said something about how marriage is hard even when things are going well. That love is always a risk. Which is when Rachel said, 'Yeah, that's why all of the rest of us are crazy, too.'"

"That's good."

"Right? I hope the headline isn't 'Caroline Lang Thinks All Actors Are Crazy!'" She smiles.

"The love being a risk thing is . . . ," I trail off. I don't actually know what it is.

"You know what's really shitty? I feel—fine. Comfortable? No, at home. I feel at home in all this." Caroline shakes her balled-up fist over her chest. "Sometimes I think I'm better at being the unhappy, struggling version of myself. I'm sure it's got something to do with my less-than-great childhood, blah blah blah . . ." Caroline rolls her eyes.

"Yep."

"When I'm happy, it makes me feel like I'm missing something. Like there's this looming thing that's going to take it all away. And it'll somehow be my fault that I didn't see it coming."

"This isn't your fault. Max made a choice."

"Yeah, but one could argue—and I assure you, my therapist has—that making the choice to marry Max made this all my fault."

"Your therapist definitely never told you Max cheating was your fault."

"Yeah, but she's thinking it." I laugh. "One of these days, she's going to unwind all those flowy scarves, and tell me what she really thinks of me." I'm about to argue with her when she interrupts: "I knew. Come on. We hope they'll change, but you know."

My face gets hot. Does she know about Adam? Can she sense it?

"You can't control who you fall for," I say, my voice a breathy, choked squeak.

"Can't you, though? I don't know. I think somewhere I knew that Max would give me what I wanted."

"And what's that?"

"To be unhappy. I know that sounds dramatic, but I'm just better when things are hard. You know the really sick thing?"

"You mean, besides you thinking your husband cheating on you is your fault and you don't get to be happy?" My voice

is too loud. Too intense. I'm taking everything too personally. I'm right on the edge.

"It makes the Oscar stuff a little less scary. Sure, a great
and amazing thing is happening, but if I just focus over here
at the slaughterhouse that is my personal life"—Caroline
looks me straight in the eye—"it balances it out. I won't ever
feel too happy." Before I can answer, Caroline's eyes go from
me to just over my shoulder. I turn around and see that Richard is pulling up just beyond the parking lot. "Today was
perfect. The kids are beautiful and it was exactly what I
needed. I actually talked to someone on the board about getting more involved." Caroline pulls her purse higher up on her
shoulder and gives Richard a wave. He steps out of the car,
opens the back door, and waits.

"I'm glad," I say.

"But, now? I want a bottle of wine. Or two. I get to do
that, don't I?"

"You do."

"Good. I don't have to be on set again for another two
months. I can let loose a little."

"There's awards season."

"Yeah, we'll see about that." Caroline gives me a sly wink,
pats me on the shoulder, and starts to walk toward her car.
"Thank you." I nod.

"Text when you get home," I say.

"I will," she says. Richard closes the door behind her. I
wave. He does not. All business. One of these days, Richard.
One of these days.

I get a text from Leah. She's running late for our happy
hour tonight. A happy hour we've already rescheduled twice.
Which is fine. A little too fine. We sometimes go weeks with-

out seeing each other, our friendship only surviving through texting. It just never evolved or deepened. Why is that?

I look up just in time to see a little boy throw the football to Ben. He catches it, of course. Ben motions for the little boy to go long! Go long! The little boy, dressed as a policeman, excitedly skitters across the parking lot. Ben threads his long fingers on the white laces of the football, drops back, pumps his arm, moves around in the pocket, and here we are again: uncomfortably reliving the past. Yes, this is very cute. Yes, Ben is so handsome and oh, look at the little boy. Isn't that adorable? I can't help but roll my eyes.

This is the kind of shit that made my entire adolescence unbearable. I'd blow up every enchanting thing Ben did—no matter how infinitesimal—and make excuses for everything else. Awww, he's not a total asshole! He just did something moderately decent and yeah, sure he slept with three cheerleaders in one week that one time in junior year, but you know, I heard it was mostly hand jobs and one of them blew him and even so, he's just looking for someone to love, you know? He's just scared. HE'S JUST SCARED.

Isn't that what I've been doing for myself all these years? Making the same excuses for why my awfulness was not actual awfulness, it was just another by-product of tightening the tourniquet, so I could start my new life.

So am I still awful, or is my new life just populated by relationships that, like with Leah, have never deepened or evolved enough to make me lash out the way I used to?

Ben throws a perfect spiral to the little boy and everyone cheers. Naturally. I dopily smile. No. NO. One delightful game of catch with a cute kid does not a good man make. This is Ben Dunn. "You've been done by Ben Dunn" Ben Dunn. He

may be older and just as funny and awesome as you'd thought
he'd be and a great kisser who has amazingly strong hands or
whatever? But, yeah. That kiss, though.

Yeesh.

"This is ridiculous," I say. Ben picks the little boy up and
hoists him on his shoulder.

"So, I'm heading out." Gus bounds up behind me.

"Oh my god, you scared me," I say, feeling as though I 100
percent got caught fantasizing about Ben. Which I kind of
did.

"I'll text when I get to my parents'," he says. "Gotta take
this back to the costuming lady." Gus gestures to his superhero costume. "They'll kill me if I take off with it."

"Okay." Gus lunges into me for another hug and I see Ben
looking over. I pat Gus's back as he squeezes me tight.

"Thanks again."

"Okay." One last smile and he sneaks out into the mob of
fun-sized candy and super-amped kids who can't wait to sep-
arate the top-tier offerings from the less valuable ones. I can
already hear the candy negotiations going on. As Gus disappears, the world around me snaps back into focus. Before I
cave in to letting Ben's kiss overwhelm me again, or think
about how I've somehow traded being awful for being a boring, numb robot, I speed home to change before my happy hour
with Leah. I do not say goodbye to Ben or wonder how warm
and lovely their hamburger night will be, followed by a dessert of five cakes.

I pull up to the valet at Otis Bar, freshly showered and blissfully de-Grooted. I hand over my keys and walk inside the

restaurant scrolling through my phone, checking on how the public is reacting to Caroline's divorce. There is definitely a huge—and quite vocal—"she deserves it" camp. Although, these are also the same people who punctuate their every thought with gifs of kids falling or some reality star crying. I've always been baffled that these same women identify with the characters that Caroline plays, but not the actress who brings those characters to life.

I scroll through Twitter and find the following doozies:

@GGGirrrl14 says, "ha! Blonde bitch now alone with skiny azz."

@SherriHeartsLove says, "he was always 2 good 4 her."

And my personal favorite:

@PepperPeepers420 says, "Caroline Lame maybe #lovewins."

I'm still shaking my head about "Caroline Lame" when I see Leah wave from one of the high tables over in the corner. As I walk over to her, I pass tables full of costumed revelers and already drunk groups of friends pre-gaming before walking up to Old Town Pasadena for a night of Halloween fun. It being Halloween will help diffuse the Caroline bombshell. People are going to be out and busy and with every day that passes, our gossip moves further down the feeding frenzy. Of course this was all intentional.

Leah already has a drink in front of her, as well as two people I've never met. She does this all the time: consolidates friends like items on a to-do list. This doesn't help assuage my fear that everyone in my fancy new life was chosen because they'll never go deeper than an acquaintance. Like Caroline was saying, we know.

"Hey, you!" she says. I pull out a stool and slide up onto the seat as elegantly as I can manage, which is not elegantly at all. High barstools are the great equalizers. No one looks good climbing onto them. And now that I'm finally seated, I'm a full two feet away from the table. Unless I commit to hop-hop-hopping the barstool and me forward, this is where I'll stay. I get inordinately angry at the thing and feel the rage building in my shoulders. There's a very real possibility that I might throw this barstool through one of the windows behind Leah very soon. But, there's also a very real possibility that this rage isn't about the high barstool at all. I wrap my purse over the chair back and collect myself.

"Hey!" I finally chirp.

"Olivia, this is my yogi, Elijah." Leah turns to Elijah. "I talk about you constantly." Leah has never mentioned Elijah once. I extend my hand across the table to the toned wisp of a man. Between the long blond hair, the waxed handlebar mustache, and the bushy blond beard, I can't help but wonder how he doesn't asphyxiate during downward dog.

"Namaste," Elijah says, reverently closing his eyes, bringing his hands up in a prayer position, and bowing slightly. Okay. I'm going to need to get out of here right the fuck now.

"And this is Jillian. She's a stylist we work with some-times." Jillian is wearing gold gladiator sandals with jean shorts that are so small the pockets are hanging out of the bottom. She's paired this tasteful ensemble with a white halter midriff-baring top that is—at this very moment—undoubtedly being worn by some rebellious teenager, much to her father's chagrin. I may not even order a drink before an "emergency" mercifully calls me away.

"Nice to meet you," Jillian says with a nod.

"Nice to meet you." I smile. "Shouldn't you guys be at some super cool Hollywood Halloween party?"

"That's later." Jillian sighs.

"Oh. Right."

"Can you imagine a party starting right when it gets dark?" Jillian says, laughing.

"Oh, I can imagine it and then be horrified by it," Leah says. The last gathering I attended at her house started promptly at dusk.

"Like a horror movie," Elijah says.

"Because horrified," Jillian says, nodding. I watch this back-and-forth as if it's some kind of Centre Court finale at Dumb Wimbledon.

"We've already ordered a pitcher of sangria and were waiting for you to decide which appy we're going to have," Leah says.

"The tuna is always good," I say, trying to move this happy hour along so they can all get to their cool midnight Halloween party and I can stop being confronted by how far I've fallen.

"I once ate so much tuna, the guy at Whole Foods told me he couldn't sell me any more," Leah says, laughing. "Mercury poisoning, he said." Leah puts giant air quotes around the words "mercury poisoning."

"But you can still have sushi, though," Jillian says.

"Just not with ahi, sure," Leah says.

"But ahi is the same as tofu." A confused look from Leah. "No, trust me. I'm vegan and I have sushi with ahi all the time," Jillian says.

OH MY GOD.

"Ahi is tuna," I say.

"No, it is not," Jillian says, crossing her long, tanned legs. "There's sushi with tuna and then there's sushi with ahi. One is vegan and one isn't. You're getting them mixed up."

"Ahi and tuna are the same thing," I say, pulling my phone from my purse and Googling "Is ahi tuna?" It immediately pulls up a picture of a giant tuna and the full definition. I show Jillian my phone. It's like watching a toddler grapple with "I got your nose."

"Is that for real?" Jillian asks.

"Maybe you're more of a pescatarian," I say, pulling my phone back.

"A pesca . . . what?" Jillian stares at the phone as I turn it over on the table. "No, I'm vegan."

"If you're eating sushi with ahi in it, you are not vegan." I look around for the waiter. I wave him over.

"Just let her think she's a vegan," Leah says, only half kidding.

"What? No," I say. Leah's eyes narrow. "Vegans don't eat fish. Jillian eats fish, ergo she's not vegan."

"But, I don't eat fish," Jillian says, annoyed.

"Let's just order, okay?" Leah suggests, her voice tight.

"I wonder what they have that's vegan here," Jillian muses, looking over the menu.

"Apparently everything," I say.

"Wow, someone has an overstimulated fifth chakra," Elijah says, jumping in. He puts his knobby elbows on the table and leans across the table toward me. "Do you ever feel strangled, Olivia? Choked up?" He wraps both hands easily around his swanlike neck. I try to force myself to look as passive as possible, because goddammit if Elijah's diagnosis hasn't hit the nail squarely on the head. Elijah's clear ice-blue eyes bore into me as he stops faux-strangling himself long enough to reach across the table. He curls his fingers around my hand and shockingly, I let him. The table falls silent and I must be truly desperate, because I find myself actually waiting for enlightenment from this mini-mustachioed guru. "Hum." Elijah closes his eyes. I tilt my head, my brow furrowing. "Huuuummmmmmmmmm!" I pull my hand back as the fugue state dissipates. And then the little weirdo starts humming. Loudly. Leah sways in time. Jillian beams. The other people in the bar rightfully stare.

"Is that 'Dream a Little Dream'?" I ask. Elijah's hums only get louder. "Okay. I get it, I need—" Elijah begins to hum even louder as our waiter appears.

"Hiya, so sorry to interrupt. My name is Mike and I'll be your server this evening. I see you've ordered the sangria, can I get you something to start? Brussels sprout salad? Maybe the deviled eggs?" Mike's pen is poised, waiting.

"The sangria will be fine for now," I say.

"Ooh, deviled eggs," Jillian coos.

"That's perfect," I say.

Despite Elijah's pleas for me to "stay in the moment," I tune out the rest of the ordering process and pick up my phone. I read through Ellen's report of the online reaction to Caroline's divorce. She's aggregated all of today's content into one spreadsheet that's broken down into different categories of researchable data. The word "bitch" was used the most. Followed up by "stuck-up," "rich," and "skinny." On the other end of the scale were the posts about "love dying," "feeling sorry" for the super couple, and that they should have known the marriage was doomed as no one could ever figure out how to join their names into one cloyingly adorable couple name: Carolax was bandied about for a while, Maxoline never quite caught on, and my personal favorite, Wang—a combination of Walsh and Lang—died the same day it was suggested. #RIPWang.

On the other side, the posts about Max are lousy on the ground with people happy that he's now single. The word "free" is used a lot. Willa Lindholm is mentioned so little it barely registers. I thank Ellen for her diligence and say that we should probably talk later. She agrees and adds that despite what the research shows, Søren insists it's not as bad as we thought it would be. I nod and text back that I'll call her within the hour.

"Olivia?" Leah asks.

"Hm?" I ask, not looking up from my phone.

"We ordered the Brussels sprout salad while you were on your phone like some kind of millennial."

"I actually have to head out. So sorry," I say, not sorry at all.

"What? You just got here," Leah says, her smile faltering.

"It's been a long day and I still have a ton of work to do," I say, holding up my phone.

"Is this about Caroline Lang?" Jillian asks.

"So sad," Elijah says.

"Not that I said anything," Leah quickly adds.

"What about Caroline Lang?" I ask, completely thrown that Leah's repeated something I thought was said in confidence. For everything that she is, she's never done this before.

Of course, she has. It's just no one has ever been dumb enough (e.g., Jillian) to repeat it.

"She filed for divorce today," Jillian says.

"Did she?" I ask, hopping down from the barstool.

"You know she did, Liv," Leah says, her voice hard.

"I think I saw something about it on Twitter, now that you mention it." I sigh. "It was lovely meeting you two." My voice is laced with all the civility I can muster. Elijah leaps off his barstool and takes a long deep breath, one hand placed on his stomach and the other gesturing as if he's scooping up his own deep breaths.

"If humming isn't your bag?" he asks. And then we proceed to stand in awkward silence for what feels like hours.

"Okay," I say. "It was lovely meeting you, Jill—"

"Speak your truth!" Elijah blurts, his voice sounding like he's channeling some being from the great beyond. He opens his eyes dramatically and whispers, "Speak your truth."

"I'd rather hum," I say, the wind slightly knocked out of me. He brings his hands up to the prayer position and bows disappointedly.

"And my name is Jillian, not Jill," Jillian says, with what I'm sure she imagines is a particularly cutting inflection.

"Let me walk you out," Leah says.

As I wait by the door for Leah to apologize for what a bitch her friend is, I can't help but feel a little bit sorry for Jillian and oddly thankful that I wasn't always considered beautiful. My time as an Invisible allowed me to find other things at which to excel. I think we're simple beings and once we feel validation for one trait, we lean into the thing that earned the accolades, and the other qualities recede. In essence, we continue to put our best foot forward.

I was always the smartest. The quickest. And I was always the most comfortable being those things the loudest and first. I was first to raise my hand, first to answer the question, and first to steamroll over those who were less so. The validation I received, however, was a bit complicated. I was rewarded for giving the right answer, but always with a suggestion that I should be slightly more demure in my delivery.

But, I continued to be the smartest and the quickest, because above all else, it earned me the most attention and praise. Had I been beautiful, I wonder if that would have been the case. While I may hate that I was once fat, I am absolutely thankful that I grew up relying on something other than beauty.

What I fear is for women like Jillian, being pretty is enough . . . for a while. We've all seen what happens to women who don't know how to not be pretty, adored, and valued by men as they age. It's a cruel discovery and one oftentimes made too late.

I think about the teenage fantasies that have become my reality over the last ten years. The swell of pride I felt as that intern envied me, even as my marriage bumped and swerved. Sure, I felt lost—but I looked great. And that made me feel better.

Wait. Shit. How am I different from Jillian? Oh my god. No, really. How am I different from the Fish-eating Wonder Vegan Jillian?

"You ready?" Leah asks, finally joining me by the door.

"Yeah," I say, slightly haunted and rechecking the math in my head. No. It can't be right. Do the work again. I am NOT Jillian. First and foremost, I know what a goddamn vegan is. And besides, beauty was something I needed so I could be above reproach. Unassailable. It was the last piece of the puzzle, not the only piece. That's not all I am. Leah and I walk in silence toward the valet. I mean, sure I like that people see my life and want it. I like the feeling I get when I walk in somewhere on Adam's arm and feel people coveting what we have. It makes me feel good. It feels a whole helluva lot better than being ignored for twenty-two years, that's for sure.

"What is going on with you?" Leah asks, as I hand my ticket to the valet.

"It's been a long day," I say.

"You didn't have to be so rude. Jillian may be a bit—"

"No one is that stupid."

"What harm does it do to let her think she's a vegan?" Leah asks, laughing.

"It makes her look like an idiot."

"She is an idiot."

"Very nice."

"Well, she is. She's an amazing stylist, but dumb as a post."

"Wow."

Leah shrugs. "It's the truth." A smile curls across her face. "Ahi isn't tuna," Leah says, giggling. She ends with a satisfied little sigh. "I can't wait to tell that one to Gregory."

"Ew, you like that she's super dumb," I say.

"What?"

"You like that Jillian's so dumb."

"That's bonkers." Leah waves me off, still smiling.

We stand in silence.

What I don't say is the reason Leah likes that Jillian is super dumb is because Jillian is way hotter than Leah. And younger. The super dumb thing evens the field a bit in Leah's mind. So she lets Jillian say insane shit like ahi isn't tuna and gets that swell of superiority as she and Gregory make fun of her later. I'm sure this is Leah's elaborate, yet entirely unintentional, plan to feel assured that whenever she feels like Gregory is taking a bit too much interest in Jillian, she just has to remind him how monumentally stupid she is. As if that's ever mattered to Gregory.

Goddammit. Another wave. Now how am I any different

from Leah? I love that I'm smarter than all my pretty idiot friends. As I've recently, and quite inconveniently, uncovered, there will never be a time when they challenge me in any way.

This afternoon comes rushing back. Ben confronting me with the terrible things I said to him. How that felt. That sickening feeling. My entire body fighting my visceral reaction to him. I haven't felt that in years. That . . . exposed.

My face prickles with memories of Ben, and I immediately feel guilty. But, isn't what's good for the goose good for the gander? Or . . . flip it. Can't what's good for the gander be good for the goose, too? Especially since this goose really liked kissing that particular other gander? Shit. No. Because the goose has to be the good one and is currently waiting for her gander to get over this philandering phase and come home so we can start the next chapter. And when that happens, the goose can't have philandered with other ganders because then the goose can't be as smug and self-righteous as she so wants to be when that moment finally comes.

"Okay. Whatever. You're just tired." Leah backs us up until we're underneath the shade of the valet's umbrella.

"Why did you tell them about Caroline?"

"They knew most of it already. Jillian dressed Max's leading man for the Toronto Film Festival last year and he was majorly bummed that Willa was into Max and not him," she says with a sigh. "And they hadn't even slept together yet, so . . ."

"Wasn't that guy in his forties?" I ask, noticing my car pulling out of the parking garage.

"Fifty-three, actually." The valet flips a U-turn and is idling behind a few other cars in line waiting to be parked. "Oh, how was that Halloween fair today?"

"It was good," I say, getting my dollar bills ready for the tip and not looking at her just in case the flush of my face betrays me. "Wait. How did you know about that? I haven't talked to you in forever."

"Gregory and I bumped into Adam at lunch yesterday." Leah runs her finger along the valet stand for a long moment. "Adam mentioned you've been super busy with it."

"I haven't been all that busy with it," I say.

"Oh, I'm sure it'll be fine."

We are quiet.

"I didn't know he had a lunch yesterday," I say. Leah's face colors and she lets out a little half-laugh.

"Yeah, at the Lake House. Remember we went there and you hated it so much you signed up for Yelp just so you could leave a bad review?" Leah's talking faster and faster. "What was it you said?"

"I said, 'more like the Fake House.'"

"That's right," she says, laughing. "So funny." Even I know that's not my best work.

"Who was he having lunch with?" I ask.

"Uh, some woman. Another doctor, I think."

"Oh—"

"Nice enough," Leah adds. The valet hops out of my car and holds the door open for me.

"Sorry to skip out on you," I say, giving her a quick hug.

"No, you're not."

"You're right." I hand the valet his tip and climb into the driver's seat. As I pull away from the curb, I feel exceedingly angry, which makes sense given the last thirty minutes or so. But my anger has this furious tail on it that I'm having trouble controlling.

Is it the fear that spending extended periods of time with the likes of Jillian and Elijah will suck actual brain cells out of my head? Or is it Leah's insinuation that I've been too busy to be a proper wife to Adam? Maybe it's the cool Halloween parties everyone's going to while I hunker down for another evening of work. It could also be the lingering effects of my day at the fair trapped in a tree, reliving every painful moment of my Sweaty Marble adolescence. Maybe I just feel guilty about how much I liked kissing Ben. I wait at a red light, my jaw tight, my breath becoming ragged.

The light turns green.

It's the lunch. I wasn't always aware of every item on Adam's daily schedule. But because of the now-infamous Failed Calendar Project, it strikes me as odd that he'd never mentioned his lunch at the Lake House yesterday. We sat at the dining room table and I sifted through all of the slips of paper, backs of envelopes, and receipts where he'd scribbled the various appointments and events he'd absently shoved into the "Desktop Papers" basket by the microwave. We went through the calendar on his phone and even added the stuff he'd put in the Notes app, as well as the terribly naive scheduling app I'd downloaded for him earlier this year.

So, what's the big deal about a perfectly innocent lunch? Why didn't he mention it?

EVEN IDIOTS CAN BE RIGHT ABOUT FIFTH CHAKRAS

I'm driving down Arroyo Parkway in a dangerous haze, picking at Adam's lunch like a hangnail. Come on, it was a last-minute lunch with another doctor. So what? Why am I making such a big deal out of this? I snap out of it just in time to realize the Lake House is right across California Blvd. on South Lake.

I bet it's open right now. It'll be a madhouse because it's Halloween and a Friday night, but . . . maybe I can use that chaos to my advantage. Jesus. Stop. Get ahold of yourself, Olivia. Really? This is the hill I'm going to die on? Adam has cheated on me for our entire marriage, but yeah . . . he doesn't tell me about one totally normal lunch and all of a sudden I'm Sherlock Fucking Holmes.

Okay, but why not just put it on the calendar? I get into the turn lane. It's going to bug me all night, and because I'm being dramatic and no, YOUR fifth chakra is overstimulated,

Elijah. I come to a stop as the two cars in front of me make their lefts. The light turns red. I wait. My mind is now empty, save the click-click-click of my turn signal.

As I zoom down California Blvd., my mind boots back up. Am I even sure he was there with Nicola? I guess that's what I need to know: Did Leah just admit that she and Gregory stumbled upon my husband having lunch with a woman that wasn't me? Will they assume she's just a work friend? Or will they suspect something more salacious? Do they now feel sorry for me? Do they think she's prettier than me? Have they been talking about it ever since? Is that why she invited Thing One and Thing Two to happy hour? Because she felt awkward and didn't want to talk about the crumbling state of my marriage? I make a left onto Lake Street.

The so-called South Lake area is a section of Pasadena loaded with high-end boutiques and restaurants. It's walkable. It's adorable. And tonight it's bustling and alive with people in costumes and packs of trick-or-treating kids as I inch my way toward the Lake House. I practice my speech. I build the backstory. I am ready for anything.

With absolutely no parking available, I pay way too much for a valet that I'll need for approximately five minutes. I grab my phone and purse and am immediately boomeranged back into the car. My phone is still plugged into the charger. I crawl back into the car, unplug my phone, and stand back up, collecting myself as best I can. I smile at the valet and begin to walk toward the restaurant.

"I need your keys," he says, running after me. I open my hand to reveal my keys and shrug back toward the young man.

"For Halloween, I'm going as a train wreck, apparently," I say to the poor man. He nods and offers a bewildered, strained smile. "I won't be that long." Another nod. Leave it, Olivia. He's not going to be sold on whatever forced sanity you're trying to shove down his throat. "Bye." In response, the young man just furrows his brow.

What is it that I think I'm going to find here? I know Adam is cheating. I know Adam has been cheating since the beginning of our marriage. Hell, Nurse Brenda knows Adam has been cheating since the beginning of our marriage. Do I really need proof positive that Gregory and Leah are privy to his cheating as well? Shouldn't I have figured out by now that, besides that one terrified intern at work, everyone else knows that I am a cuckold? Can women be cuckolds?

Shit, maybe I just don't want to go home to a dark house and another night alone.

I push my way through the front door and the rage in my shoulders hurls it open a lot more energetically than I was expecting. I need to calm down. I take a deep breath as I pose the question I came here to get answered: Do Leah and Gregory know about Nicola, and, if so, do they think I'm a silly fool for allowing my husband to philander so brazenly? I mean, what kind of woman would know about her husband's affairs and do nothing?

Indeed.

I shove past the crowd and find the teenage hostess safely behind a podium, talking on the phone. She's wearing sequined devil horns. I am just about to say something and she holds up a single, manicured fingernail. I notice her nail has a tiny panda painted on it. Her other nails are all painted to look like bamboo. I look away thinking that there is no way this woman is washing her own dishes. Just then a group of young women dressed in multicolored leotards with the word

"Crayola" emblazoned down the front of them crowd inside the restaurant.

I settle in among the Crayola girls and scan the restaurant. Just like in Escuela, I play the "Guess Who's on a First Date" game. Which ninety-seven-pound girl is eating her weight in pasta, thinking the best way to ensnare a man is by acting like you're an effortlessly sexy robot who doesn't sweat, poop, diet, or nag?

Hell, I did it.

Wanting a fresh start, I decided to move to Washington, D.C., once I'd lost all the weight. There was no way I was going to officially become the New Olivia Morten as long as I stayed in my hometown. It was easier to reinvent myself back then, the Internet and social media hadn't really taken off. A new town offered me something I never thought I could have: a new identity as someone who was never fat.

I remember riding in the shuttle on the way to the airport and at every turn being amazed at this big new life I could have. I thought receiving male attention for the first time ever or being able to buy clothes off the rack would have the biggest impact on me. Instead, I got emotional at just being able to climb into the backseat of the shuttle bus without a hitch. As I crawled over the outstretched legs of an older businessman, I was overcome.

Being fat had whittled my freedom away one pound at a time. The bigger I got the safer I played it, until my life became heartbreakingly, unrecognizably small. I'd never noticed how much time and energy I spent scanning the horizon for potential difficulties; most times I opted out altogether. My rallying cries of my life as a fat person were always, "Do I have to walk there?" and "Will I stand out?"

And traveling was always the worst.

Red faced and winded, was it too far to walk? Would people notice how out of shape I was? Would I have to run through the airport in order to make my flight? Would I be able to fit as I walked down the aisle of the plane? Would I fit in the seat? If I didn't fit in the seat, could I ask a flight attendant for a seatbelt extender quietly enough, so no one would hear? Would anyone see her handing the seatbelt extender to me? Could I hold off on any bathroom needs so I wouldn't have to shove myself back in the seat? Could I fit through the door of the airplane bathroom? Once I got to my destination, how much am I missing out on because I'm too fat—sitting out by the pool, riding on the backs of motorcycles, magnificent views from the tops of ancient buildings, tight restaurants with tiny parlor chairs, cobblestone streets and steep hills, etc., etc., etc. . . . ?

My mind was such a tornado of all the things I'd simply accepted as part of my life, that by the time I boarded that flight for D.C. and sat down comfortably in my seat, I openly cried when the seatbelt clicked easily into place. I told the man next to me I was crying because I was a nervous flyer.

"We'll get through this together, then," he'd said. That was Adam. We'd talked throughout the whole flight. It never occurred to me he was flirting. I thought he was just being nice. I couldn't believe that this was how people actually lived. Whenever I'd flown before, I never looked directly at anyone. Eyes down. Don't look at me and if you do, I'll apologize immediately for taking up too much space.

On that five-hour flight from LAX to Dulles, emboldened by Adam's attentions, I became her. This. The New Olivia Morten. When I returned to my seat, I was the Olivia Morten who played competitive tennis in high school, did some catalog modeling on the side, and was homecoming queen. Twice.

When Adam asked for my phone number just as the flight attendant told us to buckle up for our descent into D.C., I stifled the giggle that bloomed in my chest and coolly said, "Sure." The freedom of playing this version of Olivia Morten was intoxicating. Her voice was silky and confident. She moved with elegance and allowed men to look at her like she was a piece of priceless art in a museum. Her eyes were never cast down. I naively thought that all I had to do to pull this off was toss my fat history out like trash. I couldn't make the deal fast enough.

"One?" The teenage hostess sighs.

"What?"

"Is there just one of you this evening?"

"No. What? No." The hostess sighs. "I was looking for someone, but—"

"Oh." The hostess types something in her tablet and I hear a buzz just behind me. A young couple appears with a flashing red buzzer that tells them their table is ready. "Right this way." I tuck in once again behind the Crayola girls, when another hostess comes up to the podium with a stack of menus. This hostess's Halloween costume is simply a little gold halo. I know I should leave. But, I have to know if Leah went back into that happy hour and told her two dipshit friends that she may have just said something she shouldn't to her poor friend whose husband is cheating on her. The idea of Jillian and Elijah feeling pity for me both enrages and sickens me. It's one thing to know that Adam is cheating. It's something else entirely that his infidelity is being gossiped about behind my back by all of my supposed friends.

"Hi, I'm so sorry. I know it's super busy, but my boss—you know how bosses can be," I say.

"Oh, absolutely," the hostess says.

"Well, he wanted me to come down here tonight of all nights."

"On Halloween?"

"I know! Anyway, he had a lunch yesterday and his companion left her purse."

"That's awful!"

"I know!"

"What's the name?" she asks, conspiratorially.

"It would be under Farrell," I say, my voice dipping to a whisper.

"Sure, they come in all the time."

"Oh, good. What a relief," I say. Black speckles crowd the corners of my eyes. The restaurant blurs. My mouth goes bone dry.

"So is the purse Mrs. Farrell's . . . oh wait, she's a doctor too, so is the purse lady Dr. Farrell?" She scans her tablet, pressing a few buttons as the restaurant mutes and blurs around me.

"Oh, uh . . ." I blink back the panic, my fingers curling around her little hostess podium as I pitch a bit forward.

Everyone knows.

I feel like I'm going to be sick. I push my way through the crowd and out the door. Leah and Gregory know. I swing wildly between being furious and feeling utterly humiliated. How can I show my face? How long, exactly, have I been the butt of everyone's joke? How do I act like I don't know? I hand the young man my now crumpled-up valet ticket.

"Oh, it's right here," he says. He hands me my keys and shakes off the money. "Don't worry about it."

"Thank you," I say. I hear the pain in my voice and it unsettles me. The young man nods and closes the car door behind me. I sit in my car. Robotically put on my seatbelt. Check the mirrors. Put the car in drive and once it's safe, pull out from the valet. I drive up Lake Street going the exact speed limit. Safely signaling. Stopping at the red light to let the Halloween partiers cross the street. All of them smiling and laughing. Enviably carefree as a night of fun and possibility spreads out in front of them.

My hands tighten around the steering wheel. I shake my head as my last question thunks and whirls around my brain. How do I act like I don't know? What I actually mean is, how do I act like I don't know about this new thing, on top of all the other stuff that I'm already acting like I don't know about? And it comes to me, I finally understand that saying: the straw that broke the camel's back. You know, if that last straw is an entire fucking building and the poor camel has been lugging around hundreds upon thousands of pounds of straw for years—just waiting for a time when she could be free of it all.

"Oh my god," I say. My voice is tight and strained. "What am I going to do?"

I've been a fool.

Someone honks behind me and I give a little wave, pressing on the gas pedal. I don't know what to do and the pain and all the lies are slithering up my throat like a boa constrictor. I feel like if I unleash this hurt, I won't be able to control it. Whatever is crawling up my throat right now feels so big and vast, I don't know if I'll survive it once it gets free. I'm frightened. And desperate. I remember Elijah's words: "Do you ever feel strangled, Olivia? Choked up?"

Strangled. Choked up.

I start humming "Dream a Little Dream of Me." Quiet, at first. The queasiness rolls through my entire body, so I roll down my window. The balmy October night feels good on my face. I signal. Turn. Make it home. Just make it home. And I hum. Louder. And louder. And LOUDER. AND LOUDER.

Somewhere along the way I remember that tomorrow is the day Adam and I are supposed to take our Christmas card picture with that fancy photographer Caroline recommended. Something about this soothes me. It's a plan. It's the next right thing. I may not know how to fix this, but at least I can control what's going to happen next. See, Nicola? You may have him for some dumb lunch at the Fake House, but I've got him for Christmas cards that go to all of his colleagues, extended family, and the entire fucking world.

Focus on tomorrow, Olivia. The photo shoot. This can tip the scales back in my favor. Remind Adam of what he has and that what we have is best for both of us. It's good for business. I mean, I could breezily remind him how much Jacob likes me and how detrimental it would be to his status, not only at the hospital but in our private circles, to be That Guy who got caught cheating.

Oh my god.

What am I doing?

Am I honestly thinking about threatening my husband with social ruin if he doesn't behave? Is this what my marriage has become? A series of ultimatums and threats that paint me as some key-jangling warden. I think back to our wedding and my heart seizes as I rewrite the vows that I so lovingly repeated that day:

I vow to monitor you like a prison guard until both our spirits break.

I vow to settle for a loveless marriage just as long as I don't have to be alone.

I vow to act like I'm not miserable, too.

I vow to put on a good face for friends and family, never speaking ill of a marriage that I still need everyone to envy.

I vow to keep telling myself that this is a phase.

I vow not to remember how in love we were in the beginning.

I vow not to notice when your indifference toward me turns to disdain.

I vow not to notice that I don't make you laugh anymore.

I vow not to admit that I am no longer attracted to you either.

I vow never to admit that marriage is so much harder than I thought it was.

I vow never to admit that maybe I didn't know you well enough to be in love with you.

My breathing is quick and shallow as I pull into the driveway of the perfect home I always fantasized I'd live in. Packs of adorable kids dressed up as their heroes pepper the street, disappointed when they see the light on our porch unlit. I stare at it. Frozen. Unlit. No one's home. My car idles and rumbles beneath me. Minutes pass. More.

Just walk inside.

Turn off the car, Olivia.

Turn off the car and walk inside.

But, I can't move.

I can only stare at our home. The autumnal porchscape. The perfect spiraling topiaries draped with tasteful Halloween decorations. The bright red door. The black shutters. The gray paint color I scouted for months. The address numbers I hung myself. Surely, this is the house of people who have it all figured out.

I finally will myself to turn off the car. Now get out of the car. Open the door. You don't even have to grab your purse. You'll get it later when you're feeling better. Just open the door and get out. Open it. People are starting to stare. My breathing quickens. Open the door, Olivia. There are close to a thousand people roaming your street, this is not the night to do this. My hands are shaking. I press them flat against the tops of my legs to steady them. Open the door. I finally lift one hand and push it toward the door, curl my fingers around the door handle, and push the door open. My breath won't catch. Shallow. Shallow. Shallower.

If you have to crawl along the darkened fringes of your driveway, Olivia Bonita Morten, you are getting inside that motherfucking house. You are not going to have one of those panic attacks on your lawn like a crazy person in front of all these adorable kids. Trick or treat? How about a trick: You can work your whole life toward a dream and then it's taken away from you within the span of a week!

I lift my leg and put it on the ground, followed by the other. I'm beyond light-headed at this point and can only manage to stand up about halfway, so that I resemble some kind of tormented question mark. My breath won't catch and now that I've been through one, I know damn well that I'm on the verge of another panic attack.

I try, once more, to stand up straight. Nothing. Okay. Fine. Let's see how far this tormented question mark can walk toward her house without frightening the children.

I remember back to when I was in that Groot costume and all I have to do is sidestep—a sad whimper escapes my lips. Right. Okay, don't think about today at the Halloween fair. Another whimper. Ben. How about we don't think about anything until we get inside this house. Another breath doesn't catch. I'm losing my balance . . . I'm falling. No. Please. I can't fall. I can't faint in my own driveway. My eyes dart toward the sidewalk as a pack of kids come toward the house like a swarm of color and sugar highs. I'm pitched forward when it comes to me—

Speed skating.

I tuck my arm behind my back, and moving with the momentum, I slide my foot forward, catching myself before I fall. I pump my arm, letting my whole body lean with it, and slide the other foot forward. I grab my purse, bump the car door shut with my hip, and slide the other foot forward once more. I will not think about what I look like. I will let myself think that this pack of kids and their parents will just think the weird lady is waving. I'm waving. I'm waving. I will focus on getting into my house.

I catch myself absently humming "Dream a Little Dream" as I raise my arm high in the air just like I'm back on the street I grew up on. The pendulum movement of my body along with the air on my face is working. It's calming me down. My breath finally catches. And again. And again. My voice cracks with gratitude and I reach even higher, the familiar feeling of my shoulder stretching and rotating. I dig into the warmth as my quads burn. The relief shoots through my body as my breath finally steadies.

I step up onto my porch and open my hand. The keys have left a sweaty indentation. With still-shaking hands, I finally get the key in the lock and push open the door. I skate inside and close the door behind me.

"You did it," I say. I bolt the lock and lean against it. The house settles. That one creak from somewhere over the den. That same bump from just outside the kitchen. The same lights are on, ready for my solo late return. Not the overhead lights in the living room, but that one persimmon-colored floor lamp I bought from that place on Green Street with the broken spoke inside the lampshade, that no matter what I do, stubbornly remains broken. The nook light in the kitchen. The outside light by the garage. And the night-light from our en suite bathroom. Just enough light for security, but not so much that I'll feel like no one else is home.

I think back to the summer vacations I used to take with my extended family. I'd fall asleep to the sounds of the adults laughing somewhere in the house. And I'd wake up to the smell of coffee and conversations that were already in full swing. I've always thought that the sound of your family talking to one another somewhere in the house is the best lullaby you could ask for. It made me feel safe. That I was a part of something. And that when I sleepily walked down that hallway come morning, there'd be someone there to wish me a good morning.

I've gotten used to thinking I don't need that anymore. That a nice tablescape with gourds is just as comforting as the sound of voices in the house. And the smell of coffee percolating can now be achieved just by buying the proper coffeemaker. I walk cautiously over and sit down in the houndstooth slipper chair I lovingly chose but have yet to sit in.

"Ugh, so this is super uncomfortable," I say, shifting around.

I scan my house—with its planned, left-on lights and the bumps and creaks to which I've become accustomed. It's perfect. My phone rings from deep inside my purse. Perfect and cold. I lift my purse onto my lap and dig through it, finally pulling my phone from its depths. It's Caroline.

"Thish one mom she tole me imma—I mean, she tole me I shu-go as elsafromfrozen for Haylo . . . ," Caroline trails off. "Hayloweeeeeeen."

"What's going on?" I ask, my voice ragged and soft.

"Thish one mom she tole me imma—I mean, she tole me I shu-go as elsafromfrozen for Hayloweeeeeeen."

"Someone told you to go as Elsa from *Frozen* for Halloween?" I ask.

"Thash wha-I been tellin' you," she slurs.

"Who?"

"Thish bishy mom in some kinda coat with the . . ." And then silence.

"Caroline?"

"She a bish. Tellin' me to letitgo, ohhhhh I'll letitgo. In her faaaace."

"Are you handing out candy to trick-or-treaters?"

"Yesh."

"Are you drinking?"

"Yesh."

"Have you been drunk while giving out candy to trick-or-treaters?" My entire being is now thankfully completely focused on the task at hand.

"She said I shu-be elsafromfrozen. I . . . turn tha light out, shhhh. Then. THEN. I drank some wine."

"So you didn't—at any point—hand out candy to children drunk?"

"No, what? No . . . thash weird . . . who . . . who wu-do thash."

"Indeed."

"INDEED." Caroline repeats the word, but this time with a cartoonish British accent.

"Where are you—"

"Indeed!" Another exclamation.

"Okay."

"Guvnah!" And then Caroline crumbles into a fit of giggles, her phone cracking to the floor. I wait. She meanders around the house trying to find the phone until finally squealing, "Where youuuuuuuu go! There you go!" She picks up the phone. "Hello?"

"Caroline? Honey, can you—"

"Ooooooooh, honeyyyyyyyyyyyyyy."

"Caroline . . ."

"Who is thish?"

"It's Olivia."

"Oh, hello." My head drops into my hands.

"Is it time for bed?" I ask.

"Is that why you called?" Caroline whispers.

A beat.

"Yes." I raise my head.

"Oh."

"So, time for bed?"

"Sure, yeah, okay."

"Do you want me to come over? Make sure you're okay?" I hear a rustling and some distant mumbling. More rustling. "Caroline?" A door. Open and close. Another door. Some more rustling.

"Olivia?" A man's deep voice crackles through the line.

"Richard. Oh, thank god."

"I've got her. She's fast asleep on some patio furniture."

"Oh, good. Can you do me a favor?"

"Yep."

"Can you get her up to bed and then take her phone?"

"Yep."

I catch myself. "And you know, make sure she doesn't choke on her vomit and die, but . . ."

"Mostly the phone."

"Yeah."

"Will do."

"Keep me posted?"

"Copy that." Richard hangs up without a sign-off. I guess former Navy SEALs don't really feel the need to say adorable polite farewells.

Before I get into some weepy monologue, I stand and walk into the kitchen. I haven't eaten much of anything all day and would like to get something down before I turn in. I get out the fixings for my chicken salad. I grab a glass and find a bottle of club soda in the fridge, hoping it will settle my stomach.

I sit down at the dining room table, flip my napkin onto my lap, and look down at the salad. This is essentially the same salad I've been making for myself ever since I started losing weight. In the very beginning, I experimented with different meals and, after trying to do some weird, healthy hash thing with a sweet potato and black beans, gained two pounds in one week. I freaked out and went straight back to my beloved chicken salad for dinner. Within two weeks I'd lost four pounds—the two that I'd gained from the Great Hash Incident plus two more. I take a bite. Wash it down with club soda.

Another bite.

This same salad. Chicken. Cherry tomatoes. Goat cheese. Olive oil. Balsamic vinegar. Field greens. If I'm on my own, this is the dinner I make. Another bite. I'm even still using the same *Barefoot Contessa* recipe to cook the chicken.

I look over to the kitchen. I make the same smoothie for breakfast every morning. Hemp milk. Handful of baby kale. Vegan protein powder. Half of a frozen banana. Almond butter. It's changed a little over the years. Skim milk to almond milk to hemp milk. Greens to baby spinach to baby kale. I changed the brand of protein powder to one Leah told me about that wasn't as grainy. And the tablespoon of almond butter is new once I swapped out the avocado. Like within the last few years.

Another bite.

I also eat the same lunch every day when I'm not out with a client. Small curd cottage cheese. Cinnamon. Fresh berries—preferably blackberries, as they have less carbs than raspberries—although I enjoy raspberries more. Another bite.

Same smoothie. Same cottage cheese lunch. Same chicken salad dinner. Every day. For going on fifteen years. I fork a cherry tomato and pull it through a smear of goat cheese. It seems that boring, numb robot who likes to surround herself with pretty little idiots also doesn't have much of a palate.

I finish the salad, load the dishwasher, turn off all the lights in the house, and shuffle down the hall to my bedroom. I'm done processing the bullshit I've seen today. I'm going to close this day out once and for all. With our Christmas card photo shoot tomorrow, I have plenty to think about while I take my makeup off. What I'll wear. What Adam will wear. I take a long shower. Will I use a holiday background or take a more casual shot somewhere in the house? I dry off and brush my teeth. How will I act like my husband isn't a lying cheating bastard? I get into my pajamas and crawl into bed. Maybe I should go to the store and grab some pastries to set out for the photographer. Just as I'm plugging in my phone, I receive a text from Richard.

"Caroline in bed. Asleep. I have phone now."

I text back, "Thank you." And nothing.

I set the alarm and turn over on my side. Away from my phone and toward where Adam should be, but hasn't been for days if not . . . has it been weeks? I flip back over. Yes. I think I will get some pastries for tomorrow.

HULK

After making my morning smoothie, using peaches and cardamom instead of berries (take that, Boring Robot), I decide to ride my bike to the store in case I won't be able to get into the gym today. Besides, it's a crisp autumn day and I'm looking to shake off any remnants of Yesterday: The Day That Would Not End.

I roll into the parking lot, lock my bike up to a low metal gate near the market, grab my reusable bags, and stride into the store feeling strong and purposeful. I situate my messenger bag so it doesn't split my torso with one boob on either side and pull a grocery cart loose from its brethren. Just as I was leaving for the store, Adam texted that he'd be home within the hour. He didn't even make up a lie this time. I'm not sure if that's a good or a bad thing.

I bury myself in buying food for the Christmas card shoot. I feel the same vicarious joy in picking out foods I never eat as I do when I'm searching for the perfect gift for someone. The freedom to be luxurious. Something I rarely extend to myself.

I buy raspberries, juice, pastries fresh from the bakery, and various sparkling waters. I pile them in my cart and find the express lane. As I wait in line, I scan the tabloids. Infuriating headlines that taunt women as they shop for their families with promises that the perfect women they envy are on the verge of losing their man, getting older and fatter, or some shameful scandal involving all three.

We deliberately timed the announcement of Caroline and Max's divorce so it'd miss this week's magazine covers. I'm sure all of the tabloids are working on next week's cover now, scrabbling through their archives for photos of Caroline where she isn't wearing makeup and looks appropriately desperate.

The woman in front of me sets her groceries down on the conveyor belt and protectively places the plastic separator between her groceries and mine. I'm just about to start unloading my groceries when someone bumps me.

"Let me just get in front of you," the old woman says, clutching a container of soup.

"I'm sorry?"

The woman is dressed in a pair of stained sweats and an old T-shirt announcing that she was a finisher in the Fun in the Sun 5K back in 1985. She's bone thin and has applied enough mascara for a big night out, set off by pink circles of rouge on her cheeks that would make any Victorian doll envious.

"Yeah, let me just get in front of you," she repeats, now elbowing her way past me. But, there's not enough room in the narrow express lane and it's very quickly turning into the most depressing slapstick comedy bit ever recorded.

"Okay. Ma'am? Just . . . can you hold on a second?" Now everyone is staring and the woman is standing so close to me that I can smell not only the tomato soup dripping down the sides of the container but her powdery rose perfume as well. "Let me move out of your way before you—" and in the middle of my sentence she starts pushing past me once more, pulling a shelf of spearmint gum to the ground in the process. I bend down to pick up the gum just as she steps over me, sloshing her soup down on the conveyor belt.

"I've got water on my lung," the woman says as I'm picking up the gum.

"Oh," I say.

"My friends think I should go to the hospital, but they'll just admit me."

"Uh-huh." I put the last packet of gum back on the shelf.

"I just wanted some soup, you know?" I nod. As the woman tells the cashier her tale of woe, I start to put my groceries down on the conveyor belt again.

"I wish I could eat like that," she says, eyeing my haul.

"I'm sorry?" The woman hands the cashier a wadded-up five-dollar bill.

"I said I wish I could eat like that," she yells as if I'm hard of hearing.

"It's for a morning meeting." I can hear the defensiveness in my voice.

"That's what I used to say, too," she says with an elaborate wink. Her mascaraed eyelashes stick to one another and for a brief moment, she looks like some garage sale baby doll with one eye forever stuck closed.

"Your change," the cashier says, holding out the woman's money and an overlong receipt. I force myself to look anywhere else but at the woman, trying to preemptively shield myself from whatever zinger of a parting shot she has planned for me. She shoves the change and the receipt into her pocket, cradles the container of soup, and shambles out of the store without a second thought of me.

"She comes in all the time," the cashier says, beeping my groceries over the scanner. I hand my reusable bags to the bag boy.

"Oh," I say.

"Mean as a snake," the cashier says, her voice dipping to a whisper. I don't want to know the history of the Saddest Woman in the World and I certainly don't want to commiserate with this cashier about how mean she was to me. I want to buy my food, bike home, and set up a lovely spread for the photographer so I can have an even better Christmas card with the husband who's been cheating on me for the entirety of our marriage. I need this morning to go well. I need this morning to go according to plan.

"Yeah, I kind of got that," I say, pulling my credit card from my wallet and sliding it through the machine. And then, like the beginnings of a cold, I feel the tingling of the little voices asking: How thin do I have to be before no one feels the need to comment on what I'm eating? What made that woman think we were fellow travelers? Could she tell I'm a fraud?

I walk out of the grocery store without so much as a grunted farewell and hurry out to my bike. Forcing myself to get back on track, I unlock my bike, put the reusable bags into the basket, tuck my wallet underneath them, and buckle my helmet under my chin. Just as I'm kicking off, I see a run-down minivan parked across the entrance of the grocery store. That's got to be hers, I think to myself.

Despite everything telling me not to investigate, I pedal toward her. Not even trying to park in any designated spot except the one a fire truck would use in case of an emergency, the woman is now sitting in the front seat of her car drinking the soup. I need to tell her that I biked here, introduce her to Luz Alcazar—yes, THE Luz Alcazar—the world-famous photographer who will be taking our personal Christmas card portrait. I can see myself now, bicycle helmet askew, screaming my accomplishments into her smoke-stained window, the smell of tomato soup saturating my impromptu, parking lot keynote speech.

Instead, all I feel as I pedal past is this chilling recognition of something familiar. Something inevitable.

I will not end up like you, old woman.

I won't.

I bike home faster than I've ever biked. It feels good and momentarily washes me clean of whatever stink that woman left on me. I'll never be able to eat tomato soup again, I think, as I pull into our driveway.

I set out my breakfast spread, get showered, and as I'm blow-drying my hair, I hear Adam come in.

"Liv?" he calls out. I hear his keys clatter onto the table. "I got you a coffee from that place you like." I walk out of the bathroom, my towel tied tightly around my body.

"Thank you, sweetheart," I say, giving him a long kiss. I can feel his confusion as it takes him a few seconds to really kiss me back, but then he pulls me in tight and for a few blissful minutes we're us again. His strong hands weave through my wet hair—then a flash of Adam and Nicola clinking glasses with Leah and Gregory. I shake it off. My hands tighten around his waist, his crisp oxford cloth shirt beneath my fingers—did he sleep with her last night? Another shake. I dive into him more and in some altered state start to unbuckle his belt right there in the foyer of our house not half an hour before Luz Alcazar and her crew are to take our highly respectable Christmas card photo.

"What's gotten into you?" Adam asks.

"I just miss you," I say. I lunge into him again and this time I feel this intense wave of yearning sweep through me. I've never felt . . . this need. For him. "I need you." I look up at him and am almost undone by the heat of my own openness. I unbuckle his belt and feel this fantastic animalistic freedom tingle all over as I quickly untuck his shirt, my hands sliding up his perfect torso.

As we get more and more lost in one another, I can't keep my mind from inventorying how well lit this foyer is. Can I get him back to our bedroom, or maybe we could go back into the shower, but our en suite bathroom has got all the lights on and . . . no, we could go under the covers or . . . oh, wait! I realize that I'm naked under the towel and I can just keep it on and it can be super spontaneous and he won't even notice that he's not seeing me naked, because he'll be so swept away in the sexiness of the moment. Maybe we can even do it standing up? In all of our years together, we've never tried it that way. I had a whole "could he lift me" thing. But, now is as good a time as any . . .

I pull away from him and huskily tell him that I'm naked under my towel, which, I know, is obvious, but in the moment sounded super hot. I pull him toward the wall—without the seasonal wreath I bought for the holidays on it—and wrap my leg around him just like I've seen women do in the movies. I dive into him again, my hands now fumbling with the zipper of his pants.

"Liv," Adam says, pulling away.

"It's okay. Luz won't be here for another half hour."

"Liv." His voice is more forceful.

"What?" I ask, looking around for what could possibly be making him stop the super spontaneous proceedings.

"It's been a long night," he says, taking my hands in his. Stopping them from any further investigations. He looks down at me. Waiting for me to get it.

"Oh," I say, feeling like I want to crawl into a hole and die. Adam zips his pants back up, tucks in his shirt, and buckles his belt. My face is hot from want. My entire body is tingling. My hands are shaking and my breath is fast. I focus on him as he buckles his belt and there's nothing. His hands are calm. His breath is steady. His face pale and serene.

"Now, why don't you finish getting ready," he says.

"Why?" The word comes tumbling from my mouth before I even know what I'm asking.

"Why should you finish getting ready? I don't know, Livvie, I'm not sure my parents would really take too kindly to a Christmas card with my half-naked wife on it, although . . . ," he says with a wry smile as he walks into the living room.

"No. I mean why don't you want to have sex with me?" My entire mouth goes dry. Adam turns around.

"What?"

"Please, don't make me ask it again," I say, walking toward him.

"I'm just not in the mood right now," he says. "That's okay, isn't it?"

"We haven't had sex since Valentine's Day."

"That's—"

"Of last year."

"I don't think—"

"That's almost two years of you not being in the mood."

"Okay," he says.

"So . . ."

"So?"

"Why?" I ask again.

"Do we . . . are we thinking right now is the best time for this conversation?" he asks.

"Is there ever a best time?" Adam crosses his arms over his chest. I walk over to him. "There's never a good time for a talk like this." I tighten the towel around my body. I see a flicker of something in his eyes. A flash of something new. "What? What was that?" Adam shakes his head. "Please."

"I was just . . ." He motions to my towel. "I mean, God forbid, your own husband sees you naked." I watch him, scanning his face for some hint that he's kidding.

"What?"

"You asked. That's what I was thinking."

The towel now feels like the Groot costume.

"What does that have to do with why you don't want to have sex with me?" Adam shrugs his shoulders. My mind is a riot. "Okay." My fingers inch to tighten the towel once more. No, by all means, don't touch the fucking towel again, Olivia. "Okay, you're saying shitty things so we don't talk about what's really going on," I say, trying not to act like that wasn't a direct hit. I was right. This is all my fault. The hurt falls through a trapdoor and lands squarely between anger and rage.

"Maybe that's why I haven't been in the mood," he says.

"Okay, so this is where we need to check ourselves before we say things we can't take back." I stand there more aware of the towel than ever. Why did I think he didn't notice? Of course, he noticed he's never seen me naked. I mean, he's seen parts of me, of course, but in the ten years we've been married I've never stood in front of him bare-ass naked with the lights on.

"I thought you'd come around."

"Come around?"

"Get more comfortable with your body." I want to go back before this conversation started. I want to never have asked him why. I want to go back. "But, you never did." Adam watches me. He tilts his head and uncrosses his arms. His hands lazily drift into his pockets.

"I was hoping you'd come around, too."

"Shit, I'll get naked right now and no one can stop me," he says, unbuttoning his shirt. I laugh and he smiles. I can't help it. There's another new flicker in his eyes. Something I've never seen. It's up in the air whether it was there and I never noticed or this is the first time he's done it. This time, instead of asking him another land mine of a question, I take half a second to dissect it my goddamn self. He's pleading with me. Let's stay here. Don't do this. Put down the shovel. Stop digging. "Go on. Go get ready. Let's be done with this now," he says, walking toward the kitchen.

But, I don't move. He hoped I'd come around? You know what I hoped he'd come around to? Not cheating. I thought if I waited him out and didn't let myself fall into some caricature of the nagging wife, he'd snap out of it. As time went on, that bargain became how I did things, simply because it was comforting to have made a decision. Sure, he was having affairs, but I had a plan. Now all I had to do was wait for it to bear fruit. I told myself that life is long and our marriage would span decades, and while it may not look like it some- times, we were in love and our marriage was great. These were just growing pains. Whenever I had doubts, I leaned on the three most important factors that proved my plan was working.

1. Wherever he was and whomever he was with, he al- ways came home to me; and

2. Nobody else knew about the other women; and

3. I was always his "plus one."

But, as I watch my husband plead with me to let this sleeping dog of a marriage lie, the smell of tomato soup for- ever caught in my nasal passages, I must confront the truth.

1. He is no longer coming home to me; and

2. Everybody knows; and

3. I am no longer his "plus one."

Speak my truth, Elijah? Speak my truth. How about this:

"I'M EXHAUSTED," I say. Adam is just about to push through into the kitchen, his hand resting on the door. "I am fucking exhausted." His shoulders lower. He is slow to turn around.

"You're the one who wanted to take these photos," he says. His voice is a low warning.

"I know."

"Right." This conversation now feels like a hostage nego- tiation.

We are quiet.

"That's not what I'm talking about." I take a breath, and as if it's eggnog, every drop of it coats my mouth and throat. "I know. About Nicola." Adam lets out a long breath. "And Sarah.

And Margaret. And Amber. And Kate." He is completely silent. "I'm tired of pretending like I don't know." I breathe. Oh my god. I breathe.

"I agree with you—" My heart soars. "That there's never a right time for this conversation." Ugh. "But, I can pretty much guarantee that there's definitely a wrong time for it." I am frozen. "So, how about you get dressed and we table this." Adam waits. Maybe I nod? I don't know. He turns around.

"Are you even sorry?" I ask. Adam continues into the kitchen. Did he hear me?

I quickly walk toward the bedroom as if I'm trying to get out of the foyer before my unanswered question can infect me. I close the door behind me, and then and only then do I drop the towel. I don't look at myself in the mirror as I put on the outfit I bought for this very occasion. Head down, eyes darting anywhere but at my own reflection.

I am numb.

I run a comb through my now completely dry hair. It looks kind of terrible. A hurried bit of makeup and I'm back down the hallway just as the doorbell rings. I don't say one word to Adam. And vice versa. I smooth my skirt, trying to dry the clamminess. I think nothing. I say nothing. And then I open the door.

"So happy to meet you, Caroline only says good things," I say.

"We both know that's not true," Luz says, with a wide smile.

"Right. I should specify. She's only said good things about you," I say and Luz laughs. I open the front door wide and she walks through, followed by a team of people holding cases of photography equipment, lights, huge panels of netting, and so on. She is wearing a white V-neck T-shirt, jeans, and a pair of old worn-in cowboy boots. "I loved your retrospective at the Broad." I close the door behind everyone.

"Oh, thanks."

"Adam, this is Luz. Luz, this is my husband, Adam," I say. "There's food. Please help yourself." I gesture to the items I bought this morning.

"It looks delicious," she says. Luz pours herself a cup of black coffee, grabs a croissant, and starts to guide her crew through their equipment setup.

"Good thing you didn't go all crazy," Adam says, watching Luz's team stream into our house. I look up at him. Is he making small talk? I'm waiting for him to be terrible. Waiting for him to be someone other than exactly the man I married ten years ago. Show me how cruel you can be, love of mine. Make it easier on me to be mad at you. Do something to make this all your fault. But, in the minutes and hours that follow, I have to admit that this is the same man I married. Which sends a chill down my spine. This is the man I married.

He has not changed.

Luz has taken what must be a thousand pictures. On the couch. In front of the fireplace. Standing in the kitchen "laughing." And now we're outside sitting on a bench by the fountain. It's my favorite spot that I never sit in.

"Okay, if you can just . . . yes, your arm around her and a nice candid moment, you know?" Luz says. Adam is the perfect little model. Luz loves him. Naturally. And I am an unsmiling and moody brat. Every single moment of our marriage is spilling from the recesses of my brain and being filed and inventoried. What happened? Where did this all go so wrong?

Is this just marriage? "Good. Good. Let me just swap out cameras." Luz turns to her assistants and leaves us on the bench. The temperature is maybe high seventies and there's not a cloud in the sky. The Christmas card is going to be beautiful.

I'm losing control. I can feel my temper poking and prodding. Looking for an exit. Just like when I was in second grade and upon getting called out in kickball—unfairly, I might add—I launched the ball over the fence. It was run over by a passing car within seconds. That was the first time somebody compared me to the Incredible Hulk. And it was not the last. Later, words like "intense" and "passionate" took its place. But, with each new iteration, I knew that this Thing inside me was not good.

When I became the New Olivia Morten, I knew that the Incredible Hulk had to go, right along with the Sweaty Marble. A woman coveted by men had to be effortless and easygoing. Boring and sweet. Not the kind of woman who flipped tables over when she suspected that someone was cheating at Candy Land.

Adam looks at me and brushes a strand of hair from my face.

"Do you love her?" I ask.

"Hm?" he asks, tucking it behind my ear.

"Do you love her?" An assistant looks over at us, trying not to listen. She looks at her other coworkers like: *Are you hearing this shit?* But, I don't care.

"Olivia. Later."

"I don't think you loved the other ones. Maybe that's why I didn't mind. Well, that and I thought I wasn't very good at sex. You're right about the naked thing, of course. I honestly thought I was hiding it. Which is hilarious now that I think about it." The same assistant's eyes dart away from us. Now she's trying to get the attention of another girl over by the pastries. Adam's jaw tenses. He says nothing.

"You're fine."

"Yeah, but not good enough to keep you. Right?" I'm outside of myself at this point. Luz has a new camera and turns back around to find her assistants all averting their eyes and trying to let her know that this perfect, happily married couple they're photographing is not-so-silently imploding.

"Okay, now . . . smile. That's right," Luz says. She snaps photo after photo.

"Why stay married to me?" I ask. Adam is quiet.

"Okay . . . let's just try to get a few more shots," Luz says, her voice quavering a bit. Adam smiles. Easy. Calm. This enrages me. My temper punches through.

"If I'm so terrible at sex and you have to find a thousand other women to have it with, why not just get a divorce?" Luz stops taking pictures. Her entire crew freezes.

"I'll give you two a moment," Luz says, and she and her crew stream into the house, packing up any extra gear that they won't be needing. Quickly.

"Shall I just jump past this being humiliating and maybe we could have waited to have this conversation?" Adam asks.

"Yes."

"Right. Thought so," Adam says. Luz should be taking shots now because it's the first time we've been candid today.

"Well?" I'm not even . . . I don't know where I am anymore. I don't know who's talking. I don't know who I am. My entire body is buzzing. I walk over to the spread of food I'd arranged outside, grab a handful of raspberries, and pour them into my mouth. Bright. Delicious. Sunlight. Another handful and my hands are now stained red as I pop them one at a time into my open mouth. Adam watches me. I can't feel my face and yet, as I chew and savor the raspberries, there's no panic attack in sight. A silver lining.

"I don't know what you want from me." I recognize the look on Adam's face very well. It's like the one you have while watching a little kid playing with a too-blown-up balloon. It's the bracing fear of someone readying for the POP!

Despite my years denying it, I'm the pop. I've always been the pop.

Luz comes back outside.

"I think we've got what we need. Thank you for welcoming us into your home. We're going to get going." I look beyond Luz, through the French doors, and see that the crew has already cleared out. I pull a napkin from the table, wipe my hands, and walk over to her.

"Thank you," I say.

"I'll email you what I've got and we'll go from there," Luz says. She looks past me to a now-pacing Adam. She jerkily reaches out and fumbles to grasp my arm. "Good luck." I don't know what to do, so I put my hand over hers. She squeezes. Nods. Before I can say anything Luz is gone. And Adam and I are alone again. I turn around and he starts speaking.

"What I've always treasured the most about our marriage is how much I genuinely liked you—"

I interrupt what I'm sure is going to be a rousing speech. "How much you genuinely liked me."

"Yes," Adam says, wrapping his arm around me.

"Liked me," I say, hitting the "d."

It's the lightbulb moment. Whenever I watch my cozy mystery TV shows, the great sleuth always knows when someone is the murderer when they start referring to the victim in the past tense.

It's a murderer's first mistake.

MAYBE WE START THERE

Growing up, we listen to love songs and believe that's what real love is. As we get older, what sinks in is not that those songs are a fantasy, but that they simply aren't about us.

"And four! And five! And six! Wake up, ladies, or I'll wake you up!" Barb yells, early the next morning.

"That one doesn't even make sense," I say to Mom. At the moment we're doing the grapevine to "I Heard It Through the Grapevine." Barb has said "get it?!" no less than a hundred times.

Adam slept at home last night, a feat he announced as if he ought to be awarded a medal for it. When I barely cracked a smile, the night went from awkward to downright frigid. We said nothing during dinner and our good nights were about as warm as what you'd say to the flight attendant as you deboard a plane. I left before he awoke, but I did stare creepily at him sleeping. That felt like some kind of progress.

"Shh! You're going to get us in trouble!" Mom says, whizzing past me to catch up with Joyce Chen.

"Then how come Mrs. Stanhope can just float over by the lane line?" I ask, quickening my pace to keep up. Mom looks from me to Mrs. Stanhope, who's gliding around in her pink floppy hat talking about peach pie to one of the lifeguards, and smiles. Mrs. Stanhope lazily waves.

I focus on Barb. Step, cross, step. Arms high. The water fights me. Step, cross, step. *"You could have told me yourself, that you found someone else."* Step, cross, step. *"Instead I heard it through the grapevine."* Step, cross, step. Arms high. The water splashes. My face is hot and the cold morning air burns my throat as I take deeper and deeper breaths.

Over and over and over again.

I can't keep it in anymore. I want to scream it and scream it and scream it. I'm exhausted. I know I'm not the only woman who's fucking exhausted. We work tirelessly only to be told that the things at which we excel are unimportant. Running a home and having a career, all the while keeping effortlessly slim. Being cheerleaders and therapists to men who assure us that, unlike women, they need neither. How can I help? What can I do? What more can I give you? Will this be enough? Am I valuable now? Will I ever do enough for you to tell me I'm important?

Why do I care so much? Why do I believe you when you tell me I'm crazy and emotional? Why do I let you dictate what is meaningful?

Why do I keep asking the monkeys if it smells inside the monkey-house?

I'm tired of lying and as Cher's "Believe" kicks in and Barb asks us to "high kick like you mean it," I play out a scenario where I finally say it all. Hop out of this pool, grab Barb's microphone headset, and shout, "I used to be fat and my husband has been cheating on me throughout our marriage because I never thought I deserved more than the scraps of my teenage fantasy."

Or how about this: "Being fat infected me and just like consumption, I shall tragically die from it even though I look perfect on the outside." Ridiculous. High kick. High kick. Now scissor your arms! Scissor your arms! "Attention, ladies! I am a big fat fraud! Gaze at me, your fraudulent overlord, for I have sold you a lie!"

Now Barb's instructing us to run in place, as she counts down from ten. Feel the burn, she tells us. Barb growls the word "burn" in a way that's just suggestive enough to make everyone uncomfortable.

As the balls of my feet grind into the bottom of the pool, I come up with more public confessions I can blurt out: I hold in my farts even in REM sleep! I've never loved a picture taken of me! I hate kale! Eighty percent of the time I don't mean it when I say, "I'm sorry!" The pool becomes choppy and rough as each woman becomes her own personal washing machine.

"Sunday Funday? More like Sunday Bunday!" Barb says with a cackle.

As the group transitions into wind sprints to Bob Seger's "Against the Wind," I float into the deeper waters and idly wonder how long it would take to just say it all. Unleash my secrets. Would it take an hour? Two? Days? What would that even feel like? I'd probably feel great, until I came out of my fugue state to see the women staring at me with that sickening combination of pity and glee. I careen into a woman straddling a pool noodle.

"Watch yourself, hon," the woman says, steadying me with a firm hand.

"I'm so sorry," I say, dog-paddling away from her.

I catch Mom's eye. She raises her eyebrows as if to ask, what is wrong with you? I shake my head and it's right then that she sees it: Something is wrong. A tilt of the head. A narrowed eye. And I just landed myself on her to-do list.

While we warm down, I come to the conclusion that all of my fears were pretty spot-on. My successes and freedoms as the New Olivia Morten were so fragile that they've been torn down in less than two weeks simply because of . . . wait. This is all Ben Dunn's fault. My blood rises. The water splashes around me. If I hadn't run into him in that coffeehouse, would any of this have happened? Would I—

"Olivia, we're warming down," Barb barks through her microphone. I look up and Barb's slowly sweeping her arms over her head. Apparently, I was being a bit too intense. Oh, god. It's starting again. Barb better watch out, or else I'll kick a pool noodle over the fence. Mom and Joyce Chen look over at me. I follow Barb and slowly sweep my arms over my head. Barb continues, "Good. Easy. Fluid. Be water."

I force myself to keep sweeping my arms over my head as I set my sights on Ben Dunn. He did this. Yes. This is all his fault. Ben Dunn. This is . . . uh . . . him. Then there he is. I actually sigh as he walks through my mind. His face is now so easy for me to conjure. The sound of his voice. That crackling laugh of his that seems to crumble into itself. Little snippets of memories play and replay like those dumb (read: brilliant) cat gifs from the Internet. Ben throwing his head back and laughing. Slow motion as he throws a football. The way his reddish-blond hair comes to a swirled point at the nape of his neck. Barb's voice cuts through my own personal Ben Dunn highlight reel. She's telling us to inhale.

I breathe in and pull out my favorite memory: the nano-second right before Ben kissed me. Battling my own disbe-lief and, at the same time, fearing I would erupt into maniacal joyous giggling right up until the warmth of his lips on mine grounded me to a point so deep within myself that the kiss felt rooted beneath our feet. The look on his face was so focused. On me. I let out a nervous laugh and realize I ac-tually laughed in the pool in real life. Barb beams at me. Olivia gets it, she thinks to herself. Olivia gets the joy of Swimtastics.

"Aaaaand exhale." I try to remember where my hands were when he kissed me. The brush of stubble. The way he looked at me. The way he felt. The way I felt. Inhaaaaaaale. And exhale. I always wanted him to see me. Really see me. And after all the years of anguish and yearning and pain and invisibility, I wish I could go back and tell the teenage me that it was going to be so worth it.

No. Shit. Wait. Me fantasizing about Ben Dunn isn't the point. Me blaming Ben Dunn is. I shut down the highlight reel and as it flickers to a stop, I lean into the anger. And I inconveniently hit a wall. Because, of course, my theory falls apart immediately. Ben Dunn didn't make my husband cheat on me, nor did he make me keep quiet about it.

No. All Ben Dunn did was wake up the Fat Me. I've done the rest.

Focusing back on Barb, I stand on my tiptoes and take a deep breath in. Aaaaand exhale. And another.

"Job well done, ladies! I'll see everyone next Sunday!" chirps Barb, a fist in the air as the final chords of Carly Simon's

"Coming Around Again" waft over the pool deck. We all clap and thank her.

I swim over to the side of the pool with the ladies and walk up the steps like a normal person, instead of pulling myself up at the wall. Back in high school, I'd see the swimmers pull themselves out of the pool shimmering and perfect. Effortless. I tried it once and all I remember about my exit was this desperate, frothy-mouthed, almost evolutionary crawl out of the pool as if it were primordial sludge. When Mom and I started doing Swimtastics, I made it a point to always pull myself out of the pool, some kind of gotcha callback to the old days. At the stairs, now out from under the watchful eye of Barb, the women talk and laugh with abandon. Catching up with one another, swapping recipes, asking after children and husbands. Of course, in the past I missed all of this because I was too busy swanning around, waiting for everyone to notice how fluidly I had just leapt out of the pool.

"Your suit is all jumbled, button," Mom says, flipping the strap of my suit back in place. A little pat and she's back to talking with Mrs. Stanhope about Thanksgiving. Apparently, Mrs. Stanhope's son has committed the unpardonable sin of suggesting that they try a different stuffing recipe. As you can imagine, it's wreaked havoc. Mrs. Stanhope can't figure out what she did in his upbringing that was so terribly wrong. Mom waves it off. As if he has a say. They laugh.

I wonder how many of these moments I've missed in the pursuit of righting some past humiliation. Abandoning connection and community to serve some solitary obsession. For someone who's tried her darndest to erase her past, I sure do spend an inordinate amount of my time and energy back there.

I wrap a towel around my waist and follow the other women into the changing room. Mom is lying in wait. I know she is. I can feel her eyes on me as always. But, I cannot keep one thought in my head. I'm all over the place. The threat churning just below this manic energy terrifies me. What happens when I stop cracking jokes? What happens when I can't pin this on someone else? What happens when Mom asks me what's wrong? Do I yell "Everything!" and then blow away like ash? I want to go back to the way things were. But, I hit another wall.

"Thank you," I say to the woman holding the door of the changing room open for me. She smiles and I hold the door open for the woman behind me. The changing room is now overrun with little kids and their moms getting ready for swim lessons. Little potbellies and colorful swimsuits zoom and shoot around like comets.

Amid the pandemonium, I find my locker and sit down on the bench in front of it. I just need a moment before I head into the showers. I rearrange my towel and twist my hair around so it stops dripping down my back like some kind of torture. I need to find something that's been real over the last ten years. Something has to have been real.

The memories flip and flicker like an animated movie. Each memory used to be a flawless drawing of a single frame, colored inside the lines and perfect from every angle. But now, it feels like someone is going through all of those memories frame by frame and drawing in a new layer. Altering them forever. Fat Me has been very busy vandalizing each of these moments with the hard truth. Now that she's up, she thinks it's time I see what was actually happening, and not the fantasy I've been building this whole time.

As the women chatter and get undressed around me, I force myself to find a memory that remains somewhat intact and free of Fat Me's graffiti.

My wedding day. The way my wedding dress felt as it zipped up easily. Seeing myself in the mirror. The disbelief that this was actually me. Walking down that aisle. Everyone standing as I entered. Oohing and ahhing at how beautiful I looked. Taking pictures. Waving. Trying to get my attention. I couldn't stop smiling. I wanted that moment to go on forever. Basking in being seen. Seeing Adam at the end. Someone had chosen me. And he was beautiful. He was everything I wanted.

I remember the look on my mom's face as she watched me walk down the aisle. Love. Overcome with it. Unconditional. Her appearance was altered by it. And now in the glare of whatever this new hellish clarity is, I finally compare Mom's look with Adam's. Of course, I had never seen it before. Never allowed myself to. I'd always thought Adam's look as I'd walked down the aisle to marry him was one of love. But now I'm not so sure. Did I even demand that of him? He just needed to be someone who chose me and someone everyone at the wedding would covet. Someone who would make people envy me. I'd never thought to check whether or not he was overcome with love.

I focus in on him. The memory. His face.

He genuinely likes me.

But, love?

Maybe not.

One flash frame of Adam's face and I force myself to look away. I lean forward, absently zipping from one number to the next on my combination lock. I pull the lock. Nothing.

Fine. I twist the knob around a few times to clear it. The flash frame of Adam's face sticks in my mind. I try the sequence of three numbers again. Is that the look of someone watching the love of his life walk down the aisle toward him?

No.

He's waiting for a lovely friend for brunch. That's the look. We're going to the museum together and I'm the platonic work friend that he laughs with during companywide meetings. I see it now. I twist and twist and twist. Denied.

"Those locks can be super temperamental," says a woman with nothing on but a towel turban. I avert my eyes and nod. "It's like they know when you're in a hurry." She's now bending over, towel-drying her hair.

"Yep." I'd better get this lock open or I'll know more about this woman than her gynecologist. I lean forward. Clear the combination lock. Shove the now-ravaged memories of my wedding day out of my head and focus. Seven. Twenty-three. Three.

Open.

"There you go," the woman says, one foot on the bench as she combs out her hair. I nod again, take the shower caddy from my locker, and head into the showers.

"What took you so long?" Mom asks, still in her bathing suit. Joyce Chen has her suit pulled down around her shoulders and Mrs. Stanhope is, as always, totally nude.

"I couldn't get my lock open." I pull over a plastic chair and set my shower caddy on it. I turn on the shower, and step under the stream and close my eyes.

Today, the hot water is a balm. I dip my head and let it hit the crown, sending hair down into my eyes, dripping. Turn around and get my neck and the top of my spine. I spin back and step in closer, letting the water rain down on all of me. The droplets bounce and careen off my slick suit. The water feels so good on my skin. I lift my bathing suit straps and let the water hit my shoulders. Pull the suit off my skin and let the water slide under the stretchy material and onto my chest and back. Twisting and contorting so I can feel the hot water on my skin. My shoulders burn from the workout and I grow frustrated with how hard this is. How much work it's taking just to feel more of something that is good.

I scan the showers. Mom, Joyce Chen, and Mrs. Stanhope are talking and laughing. It's just us. I could take down my straps. I glance over my shoulder just as Mrs. Stanhope launches into a story. Now. I'll do it now. First the left. Then the right. I turn away from the women and let the water massage the indentations on my shoulders left by the tight suit. I look down and see the tracing stretch marks just above my breasts. The little patch of dry skin over my left nipple. Another quick glance around the shower. Joyce Chen is acting out some kind of story. About a horse? Horseback riding?

I take my shower poof out of my caddy, squirt some shower gel into it, and scrub my shoulders. When I usually do this, I have to go under the straps. This just feels easy. Another glance around the shower. I absently drag the shower poof across my chest. The suds trickle and slide down the front of my suit.

If I take my suit down to my waist, they'll for sure see even more stretch marks, and that my boobs are giving in to gravity a little more than I'd like. The scars from the weight-loss surgery are healed over, but there is a weird puckering around the one on the lower left. I could pull the suit down just above that one? I turn toward the wall and pull my suit down to my waist. Immediately the water spills over my breasts and stomach and the heat and warmth of it makes me step in closer. Why this public half-clothed shower feels so much better than the regular showers I take at home, I have no idea. I scrub my body and with no suit in the way, the ease of it stuns me.

I close my eyes for a brief second feeling it all. The riot of ridicule and scrutiny is nowhere to be found. The prying eyes and stifled giggles are nonexistent. Instead of a foreign and frustrating feeling of exposure and humility, I simply feel eerily normal. Something familiar. Deep down, I know this feeling. I've been here before.

And in an instant, I open my eyes, curl my fingers around the top of my suit, pull it down to the ground, and step all the way out of it.

The water falls. Everywhere. I wash my body with ease. And as I turn around and face out from the wall, Mom, Joyce Chen, and Mrs. Stanhope quickly go back to their conversation as if they all didn't screech to a halt, taking note of what just transpired.

The freedom. The ease. The rightness of it all. It's shocking how quickly this feels natural to me. I've finally come home to my own skin. All those years. All those lost moments. An entire life tangled up in shame. Weighted down in fear.

I'm exhausted. I can't do it anymore.

"So . . . ," Mom leads.

"Everything okay?" Joyce Chen asks. She pulls the shampoo out of her shower caddy. Joyce lathers up her hair, while Mom and Mrs. Stanhope let the hot water stream over them. They are patient. They are professionals at the long game.

"Adam and I had a fight, that's all," I say, lathering up.

"What about?" Mom asks.

I try to get mad about this conversation happening in the shower, especially today, and in front of other people besides my mom—or at all, really. But, I guess this is what happens when I finally admit that my life isn't a movie. Heart-to-hearts don't happen in the adorably falling snow as Frank Sinatra plays in the background. No, big talks happen in the smallest of moments. A moment so small, you think it can't hold the significance. But, it does. Because the background becomes everything as you replay the conversation. You can't believe you were in the showers of a stupid public pool or in the aisle of a grocery store or just standing in your backyard when everything changed.

I look from Mom to Mrs. Stanhope to Joyce Chen. Utterly naked. What was the fight about? The other women. But, did it start with the other women or is it about how I'm not good at sex and he had to go elsewhere? Does this all go back to how I never allowed myself to be naked with Adam . . . literally, and then that became figuratively, too? I hold the shower poof over my stomach. I suddenly feel the urge to put my suit back on.

Or was it that look on his face as I walked down the aisle? Or does the fight claw back even further, to when I never thought to ask myself if I even loved him? He was perfect. He liked me. And he was my ticket out of Fat Me Land. Can a fight ten years into our marriage really be about how we might have never loved each other?

"About everything," I say and just then my legs go out from under me. I hit my right hip on the shower floor and quickly slip and slide, desperately trying to stand back up. "I'm sorry. I must have . . . slipped. I—" Mom walks over and carefully eases me back up into a standing position.

"Sweetheart? Are you okay?" Mom asks once I'm on my feet.

"No," I say.

I just stand there. And nod. Over and over. The choking tears are back. Once again, I worry just how out of control and vast this thing is that's crawling up my throat. I do appreciate that I've been stark-ass naked during this entire thing. That Christmas card greeting is writing itself.

Happy Holidays!
One of us is a serial cheater and the other is naked crying in public showers.
Merry, Merry! Adam and Olivia

"Oh, honey," Mom says. She wraps her arm around me. I feel so stupid and I try to shrug it off. I've said too much. I should have just . . . what? Kept lying? No. I can't do that anymore.

"I am exhausted," I say. Out loud. I brace myself. The last time I said those three words, Adam reacted as though they were a declaration of war.

The three women nod. They understand. My mom takes the shampoo from me. She squeezes some of it into the palm of her hand and hands the bottle back. I hold on to it. She turns me around, I tilt my head back, and she starts washing my hair.

"Go ahead and rinse," Mom says. I step under the water and let the water stream over me. When I open my eyes again I catch the tail end of a shared glance of concern between the three women. Catching me catching them, Mom instructs me to hand her the conditioner. I do. I tilt my head back once again as she works the conditioner into my hair. I rinse. They wait. The locker-room sounds feel so far away. Excited little girls and hair dryers and toilets flushing. Mom twists my hair and gently lays it over my shoulder with a pat. She doesn't go back over to her shower. Time passes. The showers run.

Where do I start?

"Adam has been cheating," I say. The women wait. "On me." They all nod. They don't look at one another. I want them to rage and scream, but they don't. They just listen. "For years. He's been doing it for years." Quiet. "With a lot of women."

"Okay," Mom says.

"So what happens now?" Mrs. Stanhope asks.

"I don't know," I say.

"What can we do?" Joyce Chen asks.

"I don't know," I say, tears springing to my eyes.

"Okay." Mom nods and walks over to her shower to rinse off the soap that is starting to cake on to her skin. The sounds from the locker room wane as the little kids stream out for their swim lessons.

"It's my fault," I say. The three women react in unison.

"I seriously doubt that," Mrs. Stanhope says.

"I don't think so," Joyce Chen says.

"No way," Mom says.

"I know . . . I know you're supposed to say that, but even you have to admit that . . ." I pause. They wait. I look down at my imperfect, naked body. "That all of my body stuff is kind of a lot for him to deal with."

"Honey, this is not about your . . . ," Mom hesitates. "Body stuff."

Joyce Chen shakes her head.

"Please," Mrs. Stanhope says with disdain.

"If I were more free. Confident. You know, in . . . the bedroom. Hell, if I were more free everywhere," I say, unable to look at them.

"Honey—" Mom starts.

"I was just never very good at it," I say, totally embarrassed. I can't believe I'm saying this stuff. I must be fucking desperate.

"Did you ever think that maybe he wasn't very good at it?" Mrs. Stanhope asks. Mom shoots her a look and she throws her hands up, her shower poof throwing suds across the tiled wall.

"You think he wouldn't have gone looking elsewhere even if you were 'good at it'?" Joyce Chen asks.

"Cheating is never about sex, honey," Mom says.

"Then . . ."

"Men need to be adored," Joyce Chen says. Joyce is on her second marriage. She's much happier now. They met in a pottery class. He was her teacher. It was all very scandalous for a while and Joyce loved every minute of it. Her first marriage did not end well and now I'm thinking I know why. "If they don't feel like the big man at home, they will find a woman who will oblige them."

"It's the whole secretary thing," Mom says.

"But, isn't it also about trying to find the spark again?" I ask.

"It's less about that than you'd think," Mom says. She shuts off her shower. We follow suit.

"For some men it's also the whole madonna/whore thing. You're his wife, he can't ask you to do certain things, so he dot dot dot," Mrs. Stanhope says. We grab our towels and make our way out into the emptying locker room.

"Dot dot dot?" I ask.

"I assumed you didn't want me to get into it?" Mrs. Stanhope says with a wry smile, still stark naked.

"Quite right. Quite right," I say.

"To this day, I don't know why men think we . . . aren't curious, too," Mrs. Stanhope says.

"I remember my first husband—it was right outside of my lawyer's office, just after we signed our divorce papers. I don't know if that detail is funny or tragic," Joyce Chen says.

"Both," Mom says.

"Both," Joyce Chen says, laughing. "He was trying to tell me that he had to turn to these other women because I wouldn't have been into the stuff he was doing with them. So I asked, like what?" Joyce Chen smiles.

"Good for you," Mrs. Stanhope says.

"So, even after it was all over, he was still trying to make it your fault," Mom says.

"Oh, naturally. I was so frigid and cold, Polly. You know that," Joyce Chen says.

"It's such a chore being your friend," Mom says. And they all laugh.

I didn't know any of this. They've never talked like this in front of me. Would I have opened up to them earlier if I had known, would I have shared earlier? Or would I have said nothing and felt smug about how my marriage was perfect and not like Joyce Chen's? Sadly, it would have been the latter.

"So what was he into?" Mrs. Stanhope asks.

"It was some role-playing thing. I was expecting . . . well, something a bit more daring than that. When I told him that it sounded like fun, he . . . well, first he accused me of lying and once that wore off, he just stood there . . . looking shocked," Joyce Chen says.

Standing in front of our lockers now, we all dry off, put shower caddies away, and start the process of getting dressed. Once again, the ease of it all is stunning. How did I lose this? How did I go from the freedom I felt climbing into the back of that airport shuttle to this? I've made my entire life that fucking Groot costume.

"It's the shocked thing that made it impossible to initiate sex in the beginning. I remember being so—" Mrs. Stanhope stops. Thinks.

"Ashamed," Mom says.

"Ashamed," Mrs. Stanhope repeats.

"I mean, we didn't know anything about sex before we got married," Joyce Chen says.

"I remember my mom knocking on the bathroom door, walking in, and handing me this Kotex pamphlet that said, 'So, You've Become a Young Lady,' and then just walking out. That was the sum total of my sex education," Mom says.

"All I knew is that when my Dad's boxers were on the floor in the morning, that meant they'd had sex the night before," Joyce Chen says, laughing. "Whatever that was."

"Charlene Lyle. She was this neighbor girl who completely embraced the whole seventies free-love thing. She used to tell me all about her conquests and I just ate it up," Mrs. Stanhope says.

"There's always a Charlene Lyle," Mom says.

"I still had my white gloves in the lingerie drawer along with the birth control pills I was hiding," Mrs. Stanhope says.

"So ashamed of anything remotely racy and yet this 'sexual revolution' thing was raging on, telling us to loosen up," Joyce Chen says.

"Back then, none of us knew anything about sex. I mean, I finally figured things out, but that had nothing to do with Clay," Mrs. Stanhope says with a wink. I look confused.

"Never go into a woman's bedside table, darling," Joyce Chen says. They all laugh. I still don't understand. This dawns on each of the three women just as I realize what they're talking about. Too late, of course, to stop what's about to happen. The moment is like that split second right before you trip—how everything moves in slow motion and it feels like it takes hours to hit the floor. Paralyzed. Helpless.

"Livvie, honey, have you never used a vibrator?" Mrs. Stanhope asks. Thwack. The words hit me like falling facedown on a marble floor. I can feel my face redden and almost choke on my own spit. This only makes Mrs. Stanhope and Joyce Chen laugh more. Thank god, Mom has the sense to be busy in her locker at this exact moment.

"What?" I blurt.

"We're getting a bit sidetracked. This is clearly a conversation for another time," Mom says.

"Or never," I say.

"Like Jane said—maybe it wasn't you that was bad at it," Joyce Chen says.

"How can someone else make you feel good, if you don't even know and love your own body? You getting naked is a good start, though, hon," Mrs. Stanhope adds.

"I don't know what's worse, my husband cheating or having to have this conversation about . . . ," I say, waving my hand around.

"It's called masturbation, dear," Mrs. Stanhope says, pulling her clothes from her locker and starting to get dressed.

"Oh my god," I say.

"I remember my mother talking about a friend of hers being called an 'Anybody's Girl' after she got a divorce," Mom says.

"A divorce," I repeat, dazed. The three women stop.

"Is that what you want?" Mrs. Stanhope asks.

"I don't know. Adam—"

"It doesn't sound like Adam has a problem with the marriage," Joyce Chen says.

"Sounds like it's working just fine for him," Mrs. Stanhope says.

"Has Adam talked about divorce?" Mom asks.

"No." I dry myself off and take my bra out of the locker.

"It seems like he's been perfectly comfortable being married to you all these years. Even with the . . . ," Joyce Chen thankfully trails off. I snap my bra in the back and pull my shirt out of the locker.

"A lot of marriages are more partnerships than—" Mrs. Stanhope stops. Thinks. "Him cheating doesn't necessarily mean divorce, unless you want one?"

"I thought it was a phase. We'd talked about how we were going to start having kids after we'd been married for ten years, so I thought he'd come around. I don't even know . . ."

"Honey, what about what Mrs. Stanhope asked? Unless you want a divorce?" Mom asks.

"I know that the answer should be yes. Without any hesitation, but . . . ," I say, stopping.

"None of us takes divorce lightly, but if you're . . . ," Mom trails off. Thinks. "If you're disappearing, then maybe it's time you thought about it."

"Disappearing," I repeat.

"Something to think about," Mom says.

I've never talked about this out loud before. And it's painful. What deal did I strike with the Fat Me to keep me silent all these years? What happened to me? "How did I let this happen?"

"First, you need to stop blaming yourself. Adam made a choice. A series of choices," Mom says, pulling her shirt over her head.

"But, so did I," I say. They all look at me. "I knew. I knew the whole time. And I said nothing. To him. To you. To anyone. Because I didn't want people to think that my perfect marriage was anything but. I allowed this to happen." I stop. "And I'm still allowing it." I sit on the bench with just my bra on. "I did this."

I put my hand over my mouth to stifle the sobs that finally explode. Mrs. Stanhope and Joyce Chen look to Mom. Mom sits down next to me and I crumble into her. Between heaves, I mutter "I did this" over and over. Mom smoothes my hair and tells me it's going to be okay. Everything is going to be okay. But, I'm not sure she's right this time. This could be the first time I've driven my own mother to lie.

Everything blurs around me as I cry. And all I did was simply acknowledge how I've been living for the past ten years. Is it only ten? Is that the big trapdoor at the bottom of this sobbing? That it's been going on longer than ten years? Or is it just one trapdoor after another? If I've built this entire life on secrets and lies and I've disappeared into some role like Caroline, what happens when I finally walk off the set? Am I nothing? Have I made a deal with the devil and lost my soul because I only valued outer beauty? Have I gambled and lost? What have I done?

What have I done?

"Okay . . . okay," Mom says, swaying back and forth with me.

The tears feel like opening a bottle of seltzer and the bubbles stream to the top and there's that split second where you think maybe not . . . and then it explodes everywhere and you don't know when it's going to stop and can you get to the sink and how much more can there be? It's out of control and you can't figure out where it's all coming from.

And I knew it. I knew it was going to be like this. My hope—my last thread of a hope—was that once all of it got out I'd be fine. I'd know what to do next. I'd be fixed. Just like that. See? I was good. I dealt with it. I got naked in the showers. I cried, okay? Now can we get on with it?

I thought all my problems would be solved first, when I lost the weight and then when I got naked in the shower.

I'm still making this about appearances. Still making this skin deep. It's not about the weight. It's about the shame. Thinking my imperfections make me worthless and unlovable. And cutting carbs can't lose that.

I'm afraid it's like that lamp I have in the living room with the broken spoke in the lampshade. No matter how many times I fix it or have it welded or, as a last resort, duct-tape it, it's just broken now.

The only fix is getting a new lamp.

Am I broken now? Or was I always broken? Was I that lamp with the duct tape and everyone knew it but me?

The tears subside to a manageable whimper. Mom pulls me into a standing position for the second time today. Joyce Chen hands me my sweats and Mrs. Stanhope helps me step into them. Joyce Chen threads my arms through my sweater as Mom combs my hair. They gather their things and dole out mine between them. Lockers are slammed shut.

"Let's get something sweet. How does that sound?" Mom asks.

"Good," I say, hating that the mere act of speaking unleashes an entirely new wave of pain. We walk a few steps toward the door of the locker room. "Thank you." I look at each of the women. "For being kind."

Joyce is the first to well up with tears. I imagine this is all hitting a bit too close to home. She pulls me in for a hug and just keeps squeezing. "You're going to be okay," Joyce whispers. I nod. Mom is rubbing my back and Mrs. Stanhope is keeping watch. Joyce pulls back and wipes the tears from my face. "Trust me."

"Okay," I say. And I mean it. A smile and an efficient nod and we're out of the locker room and walking through the lobby of the public pool. We push through the turnstile and head toward the outer doors.

Joyce, Mrs. Stanhope, and Mom are now talking about their weeks. It's comforting and I know that they are aware of that. It's time to not have my sobbing be the center of attention anymore. And these three are queens at pulling focus from someone who is struggling. We walk down the path toward the parking lot and I get swept away in their chatter.

I see Louisa first. She's hard to miss. She has a tiny hot pink robe on, a lime green swimming cap, and her goggles are already pulled over her eyes. Wobbling just behind her is Tilly in a fluffy robe with little brown and black dogs on it. Her robe is listing open like an old man's, revealing a black one-piece swimsuit. Her black swimming cap can't contain her red hair and her goggles are sagging down over her tiny button nose. She minds none of this as she lumbers forward. A colt of a girl is herding them both, her flame-red hair pulled up in a long ponytail.

"We're late, you two," she says. And just behind them, Ben trots up from the parking lot.

"Found them!" he exclaims, holding up a set of water wings in triumph. And then he sees us. He slows his pace. I must look like a drowned sobbing wreck of a rat. He, on the other hand, looks amazing. Once again, the intimacy of his dishevelment takes my breath away. Worn-in sweats, a T-shirt with some sports team on it, and a hoodie that's barely zipped up. His hair isn't brushed and it looks like he hasn't shaved since I saw him last. Which was two days ago. Jesus H. Christ. Has time motherfucking stopped?

"Ben?" Mom asks, stepping in front of me. Bless her.

"Ms. Morten, hi," he says. Louisa and Tilly zoom and whip around one another making swooping noises. "It's the caps and goggles. They think they're pilots."

"A child's imagination is magical," Mom says. I smooth my hair. Swipe at my eyes. But, not too much. They don't need to be any redder.

"Oh, have you met Gretchen? My oldest?" Ben gestures to the older girl. "Gretchen, this is Paulette Morten, she knows Grammy." Gretchen nods. Ben scans the other two women and me. "Jane Stanhope. Joyce Chen." His eyes fall on me. "And Olivia Morten." It's so cliché and every part of me tries to fight against it, but Ben Dunn saying my name melts me like butter.

"I think we met at the Christmas wrapping charity event at the Tournament House. Was it last year?" Mom asks, shaking the girl's hand. Ben looks at me. I make eye contact with him for the briefest of moments. The kiss bursts through me. I look away. As does he.

"I believe so," Gretchen says politely. On the little grassy knoll just beside the path, Louisa flicks up her goggles and puts her hands on her hips.

Ben and I make eye contact again. We both look away.

"Looks like we've got a problem here. A problem with the wing!" Louisa announces, motioning to a rock.

Tilly flicks up her goggles, pulls a Winnie the Pooh spoon out of her robe pocket, and barrels over to Louisa.

"Weren't you the one who was put in charge of all the hard-to-wrap items?" Mom asks. My nose is running. I swipe at it with the sleeve of my sweater. God, I hope he didn't see that.

"All those cheerleading gift-wrap fundraisers finally came in handy," Gretchen says. Mom laughs.

"Gretchen, can you take the girls on in?" Ben asks in his dad voice. I have to admit. It does something for me. Inconveniently. Gretchen nods. "We're running late," Ben explains to the three older women who he is positive are actively judging his parenting abilities. They are, of course.

"You guys ready to swim?" Gretchen says to the two girls.

"We'll have to go by foot!" Louisa roars. Tilly pockets her spoon, flicks back down her goggles, and proceeds to the pool without a backward glance. Gretchen rolls her eyes.

"I'll see you in there," Gretchen says to Ben.

"Be in in a sec," Ben says.

"It was nice meeting you," Gretchen says to all of us and runs after the two girls as they wind their way to the pool.

"She's lovely," Mom says to Ben.

"Yeah, she's all right," Ben says, laughing. "No, she's embarrassingly together."

"We'd better head on out," Mrs. Stanhope says. She and Joyce Chen say their goodbyes and continue on to the parking lot. No talk of the previous happenings. Once again— these are true professionals at the long game.

"I'll meet you at La Monarca?" Mom asks.

"Oh, sure," I say, catching on a bit too late.

"Good seeing you again, Ben. Please say hello to your mother," Mom says.

"I will," Ben says. Mom gives me a smile and walks on like nothing has happened. "I didn't know you came here?"

"I do Swimtastics with my mom and her friends every Sunday morning," I say.

"Swimtastics?" Ben asks.

"I think they think it's a blend of swimming and gymnastics, but . . ."

"Kind of falls apart."

"Maybe it's a German word that has no English translation."

Ben laughs. "I'd better get in there before the girls go off the high dive again," he says.

"Again?"

"I know I should have been mad, but there's no way I would have had the guts to do that at their age. I think I just was proud more than anything."

"Even Tilly?"

"She started it."

"I'll walk with you a little," I say. He smiles and we start back toward the entrance to the pool. We fall into silence.

I feel emptied out. Lighter, but emptied out. I don't know what's real anymore. And because of that, I don't quite know how to be here with Ben. Is this even real? Or is this just another scene from whatever movie I thought I've been in for the last however many years? I look over at him.

No. This is real. I knew Ben Dunn when I was still the Fat Me. More importantly, Ben Dunn knew the Fat Me. Knows the Fat Me. She can't vandalize these memories, because the harsh reality of Ben's and my shared history is threaded into their DNA. There are no surprises here. There is no new layer that I've missed.

Ben slows as he gets to the entrance. I want to touch him. I scan his body. The sweatshirt that's listing open, the broad shoulders, the stubbly jawline, the untied sneakers.

"You're going to break your neck," I say, motioning to his shoes.

"You sound like me," he says, smiling. People are streaming in and out of the pool.

"Next thing you know, we'll actually be found dead in a ditch somewhere," I say.

"Our mothers wouldn't know what to do first: mourn our loss or yell 'I told you so,'" he says.

Before I know what's happening, I lunge into him for a hug. His arms tighten around me and I tuck my face deep into the crook of his neck. The smell of soap and fabric softener fills me up. He puts his hand on the back of my head.

"Hey . . . hey . . . I got you," he says. I can feel his deep voice in my chest. I bury my face deeper. "I got you." I breathe. And just let myself be held by him. I don't hurry the moment and neither does he. We finally break apart, and look at each other for a moment. He leans in. So slightly. Mere centimeters. But, it's enough. He catches himself. Comes back into our surroundings. A smile. And he leans back what now feels like miles.

"Swimtastics just really makes me emotional," I say finally. And he throws his head back and laughs. I watch him and smile. "You'd better get going." He nods.

"Speaking of going—"

"That's . . . wow, you're better than that."

"Am I? Sometimes I'm not so sure." We fall into another expanding silence. "So, back to getting going. I know this . . . I have to go because Gretchen is cheerleading in it, but . . . ," Ben starts and stops. I wait. Confused.

"In the pool?" I ask.

"No," Ben says. Laughs. "Homecoming week."

"Oh."

"You haven't gotten the emails from Shannon Shimasaki?"

"Shannon Shimasaki hates me." Of course, I've gotten the emails from Shannon Shimasaki.

"Never stopped her from sending an email," he says. I nod.

"I don't think I need to remind you that high school wasn't that great for me."

His face is wary. He knows exactly where I'm going with this. This doesn't stop me. "Not all of us were the king of the school."

"Yeah, the king who flunked out of the college he got a full ride to because he partied too much, who now finds himself renting a house and driving the same car his mother gave him after his second marriage fell apart. That's right, kids. Second marriage. So, for those in the nosebleed seats, I have one child from my first marriage and two from the second. I'm not sure which I'm going to enjoy more. The looks of pure glee on people's faces as I tell them the story of my now-middling life or hearing about what a complete dick I was to people and wondering if anything has changed. What I hope? Is that someone will point to me during the game and tell some bullying little shit if he doesn't watch it he may just turn out like Ben Dunn."

"Are you seriously asking me to go to homecoming with you?"

"As friends."

"As friends?"

"Yeah."

"Unbelievable."

"What?"

"Never mind," I say. I'm too raw. Too broken down.

"What? What were you going to say?"

"On top of the fact that, no matter how shitty my marriage is, I am still married—"

"Your marriage is shitty?"

"Yeah, but that . . . that's not the point."

"Can't it be a little of the point?"

"Why didn't you ever ask me before?" Of course, I'm crying now. Because why wouldn't I round out this blissfully humiliating morning by sobbing in front of Ben Dunn. He steps closer. "Why are you only asking me now that you need proof you've been redeemed?"

"What? That's not why I'm asking you," he says.

"God, I would have done anything to have gone to homecoming with you. It's all I wanted."

"I thought you hated me."

"No." A sob escapes. Ben pulls me into him for a hug. "I loved you." I hear Ben struggling with what to say; emotion and pain keep swallowing up his words. Trapdoors are blown open. Incredible Hulks kick balls over fences. Sweaty Marbles roll around with abandon.

The Fat Me has spoken.

It was love, not hate, that transformed me into the villain I became. My origin story. It was the need to protect my heart that compelled me first, to put on the armor of the weight and second, to become the New Olivia Morten, Numb Robot. It was why I settled for genuine *like*. Love hurt. Genuine like can last ten years without a scratch, but real love scars you forever.

I break from Ben. He nods. He starts to say something. Decides against it. One last smile and he disappears into the pool entrance. And I just stand there. A group of ladies rolling pieces of luggage filled with their swimming accouterment file past me. I smooth my sweater down. Feel something. Me. I'm real.

I'm real.

I walk toward the parking lot, beep my car unlocked, and climb inside. I drive to La Monarca in a haze. I can't think about any one thing that's happened in the last couple of hours, let alone the last week. So, I just focus on the drive. Put my indicator on. Turn right. Notice that the house being renovated has built a super high fence, making a mental note to count down to when the Pasadena powers that be will demand that the owners remedy the situation. I give it a month. I turn up the music. Stop at the stop sign. See that one house is for sale. The one with the lavender growing out front. Turn on to Mission, find parking down the street a bit, and walk into La Monarca as blank and fine as I can manage. I doubt that this is a victory. But, it feels better than whatever was brewing this morning. I don't know what to do next. Now that I know whatever it is that I know.

Mom waves from over in the corner and I walk toward her.

"They haven't called my name yet," Mom says.

"What did you order?" I ask.

"Café de ollas, a croissant for me, and a cup of fresh fruit for you." I nod. Mom watches. "What did Ben have to say for himself?" she asks.

"He asked if I wanted to go to the game with him on Thursday."

"The homecoming game?"

"Just as friends," I say, unable to look at her. "Adam and I have a thing, so I couldn't go, but—"

"Olivia, look at me." I obey. "This can't be about you becoming just like Adam and staying in a marriage that isn't working and seeing Ben on the side. I will not watch you become that. You deserve better. Ben deserves better. And so do his girls." I look down at the table. "Olivia. Look at me." I am slow to meet her eyes.

"I'm not going to the game with Ben. I said no."

Mom just looks at me.

"Fine. I'm sorry," I say.

"Do better than just being sorry." Her voice is clipped and serious. She hasn't been this mad at me in years.

"Polly? Your order is ready," the girl behind the counter calls out.

"I'll get it," I say, jumping at the chance to get away, if only for a minute, from my mother's vast disappointment in me. I walk back over to the table with our order and Mom opens up her café de olla. She breathes it in like she always does.

"I don't know where to start," I say.

"Let's start with whether or not you want to stay married to Adam, regardless of Ben Dunn being in or out of your life." Mom pulls apart her croissant and takes a bite.

That's the big question, isn't it? I want to stay married to who I thought Adam was. I want to stay in the blissful ignorance of the marriage I thought I had. I want to go back to sleep. I want this marriage to be with the New Olivia and Adam being in love and not with the Fat Me and Adam being in genuine like.

"Not as it is now, no." I pull off the top of my coffee. Breathe it in.

"And what does that mean?" Mom asks.

"No more other women. And I think . . . I don't think I've ever been myself with him."

"And what is being yourself?"

I think I have the answer and then I just . . . don't. I sit there. Mouth hanging open. The wafting smell of café de olla. La Monarca bustling around us. I close my mouth. Open it again and . . . nothing.

"Um . . ."

"Right. So maybe we start there."

ALEX, I'LL TAKE GLUTTONOUS AND SELFISH FOR $400

When I get home from La Monarca, Adam's in the kitchen making his lunch. I stride in boldly, but once I'm there have no idea what to do. Do I want to take off all my clothes and make him look at me? Do I scream and rail against all the other women? Or just walk in and let out a huge fart while eating the bag of M&M's I got at the gas station on the way home? Maybe some fetching combination of all three?

"Hey," he says, turning around, holding a turkey sandwich on wheat.

"Hey," I say. He takes a bite of the sandwich. "Can you make me one?"

"Oh, sure," he says, a slight hesitation in his voice. I haven't eaten bread in years. He gets the mustard back out of the fridge, cuts a slice of fresh tomato, and adds a handful of lettuce.

I get that my marriage isn't doing well. Maybe if I tried to be my real self—whatever that is—we might have a chance. I've got to find out if my withholding is just as much at fault as his cheating. And if one is directly connected to the other. Adam's been married to the social media version of me for ten years, and maybe he deserves to see the real Olivia. Hell, maybe we both do.

All I know is, ever since I walked into this kitchen I'm feeling everything. And the electricity of it is terrifying. It's like I just got let off the leash. I don't know what's happening to me, but I think I like it. That is, until my entire life falls apart. Which . . . I'm sure is just a matter of time. But, maybe not? Maybe I can stay married to Adam and be who I really am. I mean, why not, right? Just today, I was naked in front of an entire changing room full of octogenarians. My own husband might be next. Adam puts away all the fixings and hands the sandwich to me.

"Thank you," I say, taking a giant bite.

"I know you don't like mayo."

"I don't," I say, feeling like my plan is already working.

"You have—" Adam hands me a paper towel and gestures to my entire face. "Mustard." He's laughing as he says it.

"I love bread," I say, taking another bite.

"As do I," he says. We stand in the kitchen and eat our turkey sandwiches. Adam starts in on a story about some weird door-to-door salesman who came by. "I honestly couldn't fig-ure out what he was selling. He had a catalog, but it wasn't like I could buy anything in the catalog. I thought he was selling magazines at first, but he told me that the magazines were online now. Who knows, maybe he was just casing the place and will be back later to rob us."

"Did you end up buying anything?" I finish up the last of

my sandwich and walk over to the sink to wash off all the mustard smears that have gotten all over me.

"By the end, I just felt bad for the guy," Adam says, handing me the soap.

"Thanks," I say, taking it. I dry off my hands. "Do you want to see a movie?"

"What . . . today?"

"Yeah, apparently I need to see more movies."

"Didn't you want to go through Luz's pictures? For the Christmas card?" Adam asks. I stare at him. He waits. A furrowed brow. Why is this seemingly simple question taking so long to answer? he must wonder.

Come on, Olivia. You can't solve the giant philosophical questions about who it is you've become if you don't know what you want to do on a Sunday afternoon.

I've checked my email and Caroline is fine. She was photographed at a brunch with friends and she was eating a good meal that'll make people think she's normal and handling the divorce like any other regular person would.

This is my day off. The house is clean. The laundry is done enough. The bills are paid. What do I want to do? Why is this so hard? Maybe because my entire life has become about what I should be doing rather than what I want to be doing.

A snippy voice inside my head argues that I should spend this Sunday efficiently putting an end to my marriage and begin the process of rebuilding now that I know there's a problem. I've talked about it in front of people and if I don't handle it, they'll think I'm weak. Adam is a serial cheater and he's shown no respect for our marriage. Put my big-girl panties on and handle this like I would any of my clients.

Another voice. Deep down. My gut. My instinct. I know it's

her. The Fat Me. I think I'm scared that the Fat Me is going to roll through my life and be this gluttonous blob of nihilism. Me want food! Me no want to work out! Me take whatever you throw away. And I'll immediately gain a thousand pounds and rather than being unmasked, I'll explode through my clothes like some kind of repressed Hulk. I'm afraid I won't be able to control her. And once she feels the sweet crisp air of freedom . . . freedom. I turn away from Adam.

She was free. I was free. I was free once.

She didn't care what anyone thought and that didn't make her gluttonous or selfish, it made me happy and free.

"I want to see a movie," I say. Adam nods. I look at him. "And then maybe take a walk later. There's this house that's being renovated on La Loma that I want to take a closer look at. And I love dusk. The cozy lights going on inside the homes and the night jasmine, you know? And I want grapes. I really love grapes. You up for that?" I look up and he's just watching me. He's clearly waiting for this all to be some twisted mind game. "I know we have a lot to talk about, but I don't want to right now. Is that okay?" I ask.

"Yeah," Adam says. I make my way out of the kitchen in search of my phone and movie times. I look down at what I'm wearing and, rather than changing into something less comfortable, decide that this post-Swimtastics ensemble is just fine for a day off with my husband. Adam comes out into the living room announcing some movie times and we load up into the car.

At the theater, we buy popcorn and sodas. It's a huge su-perhero movie and I love every second of it. As dusk falls, we walk around the neighborhood and I greedily breathe in the night-blooming jasmine.

Later, I sit on the side of the mattress and watch Adam getting ready for bed. Brushing his teeth. The muscles in his arm tensing and flexing with every movement. He really is stunning. And by some cruel twist of fate, he's getting better with age. A smile curls across my face as I remember this morning at the pool.

"What's . . . why are you smiling?" Adam asks, standing in front of me in just pajama bottoms. I turn away from him and pull my pajamas from the dresser. A deep breath. Ease. Freedom. No more contorting. No more Groot. I begin to get undressed. Shirt. Pants. I can feel Adam watching me. I turn around. Bra. I want to put on my pajama top before I take off my underpants. My movements hitch and stutter as I make myself take off my underpants. I throw my clothes into the hamper. And I stand there. Adam watches me. One second. Two seconds. I bring my arms up and then let them fall. No. Three seconds. Four—Adam smiles. I grab my pajama bottoms and catch my toe on the waistband, tripping myself. Gathering myself, I thread my arms into the pajama top and fasten the bottom button.

"Slower," Adam says. I know I should whip off my pajama top and launch into Adam right this very minute in some sort of spontaneous sexy mania, but instead I can only think about him growling "slower" to Nicola as she seductively strips off her clothes. I look down at the floor, button up my top the rest of the way, and crawl into bed.

"Good night," I say, turning away from him.

Ellen noticed something different about me immediately. I told her it was a new massage therapist. I didn't think it'd be appropriate to tell her that I had some sort of epiphanic, religious experience whilst sobbing naked in a public pool shower.

But, of course, as with everything else right now, it's not just one thing. Asking myself what I really want has been the most eye-opening development of all. Not running everything I do and say and wear and think through my old web of cruel filters and critical layers has made me feel happier and more free than I have in decades. I think Fat Me is learning how to live in the present day like some kind of foundling who has to be domesticated. THIS IS A SPOOOOOON. Spoooooooon, she mutters before hurling it at the wall. Oh, Fat Me. You'll get it.

Here's where I can start. The way I have been living isn't going to work anymore. The fantasy that I built—no matter how hard I tried—will never be real. I can start there. What will it look like if I decide that the way I am living won't work anymore?

I feel different. Of course I do. I made a chicken mole dish one night for dinner and then went all out the next night: I had a craving for sushi and ordered Sugarfish to be delivered right to my door. That's two nights without the old chicken salad. I haven't worked out at the gym all week. I've replaced the thankless hours on a treadmill with lovely long walks through my neighborhood at dusk. My tour of renovated houses, I'm calling it. That fence was taken down yesterday. I knew it would be. I'm even starting to say hello to people who take walks at the same time. I now know a few of their names.

When Mom calls to check in on me, I've tried to be as honest with her as I can. I'm being myself, I say. The long walks. Having Sugarfish delivered. That one movie Adam and I went to. I ordered this Advent calendar of tea I've always wanted but thought was too expensive. I bought a red sweater.

I listened to pop music the entire ride into work. I ate too many grapes and almost shit myself one afternoon, but I'm confident I'll learn moderation soon enough.

Mom listens. She says, "That sounds nice, dear," but I know she's wondering how things are going with Adam. I told her I got naked that first night after our talk at the pool and how we've been affectionate and playful like we were when we first started dating.

I told her we haven't talked about the other women, per se, but that he'd spent every night at home this week. When she pressed the issue, I told her I was going to talk to him about it tonight at the event for Jacob Peterman. "Good," she'd said. I wanted her to say more. Really badger me about it, but she didn't. We talked about some of the renovated houses I'd been following on my walks and if I'd heard anything more from Ben about the homecoming game. I hadn't. I didn't tell her I'd found the emails from Shannon Shimasaki and knew the schedule of all of the homecoming events, just to be on the safe side. Doing the legwork doesn't mean that I planned on going. It was just in case. Plus? If tonight's conversation with Adam goes well, I plan to have some "New Olivia sex" with him and the whole Ben thing will be just a memory. A very—I take a long drink of water at my desk—distant memory laced with crackling laughs and whispered "I got you's."

"That husband of yours is here," Ellen says, coming into my office.

"Oh, thank you," I say, shutting down my computer.

"How weird will I make it if I talk about how hot he is?" Ellen asks.

"You've already made it plenty weird," I say, closing my laptop.

"I know. I know," Ellen says. I see Adam striding through the office just beyond my now-open office door. I watch as the interns stop what they're doing and just gaze at him. Shared looks of disbelief and hidden smiles of exaltation ripple behind him like an earthquake aftershock.

"Well, hello there, Ellen," Adam says.

"Oh, yeesh. Hi, Dr. uh . . . Dr. Farrell. Adam. Adam Dr. Farrell."

"It's just Adam, kiddo," he says.

"Adam Kiddo." Ellen blushes. "That was a joke. I need you to know that that was a joke."

Adam smiles and Ellen shakes her head as if she wants to crawl under a rock and die.

"So, you'll text me," I say.

"I will," she says.

"Nothing is too small."

"I know." Ellen starts to back out of my office.

"I'll check in with you throughout the night," I say.

"Okay," Ellen says, now all the way out of my office.

"You ready?" Adam asks, leaning in with a kiss. "Oh, shit. Are we . . . are we kissing yet?"

"We most certainly are," I say, diving into him for another kiss. He closes my office door. "We're going to be late." He kisses me again.

"I don't think I care." Another kiss. This is my husband. This is my marriage. He sweeps me up in his arms and it's not until his phone vibrates and rings for a continuous five minutes that we break apart. "That's the car. To be continued?"

ON WISCONSIN

"Will you tell Caroline I think she's so brave? And can you ask—she did that '73 Questions' for *Vogue*? Was that in her house?" Nanette has me cornered by the open bar. She's wearing a black low-cut dress and dripping in diamonds.

"It was," I say, comfortable giving out information that is also available on *Vogue*'s website.

Tonight's gala is at the home of one of the hospital's board members. It's a giant house just south of Caltech and we're set up on the back lawn. Heaters have been strategically placed around the property along with strings of Italian café lights—my personal favorite—and baskets filled with cashmere tartan blankets, should we need them during the cocktail hour. Cater waiters and floral centerpieces pepper the landscape with color and texture. There is a string quartet set up in the corner and the lilting sounds of Bach waft throughout the party. I notice right away that there are only approximately thirty or so people here. This is an elite bunch.

I texted Mom to see if she knew the people who lived here and she texted back, "new money."

"Okay. So, Question 23? The one where the guy is asking Caroline where she prefers to stay when she's in London? Now, Jacob always tells me that we should stay at the Dorchester, but Caroline mentioned a hotel I'd never heard of?" Nanette pulls the phone out of her beaded clutch and has it at the ready.

"It's the Number Sixteen. She stayed there on her first trip to London and she's just kept staying there," I say.

"I've never even heard of it," she says, desperately typing it into her phone.

"It's down in South Kensington. Really nice place. Cozy."

"Cozy? Is that . . . does that mean . . . small?"

"Kind of."

"Hm," Nanette says, replacing her phone back into her purse. "I don't know if I'm down with small."

"Yeah." I sip my champagne so I don't crack up at the words "down with small." And then we stand there. In companionable silence. As Nanette is wont to do. She smoothes her hair down. Poses a little. Looks down at her dress. I watch as Adam makes the rounds with Jacob. Shaking hands, being charming. He's so good at this. "So, where are you from?"

"Hm?" she asks.

"Where are you from?" I ask. Fuck it, right?

"Sacramento," she says.

"Oh?"

"It's the worst."

"It's the state capitol, so there's got to be something to it."

Nanette looks over at me and rolls her eyes. Like actually rolls her eyes. It's a split second, but in that span of time I ask and answer a question inside my head. What would the real Olivia do right now? The real Olivia would ask, "Did you just roll your eyes at me?"

"No, at Sacramento." Nanette shifts from one foot to the other, jutting her hip bone out and it's in that moment that I see her for the mall rat that she must have been back in Sacramento. Shopping for hair things and eating pretzels that smelled way better than they tasted. "I couldn't wait to get out of there." Nanette sees someone she knows—or maybe it's just her own reflection or a shiny light—but, she meanders away, just as dinner is announced, finally leaving me on my own.

We file into the house and are led into the formal dining room. Once there, I understand Mom's "new money" comment. There's a lot of white silk. A large wooden table extends down the center of the room, covered in white china and white roses and crystals, with three large chandeliers hanging just above it. There are also hot pink, oversized wingback chairs at each end of the table. Along with a zebra-print runner that assaults the eye as we walk in. The servers see us to our reserved seats. As it's customary that husbands and wives do not sit with each other, Adam gives me a look of "holy shit with this room, right?" from across the table. Once the women are seated, the men sit and we all arrange ourselves around the table.

The people around me know each other and fall quickly into conversation. I don't mind. I'd rather that than Nanette and her vacant-eyed game of twenty questions about Caroline Lang. As the first course is set before us—some kind of

raw salmon atop what looks like grapefruit—I take the opportunity to excuse myself to the ladies'. I don't have to go,
but I want to check my phone for updates from Ellen. I wind
through the house and find the powder room right off the
foyer. I read through Ellen's texts. The movie was well received and this Q&A is, according to Ellen, way smarter—or
more pretentious maybe—than the others, because it's an industry panel rather than just a regular Q&A at some theater.
The questions are about craft and process. Not about who
Caroline's husband is having sex with. I text back that it
sounds like it's going well. She tells me to enjoy myself. I drop
my phone into my purse and walk back through the house
and into the dining room.

I sit back down, return my napkin to my lap, and dig into
the first course. The young couple sitting beside me introduce themselves.

"We sneaked sitting next to each other." She is rosy cheeked
and looks like she should be gracing the outside of a butter
package. Wholesome and lovely.

"There were name cards, but we were a whole three
seats apart," he says. He is nerdy and bespectacled and looks
like he weighs seventy . . . maybe eighty pounds with his
shoes on.

It appears they are newly engaged and are now excitedly
talking about their big Santa Barbara wedding plans. I look
to the woman just to my right. She's probably my age and
has one of those pixie cuts that many women feel emboldened to give a try, only to regret it immediately as they're called
"sir" until it grows out.

"Santa Barbara is lovely," I say, taking a sip of my champagne.

"We're from Wisconsin originally, so anything with sun and ocean is . . . ," the bride-to-be trails off.

"More than anything we ever could have imagined," her fiancé finishes. They beam at one another. Oh, good. I'm seated next to the Impossibly-in-Love Couple. This is going to go really well, I can feel it. I slide my champagne glass away from me and when the waiter asks if he can top me off, I say no. The last thing I need is to be tipsy right now.

"Liv—" A hand gently squeezes my shoulder and I jump. Adam.

"You startled me," I say, trying to temper my voice so it goes from slightly alarmed to effortlessly coquettish.

"A word?" Adam asks, stepping away from the buzzing table.

"Must be a dinner party emergency," I say to the people around me. The Super-in-Love Couple laugh, but Ms. Pixie Cut barely cracks a smile. Oh, I'll win her over by the end of the night. I place my napkin on the table and follow Adam into a quiet corner of the dining room. "Is this about that weird grapefruit thing? I think it was salmon, but—"

"So, we're going to keep it together, right? You . . . you're going to keep it together?"

"If this is about the eye-rolling thing I said to Nanette earlier—"

"I just need to know you're not going to make a scene."

"Of course I'm not going to make a scene. My family has been not making scenes for hundreds of years."

"Good."

"Maybe a glass of wine? Loosen you up." I pat Adam's arm and walk back over to the table.

"My husband is concerned I'll make a scene," I say to Ms. Pixie Cut, smoothing my napkin over my lap.

"Oh?" she asks.

"But, there's a time and a place," I say with a sly wink. Ms. Pixie Cut says nothing. I shift my focus back to the Super-in-Love Couple.

"Where in Wisconsin are you from?" I ask.

"Milwaukee," they say together. And then crumble into giggles. Ugh. I move my champagne glass back toward me and eye the waiter. He obliges and fills it back up. I see Adam across the table shoot me a look of concern. I just smile. It's fine. I'm a professional at these events, remember?

"So, the wedding is going to be in Santa Barbara. Do you know where?" I ask.

"Wherever they'll have us!" the bride-to-be says. Okay. That's not quite how planning a wedding works, Ms. Wisconsin. I still have my binder from mine and it is a thing of organizational beauty.

"And the honeymoon?" I ask.

"Somewhere wonderful?" the bride-to-be says, sipping her water. No alcohol and she hasn't touched the raw fish, either. Is Ms. Wisconsin already pregnant?

"Big Sur is amazing," I say. Ms. Pixie Cut nods as she finishes up her first course. A waiter sweeps in and clears her plate. "That's where I went on mine."

"Oh, wow," the bride-to-be coos. I let the waiter know that I'm done picking at my first course and he takes my plate as well.

"Isn't it just camping there?" Mr. Wisconsin asks.

"You should look into the Post Ranch Inn. It's kind of expensive, but for one night . . . ," Ms. Pixie Cut trails off.

I look from Ms. Pixie Cut to Adam. Time stopping. Urgent whispers of not making a scene burst through my brain like fireworks. Okay. Hold it together. Wait. Is Ms. Pixie Cut, Dr. Pixie Cut? Am I sitting next to Dr. Nicola McKesson? No. No? The Post Ranch Inn is one of the most famous places to stay in Big Sur. You mention Big Sur, someone is inevitably going to bring up the Post Ranch Inn. Adam watches me.

"You've been to the Post Ranch Inn?" I ask, as a waiter sets the second course down in front of me. It's some kind of white soup with a piece of cracker bread across the top of the bowl. Potato leek maybe?

"Just went for the first time this past month," Dr. Pixie Cut says. She's busy thanking the waiter for her soup and doesn't notice me narrowing my eyes at her. Adam does, though. I hear him clearing his throat and turn to look at him. I raise my eyebrows and he just stares at me. I pick up my spoon and take a sip of the soup. I want to look mad, but the soup is cauliflower, not potato leek. The bitterness makes me wince, so instead of looking steely, I just look like a baby that's been fed a lemon.

I see Adam try to get Nicola's attention and it enrages me. Oh, are you trying to warn your ladylove that the monster's at the gates? Just ignore her! Don't make eye contact with the poor wretch! She'll shuffle on to the next fair maiden if you throw her a scrap of bread!

"What brought you to the Post Ranch Inn? Celebrating something?" I ask, my voice measured and careful. Mr. and Ms. Wisconsin are discussing the soup. They're not fans.

"No, just a little getaway," Dr. Pixie Cut says with a slurp of her soup.

"Uh-huh," I say. The waiter tops off my champagne and thankfully relieves me of my soup bowl. From the head of the table, Jacob Peterman stands clinking his knife against his

Baccarat wineglass. I see Adam let out a sigh as the guests turn to focus on the man of the hour.

"You all knew I wasn't going to pass up the chance to hear myself talk, right?" Jacob says. Everyone laughs. I am now openly staring at Dr. Pixie Cut. Is that really Nicola? She's . . . oh, god. She's Pageant Plain. For chrissakes, she's goddamn Pageant Plain. I knew it! I sit back in my chair and nod my head. Staring at her as Jacob blathers on in the background. "So, thank you to all of you for making this old man's life something to be proud of." Jacob raises his glass.

"To Jacob," they all say. I don't. I'm currently having a rage blackout. I down my champagne. The next course is served— another kind of fish? Come on. With the amount of alcohol I'm drinking, I'm going to need a helluva lot more than these eensy-weensy fish courses.

"Can you pass the bread?" I ask Ms. Wisconsin.

"Oh, sure. I didn't know L.A. people would want bread," she jokes.

"That's our secret. We always want bread, we just don't eat it," I say, pulling a warm roll from the basket. Ms. Wisconsin nervously titters. "And the butter?" She obliges.

"Do you know of any—" Ms. Wisconsin starts.

"So, was this trip to the Post Ranch Inn with a former flame, or . . . ?" I ask Dr. Pixie Cut. She's got to know who I am, right? Is she actively fucking with me or is she just as in the dark as I am? Oh, god. What if it isn't even her?

"I'm sorry?" she asks.

"This trip to the Post Ranch Inn. Was it with a former flame or someone you're still seeing?" I ask. I shove the buttered roll in my mouth. "I mean, assuming you didn't just go to the world's most romantic place by yourself, that is."

"No, I wasn't by myself," she says. I take a bite of my fish. My fork scratches against the china, causing the man across from me to give me a look. I roll my eyes at him. Which is when Adam excuses himself, stands, and walks over to me.

"If I could borrow my wife," Adam says. Dr. Pixie Cut doesn't even look up.

"You knew," I say to her. She won't look at me. Adam places his hand on my shoulder, but this time I lean forward and his hand slips off. "Look at me." She clears her throat. "You're having an affair with my husband, the least you can do is look at me." She finally turns and her eyes meet mine. A rush of cruel insults floods my brain. She could be thinner. She could be prettier. She's one of many. He'll cheat on her just as he's cheated on me. Nicola looks from me to Adam as I struggle to find my words. "Do better." A scoff. She looks away. "Be better."

The conversation at the table has come to a halt. A drunken idiot (me) has just hurled an accusation at a well-respected doctor (Dr. Pixie Cut), like some hysterical little girl at the Salem witch trials.

I wouldn't change a fucking thing.

"Excuse us," I say with a smooth lilt. The table breaks into conversation as the third course is swept away and the main meat dish is set in front of the guests. Adam gives a final look to Dr. Pixie Cut. A look that says, "Let me handle this." The "this" being me. The "this" being some small unpleasantness on par with a wild bear who's approaching the open window of your car. I toss my napkin on my chair, grab my purse, and walk out of the hot pink and zebra-print dining room that's become the second tackiest thing at dinner tonight.

We wind through the house and find ourselves back outside by the Italian café lights and baskets full of cashmere blankets that no one ever used.

"The balls it takes to discipline me about causing a scene when you're the one cheating. You're the one—"

"You said you knew about Nicola."

"I said I knew about her, not that I (a) knew what she looked like, or (b) would be comfortable sharing a meal with her," I say. My breath is catching and I feel that tightness in my chest again. I sit down on a stone wall. It's cold. Too cold. I pull a tartan blanket from the basket and wrap it around me.

"I didn't know she was going to be here." He's looking right at me. I need him, in that moment, to not be able to make eye contact with me. I want him to be ashamed. To look down. I want him to get that what he's done is wrong.

"Are you still seeing her?" I ask, the words getting caught in my throat as the breath clunks around my chest.

"Yes." It's such a simple, unadorned word.

"Yes," I say, repeating it.

"I don't know what you—"

"Expected? Wanted? Needed?" I offer.

"Any of those," he says, letting his hands slide into his pockets. I can see his breath in the night air.

"I expected you to stop seeing her. I wanted you to love me. I needed you to be all in in this marriage." I look up at him. Adam looks around. He stops a waiter.

"Do you have bourbon?" Adam asks.

"Yes, sir," the waiter says.

"Can you bring me a glass? Neat."

"Do you have a preference as to what kind, sir?"

"Not tonight I don't."

"Yes, sir."

"Thank you." Adam sits down on the stone wall next to me. After a few seconds, he reaches over into the basket and pulls out a tartan blanket of his own. He puts it over his lap. We are silent. The waiter returns with a glass of bourbon. Adam thanks him. He downs it. And replaces the glass on the waiter's tray.

"Another, sir?"

"What do you think?" Adam says with a beleaguered sigh. The waiter nods and retreats. Adam takes a deep breath. He takes my hand in his. "You are my wife. Nicola means nothing to me. She knows that." The waiter reappears with another glass. Adam takes it. "Thank you. That'll be all." The waiter nods and disappears. Adam takes a sip of his bourbon and cradles the glass in his long fingers. The caramel liquid glints in the light. I lean into him and kiss him. Nothing. The bourbon on his lips tastes smoky and sweet like molasses. Another kiss. Nothing. He leans into me as I pull away. I rest my hand on his. My hands are shaking. From the cold. From what's about to happen. From all of it.

I always thought my rock bottom would be this extremely painful public spectacle. But that's not how it happens. I simply close door after door and go on to live in the easier rooms of myself. Happily and voluntarily trapped in a cage I don't even see. My rock bottom is private and comfortable. There's no pain, because there are no feelings. It's nice here. Turns out, it's out there that's hard. My mind is clear. The alcohol has evaporated and I find my voice.

"I'm going to go." I stand, unwrap myself from the tartan blanket, and set it on the stone wall next to Adam.

"We were happy, we can be that again," Adam says, taking my hand in his.

"You're right, but not together," I say. I pull my hand away and stand tall.

"So, that's it?" Adam stands. I look up at him. He steps closer.

"Did you ever love me?" I ask.

"Yes," Adam says. He's telling the truth. We are quiet.

"Did you ever love me?" Adam finally asks. A long moment.

"I thought I did."

Confusion. A flare of anger. An arrogant flash. Adam tries to say something. His mouth opens and closes.

"My best to Nicola." I turn around and don't look back.

I walk out through the house and the valet calls the car that Adam set up to drive us here this evening. I don't worry about how he's going to get home. I climb in the back and tell the driver our address. Shit. No. We're no longer an "our."

As we pull away from the house, I can't help but think how boring the moments are just after such a huge decision is made. This is what change looks like. Sitting in the back of a town car listening to the driver talk to his dispatcher over the sounds of smooth jazz. I am getting a divorce. My marriage is finished. I didn't play it cool. I didn't come off as flinty and plucky. No, I just came off as wretched and snappy.

But, it was all me. I let out a laugh. That was genuinely me being myself. That's a small victory, at least. Those will be the kinds of greatest hits I can look forward to as I move through this life alone.

"Oh, god," I say aloud. The driver flicks a concerned glance in the rearview mirror.

It all comes racing back. The whole life before. I was hard to like. Ben wasn't the only person who found me difficult. I was prickly. Arrogant. Wait. It's not *was*. It's *is*. I kept acting like when I lost the weight I learned how to be a better human being, but that's not true. I was terrible in the run-up to my wedding. To good people. The only thing I've been faking is that there was ever a time when I earned anyone's goodwill. I've been kind of awful. I shift in the chair and the leather seats squeak and fart beneath me. The seatbelt is constricting. This dress is too tight.

I was content with Adam because he never asked me to be a better person. He was kind of awful, too. God, we were terrible. In all these years of wanting to be envied and coveted, I never asked the simple fucking question of whether or not I was good. Just good. Am I a good person? Because, it was never about people liking me. I never gave a shit about that. That's why I was so free. I never cared. I've been so wrong. About Adam. About me. About everything.

I sit in stunned silence. My phone is buzzing in my purse. I blink back to life. I see that there are texts from Ellen, but instead I switch over and text Mom.

"Can I stay with you tonight?" I text. As I wait for her reply, I look out the window. My mind is filled with everything and nothing. I'm not angry. I'm not sad. I'm not anything. I'm just stunned.

"Sure," Mom texts back.

"Thanks," I text.

"Everything okay?"

"I left Adam," I type. I look at it. There it is. Three little words in an adorable blue text bubble. Is there an emoji for this, I wonder? Probably. The broken heart? The thumbs-down? Or is it just a series of poop emojis along with the little yellow sobbing happy face. How do you communicate that your marriage of ten years is over. Not even over, never started.

Oh, good, there's the anger. I press SEND and my text swoops out into the ether. I let out a scoff. And another. The anger's building. Swelling and rolling through me like a series of tidal waves.

"I'm so sorry, sweetie," Mom texts back.

"I know," I text back. And before she can reply, I text, "My battery is almost dead, we can talk when I get there in about an hour. Is that okay?"

"I'll be here," Mom texts. The anger bleeds into hurt. I can't even reply to her text without tapping into what I'm certain is that same vast pain from earlier in the week at the pool and the lovely added guilt of how terrible I've been over the past several decades.

I switch my phone off and put it back in my purse. Don't think about anything, Olivia. How about that? Just look out the window. The houses. The other cars. People bundled up, walking along the streets. My breath fogs the window. I think for a minute that I'd like to draw something. I raise my finger and it just hangs there. Finally I draw a circle. Two eyes. And a smile. I sit back and close my eyes.

"Ma'am? We're here."

"Oh, thank you," I say, completely sobered up now. I grab my purse and am opening the door, when the driver opens it from the outside. I step out into the cold night air and he closes the door behind me. I tip him and he thanks me.

"Do you need anything else?" he asks. How about don't go back and pick up my husband and his pixie-cutted lover? Leave them stranded there to maybe stay the night in some terrible hot pink and zebra-print guest room of the host's choosing.

"No, thank you," I say. I walk up the pathway and into the dark and empty house. In a haze, I throw clothes into a bag like I'm taking a business trip. And then I grab this wooden seal of my grandfather's and a picture of Mom and me at my wedding. I throw that into the bag as well. I walk into the bathroom and grab whatever toiletries I'll need for however long . . . forever? I take my pillow off the bed and the quilt my grandmother made. I zip up the luggage, heave the pillow and quilt under my arm, and shuffle down the hallway. At the front door, I look back into the house. The lamp with the broken spoke. Hm. Hitching the pillow and quilt up under my arm farther, I walk over to the lamp, unplug it, and take it with me.

I load everything up in the car and drive over to Mom's. The porch light is on as I pull into her driveway. I tug and pull the bizarre assortment of things I decided to pack out of my car and walk up to the front door of my childhood home. Mom opens the door in her pajamas, robe, and slippers. I walk in and she closes the door behind me, locking it. She doesn't ask about the lamp.

"I took the waffle iron when I left," she says, walking up the stairs toward my room. "I hate waffles." She opens the door to my room. I walk inside. "I bought you some jammies for Christmas. They've got pugs on them. Thought you might think they were funny. They're on your bed."

"Thank you," I say, my voice a grumbling mutter.

"I love you, my little darling. And you're going to be okay." She hugs me. I'm still holding the damn lamp. I start crying. Of course.

"Am I awful?" I ask.

"No, honey."

"You have to say that," I say.

Mom smiles. Wipes my tears away. "Get some sleep. We'll talk in the morning," she says, finally loosing the lamp from my grip. I stand in my childhood bedroom, take off the too-tight dress, and try not to spiral down into a world where a week of eating chicken mole and sushi led to my gaining all the weight back in record time. I get into the pajamas Mom has laid out for me. I put my pillow on the bed and lay the quilt on over the covers that are already there. I switch out the light and crawl into bed. I fall asleep to the glow-in-the-dark stars on my ceiling.

"Olivia? Honey? Olivia?" says Mom. Sunlight streams in. Oh, shit. Shit.

"What time is it?"

"It's just 6 a.m."

"Friday, right?"

"Yes—honey, Ellen is here. Something happened with Caroline." I burst out of bed and am at the door to my bed-room.

"What? Is she okay?" I run down the stairs. Ellen is stand-ing in Mom's foyer with two coffees, wearing the same clothes from last night. My stomach drops.

"You need to come with me. Now." Ellen hands me a cof-fee and pulls my coat from the coatrack.

"Can I at least get dressed?" I ask.

"Caroline got away from Richard and me, so she could be in an elevator all by herself with that shitty reporter from that other Q and A. Once alone, she told him exactly what he could do with his article in a monologue that I look forward to being performed on all the late-night shows by anything from pup-pets to little kids. Naturally, not only the reporter himself, but also the elevator's cameras caught this monologue on tape. You should have answered any one of my hundred texts from last night. But, you didn't. So now we're here. What do you think? Do you have time to at least get dressed?" Ellen asks, holding out my coat.

"No. I don't," I say, grabbing my coat.

YOU LOOK WAY DIFFERENT IS ALL

"Hi. Yeah. Remember me? I have some questions for you. Oh, no, you are going to answer them because it's my turn and I want you to feel what it's like to have some annoying turd ask you hurtful, personal questions, you nameless ball bag. First: Is this what you dreamed you'd be doing when you were a child? Kid next to you says he wants to be a fireman. Another says she wants to go to the moon. And you raise your tiny baby hand—which hasn't grown a fucking inch, if you know what I mean—and squeal that what you really want to do is shit on people's dreams for a living and when you can't do that, you aspire to hurt people you don't even know by humiliating them in public. Do I have it right? Is that how it went down? Do you forget we're people? Do you go into some zone when you're asking about broken marriages and cheating spouses where you forget that I'm just a human being trying to get through the day? And if you say I signed up for this, you can go fuck yourself. I wanted to act because I had a shitty childhood and make-believing I could be anywhere else is how I got through it . . ."

Ellen shuts the recording off as Caroline's voice crumbles into sobs. She closes her laptop. We all just stand there.

"What's a ball bag?" Søren asks.

"I don't know. I've been watching a lot of British television," Caroline says, walking over to her refrigerator and pulling out a carton of almond milk. She pours it into her coffee, offers us some; we all turn it down. She replaces the carton. She takes a sip of her coffee. "Why are you in your pajamas?"

"Because it's six thirty in the morning," I say.

"Where were you last night?" Caroline asks, her voice clipped. I take the last swig of the coffee Ellen brought me and try to formulate an answer. "Because—"

"I'm going to stop you there. It sounds like you're about to blame me for what happened last night. That's not going to happen. You had an ex–Navy SEAL and Ellen there to watch over you, on top of the fact that you're a grown-ass woman. So, let's just not, okay?" Richard stands there acting like this is his fault. I walk over to the bin and toss in my empty coffee cup. On the way back, I pat him on the shoulder and he shakes his head. "This isn't your fault." He nods. Ellen gives me an impressed look.

"Of course it's not Richard's fault. I just really want to blame someone," Caroline says with a sigh.

"I know," I say.

"It felt good, though. The look on that little shit's face. God, did it feel good," she says. I let my head fall into my hands.

"Well, then that's all that matters," I say.

"So, there's already a Nameless Ball Bag Twitter handle.

It's currently tweeting about how misguided its childhood dreams were. It's actually kind of hilarious." We look up. Ellen clears her throat and continues. "Caroline Lang is trending on Twitter and Willa Lindholm has subtweeted something about how sad it is when old people lose their marbles or something . . . it's in Swedish, so . . ." Ellen scrolls through her phone as she speaks.

"Anything from Max?" I ask.

"No," Ellen says without looking up from her phone.

"Looks like at least one of you is listening to their publicist," I say, staring at Caroline.

"Oh, come on. I'm just so sick of it. I'm so tired. Don't I get to be tired?" Caroline asks, dramatically flopping her head down onto the counter.

"We have offers to talk from all the late-night shows, as well as several reporters and, well, everyone," Søren says, sipping his tea.

"Are you worried about this?" I ask. Søren looks up from his tea. Caroline raises her head from the counter. "Honestly."

Søren is thoughtful. He puts his tea down on the kitchen island. The expensive china echoes against the marble of the counter. "Yes and no." We all lean in. "I think Caroline should go on to one of these late-night shows. We should choose which one now, because if they film in the late afternoon, we have to . . . well, you know."

"Yeah," I say. Ellen starts typing furiously on her phone.

"We can't act like nothing happened. We can't act . . ." Søren picks up his tea and sips. "I don't know." The kitchen falls silent.

"Wait. You have to know. Søren? You have to know," Caroline says. Søren takes off his glasses and rubs his eyes.

"Leave me to it," I say. Søren puts his glasses back on and looks over at me. I nod. "I've got this."

"Okay," he says, getting up from his stool. Caroline looks from him to me.

"Ellen, if you could finalize all the late-night stuff," I say, walking her through which show we'll be doing, contacting Caroline's agent and manager as well as finalizing the arrival of Caroline's stylist, hair, and makeup who should be here within the hour. Ellen is on it. She grabs her laptop and disappears into one of Caroline's other rooms. Søren says his goodbyes and as I walk back into the kitchen, I ask Richard to give Caroline and me a few minutes alone.

"You're not going to kill her, are you?" Richard asks.

"Is that a joke?" I ask.

"Did you just make a joke?" Caroline asks.

"I did," Richard says, blushing.

"Well, well, well," Caroline says.

"Will miracles never cease?" I ask. "And yes, I am going to kill her." Richard laughs and walks down the hallway to where Ellen is set up. I walk around the kitchen for a bit and then hop onto one of the stools around the kitchen island.

"Look, I know the drill. I'll make a few jokes, fall on my sword, blah blah blah, just tell me what to say and I'll say it. I memorize lines for a living, right?" Caroline says, running her hand through her hair. "I know I fucked up."

"I don't know if you did," I say.

"What?" I am quiet. Thinking. About everything. "Olivia?"

"What if you just told the truth?" I ask after a long moment.

"About what?" Caroline asks.

"All of it."

Caroline sets down her coffee. Starts and stops several questions. Looks out a window. Back at me. "Hm."

"Fuck it, right?" I ask.

"Right," she says, smiling. The tears well in her eyes. She's just as shocked by them as I am. Then the tears well up in my eyes. And now we're both half crying, half laughing at our own ridiculousness. She reaches across the counter and takes my hand. "Thank you." She squeezes my hand. She swipes at her tears with her shoulder. "Actresses, am I right?" I laugh, and she bursts through her tears with an open-mouthed laugh that's so unguarded it breaks my heart.

Ellen walks into the room and immediately regrets it.

"Shit. I'm . . . uh . . . Caroline, your stylist is here," Ellen says.

"That was fast," I say.

"She was waiting for the call," Ellen says without looking at us. "Figured you'd need her."

"Ah, right," I say.

"Can I send her in?" Ellen asks.

"Yeah," I say, stepping off the stool. Caroline looks up at me. "Everything is going to be okay."

"I believe you," she says.

Caroline hops up from the stool and gives me a giant hug. "Yes, I'm still crying, but these are tears of joy now, okay?" she yells into the crook of my neck. I laugh.

Ellen walks in with Caroline's stylist and we stop embracing each other long enough to welcome them into the kitchen. I walk over to Caroline's breakfast nook and tuck into the banquette with my phone. I text Mom that everything is okay. She's glad to hear it. We go back and forth about if I'm going to be home for dinner, and whether or not she can tell Mrs. Stanhope and Joyce Chen about the goings-on. I play along and act like she hasn't already told them. I text Gus and confirm that we're still on for our first event since he moved out of L.A. It's up in San Francisco and is just a photo shoot for an interview that he'll be doing later on in the month. It should be a pretty painless reentry. I'll meet up with him for dinner in Mill Valley and we'll head over to the studio together in the morning.

I scroll through my emails as the stylist has Caroline try on close to a thousand different looks. We decide on an off-the-rack fuchsia Christian Siriano faille petal gown. With its three-quarter-length sleeves, high neck, and leaf appliqué, the dress looks like something a punkish girl would wear to her grandmother's afternoon tea. Caroline usually defaults to black and cream. Classic designers. Safe styles. She has never made it onto a worst-dressed list, nor has she made it onto a best-dressed list, either. This dress, with its bold color and spotlight style, marks a definite change. It's unlike anything Caroline has ever worn and it's perfect. Caroline's hair and makeup are close to being done as morning becomes afternoon. She hasn't practiced what she's going to say. She's been laughing and talking all day, completely unburdened. No lines to learn, she just has to be herself.

Just be yourself.

I know that I got broken like that lamp. And instead of trying to fix it, I decided that I should get a new me. It was easier.

The Fat Me is the Real Me.

That's the dark secret I didn't want anyone to know. I am unlikable. Difficult. Arrogant. Hard to get to know. And so uncool. No amount of weight loss or dyed hair or expensive outfits or the perfect husband is going to hide that anymore.

Thank . . . god.

I scroll through my emails and find the one from Shannon Shimasaki. The homecoming dance is tonight. And I'm taking the Fat Me as a date.

"No, I don't have a ticket, I'm . . . I used to go here," I say to the apparent ten-year-old behind the card table decorated with blue and gold streamers.

"Oh. When?" The look on her face is one of complete disbelief. Like someone my age could have gone to a school that is not now a Roman ruin.

"There. Olivia Morten," I say, pointing at a name tag. The girl looks at the picture that's on the name tag. Back at me. Back at the picture. "Yeah. I know. It's me."

"You look way different is all," she says, peeling the name tag off its plastic backing and pushing it onto my boob with the finesse of an EMT searching for a heartbeat. I pay my money and the girl rattles off directions and door prizes and all the awards and king and queen, and she's still talking even as I walk down the long hallway toward the ballroom. I'm wearing a dress that I borrowed from Caroline. Once she found out what I was going to do, she made sure I was wearing the best revenge dress ever. Never above a makeover montage, I went along with it. It's a tight red dress that looks like it should be on some pinup girl painted on the side of a World War II bomber. Am I trying too hard? I should have dressed more casual. But, I couldn't say no to the dress. Well, it was what the Fat Me wanted.

Caroline zipped the dress into its bag and I carried it right onto the lot where the late-night show is taped. Ellen and I watched from the greenroom and Caroline was funny and honest and irreverent. She sat in the chair just like she sits at home—one leg curled under her. She talked honestly about the pain of divorce, and she never got bitter and she never blamed anyone for what she said to that reporter. By the time she climbed into the car with Richard, she'd won everyone over simply by being real. She wasn't right. She wasn't perfect. She was just someone people could relate to. She was a human being.

I can hear the bass of the music from out in the hallway, as well as high-pitched titters of the teenage girls and the monosyllabic grunts of their gangly, awkward dates. Oh, god. I turn around and begin to walk back down the hallway. Why did I come? What was I thinking? I smooth the dress down and catch a pack of teenage boys looking right at my boobs. I spin around. Walk in. Back around. No. You don't need to do this. Just because you never went to a homecoming dance doesn't mean that you need to remedy this now, Olivia. Spin back around. Yes, it does. She deserves this. I deserve this. I get to go to homecoming, goddammit. I spin back around. Fine. Okay. Just walk.

I make a deal with myself. All I have to do is walk into that ballroom. See it. Just see it. Just let it know that it didn't beat me. I am you, past. And you are me. And I'm here to say goodbye. And then I can walk right out and say that I've done it. That's it. That's all I have to do. And then I can go back to Mom's and eat bean and cheese burritos and watch more episodes of the hot-vicar cozy mystery Caroline got Mom and me hooked on.

"I can do this," I say. And I walk in.

The large ballroom is alive. Hundreds of people sit at round tables, stand in clusters, and fill the dance floor. The music is loud and everyone has come here to have the night of their lives. Including me. I take a slight step back.

"Olivia Morten?" A group of women are standing just inside the doors to the ballroom. I turn to look at them. Mary Benicci, Gretchen Bliss, and Shannon Shimasaki. The three girls who made my high school life hell. They look exactly the same. They sound exactly the same. "I'd heard you'd lost a ton of weight." I smile at the women and then just keep walking. They're only important if I make them so. I've finally broken free and there is no way I'm going to tether my happiness to whether or not these insignificant women cosign my ongoing successes.

I step out onto the ballroom floor. I'll do one lap around the dance floor and then I'll leave. For good. I walk. And watch. Kids laughing. Dancing. Couples fighting. Couples hugging. Girlfriends circling the wagons around a friend who's been done wrong. Packs of kids dancing together. Taking pictures on their phones. Kids standing on the fringes being dragged onto the dance floor. I can't stop smiling. It's . . . it's everything I thought it would be.

I settle alongside the dance floor by the concessions. I let myself move a little to the music. I close my eyes and sway. It feels good. I feel weightless. Somewhere deep inside of me I hear someone saying, "This is so fun!" And the voice gets louder and louder as the Fat Me stops being my dirty little secret and starts being me being myself. A group of kids gather around the dance floor and I open my eyes. I turn to the two girls closest to me.

"This is so fun," I yell over the music.

"Right?" the girl says back.

"You should get out there and dance," the other girl says.

"Oh, I'm okay. You go! You go!" I say, getting all flustered at the prospect of being dragged out onto the dance floor by a pack of overzealous teenagers looking to give an old-timer a special moment.

The song changes over to Bruce Springsteen's "Secret Garden." I look at the girl standing next to me. I yell over the music, "I love this song!" She nods her head and then she and her friends bound toward their table before some boy asks them to slow dance.

I sway along with the song. The shimmering lights. A couple steps back. Another steps forward. They move left and then float to the right. The quiet murmuration of Easter egg–colored dresses pressed against dark-hued, ill-fitting suits. But, straight through the center like an arrow shot at the moon, Ben Dunn pierces across the dance floor as if no one else exists. An inky black suit and a crisp white shirt that lulls open with the weight of his starched collar. I watch him. All of him. Closer. His eyes on me. Closer. The song now muffled. The lights now dimmed. He stands in front of me.

"What are you doing here?" I ask, unable to hide how happy I am to see him.

"Chaperoning. Remember?"

"I thought that was just the football game?"

"Nope."

"Hm." I look back over to the dance floor and smile. Sway with the music.

"Shall we?" he asks, extending his hand. The voice that was once buried so deeply is now right at the surface of my skin. She is me and I am her. And we are finally free.

"Hell yes," I say, taking his hand. He leans his head back and laughs that crumbling, crackling barroom laugh of his.

We walk out onto the dance floor and he takes my hand in his, tucking it close to his chest. He wraps his other arm around my waist and pulls me in close. An arched eyebrow and a curl of a smile and he moves us with the music. The rest of the dance floor fades away and it's just us. I tuck in and feel his stubbly jawline against my face and let the smell of soap and fabric softener welcome me home. He leans down and brushes my face with his. I hold on to him. And we move. And sway with the music.

I've never felt more safe. And real. And seen.

When the song ends, we just stand there. Staring at each other.

"I was an idiot," he says.

"When?"

"Always." I laugh and he smiles.

"I'm getting a divorce," I say.

"That's too bad," he says, smiling.

"No, it's not," I say.

"No, it's not."

I take my time. I bring my hand to the side of his face. His arm tightens around my waist and as I'm pulled closer to him, I laugh. It's a nervous, dangerous laugh. And when he kisses me, it's a joyous riot of a kiss that doesn't scare me at all.

"I'd better get home," I say, pulling away from him however many minutes later. "I mean, I have to get back to Mom's. She's making bean and cheese burritos."

"Right. Okay," Ben says, breathless. "Oh, shit. Wait. You're shaking." I hadn't even noticed. He takes off his coat and holds it out for me. "I got you." I thread my arms into the warmth that his body left. I smile. "What? What was that?"

"I was just thinking how thankful I was that the coat fit," I say, laughing. He is confused. "At one time it probably wouldn't have." I wait for him to get it.

"Oh, right."

"Yeah." He's about to say something. "We don't have to . . . I . . ." I tilt up and kiss him. I wrap my arms around him and lean back. "You're real. That's all I need." He nods.

"I can do that," he says.

"Then we're good," I say.

I try to give Ben back his coat, but he says he'll get it the next time he sees me. And I can't wait.

The next morning, I wake early to find his coat hanging on the chair next to the desk where I did all my homework in high school. I wish I could show it to the Fat Me. Let her see that one day Ben Dunn's coat is going to be in her room. But, she sees it. She's here now. She knows.

I pad over to the coat and run my fingers along its fabric on my way to the shower. I get ready, have morning coffee with Mom, and am on my way to see Gus. Windows open. Music blasting. Maybe I played "Secret Garden" twenty or thirty times. Who'd blame me? I stop at giant gas stations and fill up on sparkling waters, hot teas, and any kind of road food I want. I throw my hair up into a ponytail and can't remember a time I felt this alive. This free. By the time I hit San Francisco, it's dusk.

As the Golden Gate Bridge comes into view, I'm smiling and crying and thankful and overcome and mournful and hopeful and excited and happy and thoughtful and nostalgic and scared and real. I'm finally real again.

I cross the bridge in reverent silence. The beautiful thunking of the bridge under my wheels is a religious thrum. The bay glistens below me and the fog rolls in above me. Once across, I find parking, pull Ben's coat from the backseat, grab my scarf, and climb out of my car. I wrap the scarf around my neck as I walk toward the bridge, the lights of the city twinkling back at me. I lean over the bridge and breathe it all in. The air is just different up here. Blasts of crisp wind cleanse and brutalize me all at the same time. And all I hear is the water, and the thunk-thunk-thunk of the wheels on the bridge, and my own breath.

I stand back up and finally replay that fateful night. Thar She Blows. I look back out at the bay. How did I never see it? How did I not see that was the night I lost myself? How did I not see that was the moment I disappeared? That it was that night when I chose to believe I was so broken that I deserved to be thrown away. That I was hopeless and beyond redemption. How could I have been so wrong? I lean back over the side of the bridge and take in another deep breath.

I am not broken.

I am real.

And I am here.

ACKNOWLEDGMENTS

I was sitting in my car. It was hot. And I was being told that my publisher passed on my latest book proposal.

Here's the thing about That Moment: you don't know it's That Moment.

If you knew it was That Moment—the Maybe I Don't Get to Write Novels Anymore moment—I . . . well, I'd disappear. I'm a writer. I write novels. I'm a writer. I write novels. Aren't I?

Sitting in that car, time slowing like molasses, sweat dripping down my face, disappearing disappearing, I threw a Hail Mary. Throat choking, I pitched *The F Word*. That was three years ago.

Marilyn Monroe famously said, "If you can't handle me at my worst, then you sure as hell don't deserve me at my best."

Here are the people who were the best when I was at my worst.

Annelise Robey was the first hand to come over the cliff. Amy Einhorn, Caroline Bleeke, and everyone at Flatiron Books pulled me up, dusted me off, and got me to work.

Sarah, Amber, Sarah, Kate, Margaret, Erik, Cecil, Javi, Jay, Tom, The Shamers, Nick, Alyssa, Jenelle, Cindi, Sarayu, Jenn, Kerri, Julia, Mark and Sara, Garrett, Kate, Garrick, Neil, Matthew, Sanjana, Rocco, BuzzFeed lovelies, and Zack. Thank you. Thank you for being there. For being kind. And funny. And so smart and talented.

And my family. Resendizs, Jasos, Petersons, and Gallaghers. Mom, Don, Alex, Joe, Bonnie, and Zoë. You are my people. It's us. Until the wheels come off. Ride or die.

The F Word
by Liza Palmer

Welcome to the Reading Group Guide for *The F Word*.
PLEASE NOTE: In order to provide reading groups with the
most informed and thought-provoking questions possible, it is
necessary to reveal important aspects of the plot of this novel—
as well as the ending. If you have not finished reading
The F Word, we respectfully suggest that you may
want to wait before reviewing this guide.

1. Discuss the novel's opening line: "There's the truth
   and then there's the lie that people want to believe."
   How does that distinction apply to Olivia's life?

2. At her dinner party, Olivia argues that celebrities shape
   our lives without our even realizing it: "Being a woman
   can be such a mystery sometimes, we unconsciously
   look to these celebrities as surrogate mentors for our
   own femininity. They appear to be so natural, that we
   look to them to set the standard.... I'd even go so far
   as to say that you owe your very marriage and current
   happiness to none other than Caroline Whatever-Her-
   Name-Is." What do you think? How are celebrities
   portrayed in this novel?

3. Olivia claims that the "ugly truth about women and
   gossip" is "we only talk shit about the women we're
   afraid jeopardize the things we have and want. That's
   why when I was fat, people made fun of me, but no
   one gossiped about me. Why? Because nothing of
   theirs was ever at risk of being taken by me, least of all
   their men." Do you agree? Discuss the various female
   friendships in this novel and how they are often tied
   up with jealousy, weight, and beauty. How do Olivia's
   friendships compare to her mom's?

4. Olivia argues, "Everyone has a story about who they are. Not just celebrities. Look at social media—we're all pushing some version of the life we want you to believe. It's all just PR." Do you think social media has changed our relationship to fame and celebrity? To ourselves?

5. For Olivia, her obsession with her weight is tied to a much larger issue: "When a woman calls herself fat, she's voicing the deep fear that she is, in fact, unlovable. It's just easier to talk about juice cleanses and Cardio Barre than the deep abiding shame we fear is threaded into our DNA." Do you agree? Why do you think there is still so much pressure on women to be thin? Why is weight so often tied to self-esteem?

6. Olivia reflects: "Caroline's Super Hobo should meet my Sweaty Marble. They've turned out to be quite the similar pair of ghosts." How do the various characters' pasts both haunt and motivate their futures? In your opinion, how important is childhood in determining who we grow up to be?

7. Ben tells Olivia: "Lou was talking with me about those superheroes and how sometimes you need a person who is kind of a villain to take out the bigger villain. And the kind of villain who is…what did she say, only bad because people had been mean to them." What does she mean by that? Are there villains in this novel, and if so, who?

8. Olivia initially describes Adam's serial cheating as "essentially the golf of Adam's busy schedule—a hobby I wasn't interested in and was happy he did with other people." For her, "In the end, I have to believe that marriages like ours last longer than the seemingly exciting, more volatile ones that soon fall prey to the whims of love." Do you think there is any truth to that? Can a marriage still work if one spouse is unfaithful?

9. Olivia's first panic attack comes when she tells Gus he needs to get out of "the monkey-house" that is L.A. What does she mean by that? How is L.A. portrayed in the novel?

10. Olivia says: "Growing up, we listen to love songs and believe that's what real love is. As we get older, what sinks in is not that those songs are a fantasy, but that they simply aren't about us." Do you agree? How important is pop culture in shaping our self-image?

11. Olivia's mom tells her: "Cheating is never about sex, honey." Do you agree? What is Olivia's relationship with sex throughout the novel? How is that tied up with her weight change?

12. Olivia admits that she isn't necessarily a "good person": "I was content with Adam because he never asked me to be a better person. He was kind of awful, too. God, we were terrible. In all these years of wanting to be envied and coveted, I never asked the simple fucking question whether or not I was good. Just good. Am I a good person? Because, it was never about people liking me. I never gave a shit about that. That's why I was so free. I never cared." What do you think? Is Olivia a "likable" narrator? Does it matter? Do you think you could do her job and be a nice person?

13. Discuss Caroline's breakdown monologue: "Do you forget we're people? Do you go into some zone when you're asking about broken marriages and cheating spouses where you forget that I'm just a human being trying to get through the day? And if you say I signed up for this, you can go fuck yourself. I wanted to act because I had a shitty childhood and make-believing I could be anywhere else is how I got through it…" Do you agree, or do you think celebrities should be held to a different standard?